I Take This Man

By Valerie Frankel

I Take This Man

Valerie Frankel

AVON

An Imprint of HarperCollinsPublishers

I TAKE THIS MAN. Copyright © 2007 by Valerie Frankel. All rights reserved. Printed in the United States of America. No part of this book may be used or reproduced in any manner whatsoever without written permission except in the case of brief quotations embodied in critical articles and reviews. For information address HarperCollins Publishers, 10 East 53rd Street, New York, NY 10022.

HarperCollins books may be purchased for educational, business, or sales promotional use. For information please write: Special Markets Department, HarperCollins Publishers, 10 East 53rd Street, New York, NY 10022.

FIRST EDITION

Interior text designed by Elizabeth M. Glover

Library of Congress Cataloging-in-Publication Data

Frankel, Valerie.
   I take this man / by Valerie Frankel.—1st ed.
      p. cm.
ISBN: 978-0-06-078555-0
ISBN-10: 0-06-078555-1
1. Brides—Fiction. 2. Kidnapping—Fiction. 3. New Jersey—Fiction. I. Title.

PS3556.R335812 2007
813'.54—dc22   2006024187

07 08 09 10 11 JTC/RRD 10 9 8 7 6 5 4 3 2 1

*Dedicated to my excellent friends
in the See You Next Tuesday dinner group—
Daryl Chen, Lauren Purcell, and Jeanie Pyun—
you are all fantastic writers, eaters, drinkers,
talkers, laughers, and listeners.*

Acknowledgments

Special thanks to Michele Cagan for the title.

Chapter 1

Penny Bracket, twenty-three, looked ghostly in white. She might as well have cut eyeholes in a sheet and thrown that over her head instead of wearing the gown.

"I'm the corpse bride," she said, staring at her ashen pallor in the vanity's mirror. "As soon as the ceremony's over, I'm stripping."

"You could take it off now," suggested Esther Bracket, forty-five, Penny's mother. "Skip the ceremony entirely."

Penny frowned at her mom's face in the mirror. Esther was seated across the jewel box bridal prep room on a damask-covered settee, wearing a smart pearl-gray suit with three-inch heels that disappeared in the carpeting. Around her wrists, neck, and fingers, Esther sparkled in diamonds, expensive and plentiful, five pieces more than she needed. But in New Jersey, excessiveness was the rule, be it big hair, loud clothes, garish decorating, large personality, violent crime, government corruption, or political scandal.

Penny was a Jersey girl. She was born a few exits up the Garden State Parkway. Sinatra was also a native. Like Frank, residents did things Their Way. The state song: "Born to Run" (which, ironically, was about escaping NJ). The state's motto: "Come see for yourself," since no one who lived here could be trusted to speak the truth. The state's role model: Tony Soprano. One of the nation's smallest states, geographically, it had the densest population. In more ways than one.

Some Jerseyites set themselves apart with decorum, dignity, and discretion. Penny just didn't happen to know any. Despite Penny's stated preference for a modest wedding, Esther insisted on a lavish Short Hares Plaza affair. Although she'd never admit it, Esther had shelled out $75,000 for her daughter to marry a man she despised just to impress the neighbors.

"Full house?" asked Penny, sweeping her cheeks with blush, doing what she could to look like a living person.

"Packed," said Vita Trivoli, twenty-three, the third person in the tight room, Penny's best friend and maiden of honor. "Two hundred of the fanciest white people I've ever seen. Why don't you go check it out, Mrs. Bracket? You probably need to talk to the wedding planner. Or greet guests. Or do something that takes you out of this room." The maiden of honor, a redhead, was not subtle. Today, she wore a magenta skintight backless, strapless gown along with every piece of jewelry she owned.

"Your makeup becomes you, Vita," returned Esther, of the razor-plucked Garbo brows and flawless nude foundation. "I've never had the courage to go garish."

"But your base coat of bitterness gives you a perfect *je ne sais quoi*," said Vita faux-admiringly.

"It's a very thin layer," said Esther, patting her chiseled cheekbone.

"By thin," asked Vita, "do you mean brittle?"

"I'm so glad you two have finally found something to talk about," said Penny, trying to defuse the tension between her mom and best friend.

"You realize you're the first person from college to get married," Vita said to her. "That means you win."

When Vita said the word "married," Esther flinched.

"I win?" asked Penny. "Getting married is like a game show to you?"

"You get fabulous prizes," said Vita, gesturing toward the heavily laden gift table, its carved legs trembling under the tonnage of wrapped boxes from Tiffany's. "You get a dream vacation—to Hawaii. You stand in the winner's circle and kiss your dreamy husband while everyone applauds. It's just like *Wheel of Fortune*."

"The wheel of fortune turns," said Esther grimly.

"You really have to shut up, Mom," said Penny.

"If you hate the gown so much, why did you buy it?" asked Esther.

"Bram wanted traditional," said Penny.

"For Bram's sake, you spend $15,000 on a dress you despise. What else will you do for his sake?" asked Esther. "What other compromises and sacrifices will you make over the years? How's your wrist today? And your jaw?"

Penny instinctively reached to touch her jaw, but she caught herself and redirected her hand to fiddle with her veil.

Esther growled and started pacing the small room. Penny watched her mom move in and out of the mirror's frame. Esther's calves were identical to her own. Long. Strong. Physically, Penny was the brunette version of blond Esther—minus the ravages of twenty years of bitterness. Penny had often wondered what her mother would look like without the black cloud over her head.

"I love Bram," said Penny serenely. "He loves me. Our relationship is based on honesty and respect. We're devoted to each other now, as we will be forever."

"Okay, even I thought that sounded canned," said Vita.

"Walk away," pleaded Esther.

"Never," said Penny, slamming down her blush brush, pink powder dusting the vanity. She swiveled to face her mom. "Leaving someone at the altar is a deplorable, cowardly, inexcusable act, punishable by death. The lowest of the low. That's the opposite of who I am."

"Does that make you the highest of the high?" asked Vita.

"Wish I were."

"Sacrifice," said Esther. "Compromise."

"I'm getting married," declared Penny. "End of conversation."

She swiveled back to the mirror. The tension was getting to her. Her head swam suddenly (just a few strokes). She looked at the mirror, and the glass seemed to ripple, like a pebble dropped into a still pond.

A knock at the door. Had to be Ms. Wistlestop, the Short Hares Plaza's wedding planner, coming to tell her it was time to walk the walk. Penny's heart beat its wings. She stood up and arranged her voluminous skirts, the ten layers of tulle and crinoline.

Vita said, "That's your cue," and opened the door.

Oddly, Ms. Wistlestop was not standing on the other side of it.

Penny said, "Morris? What are you doing here? You're supposed to be waiting at the altar with Bram."

Morris Nova, twenty-five, Bram's best man, wore a rented tux. Most men looked sophisticated in the penguin suit, James Bondish. Morris could wear a king's raiment, though, and still telegraph the same rugby-on-the-weekends never-quite-clean masculinity. He could've brushed his hair on my wedding day, thought Penny. He could've shaved.

"I have a note," said Morris. He choked it out, actually, each word a frog squirming in his tight throat.

"I'll take that," said Esther, snatching the envelope from Morris's outstretched hand.

While her mom liberated the single sheet of hotel stationery from its sheath, Penny watched nervously, a cold prickle climbing her back.

"I *will* kill him," said Esther simply after reading the note.

Vita took the sheet from Esther and handed it to Penny without looking at it.

Penny turned her brown eyes to the china white paper and read the succinct, economical, to-the-point, late-breaking news flash from her beloved.

Dear Penny,

I can't go through with it.

> *Sorry,*
> *Bram*

"What does it say?" asked Vita, reading the note over Penny's shoulder. The redhead gasped like she'd been stabbed in the lung and said, "This is the cruelest, most cowardly, despicable act, punishable by—"

"By death," said Esther flatly.

"Are you okay?" Vita asked Penny.

Morris said, "She hasn't blinked."

"Stop staring at my daughter," said Esther, swatting at the once and former best man.

Penny examined the terse message again. Bram hadn't wasted a word to throw away two years of her life. She looked at her mother, a woman who'd also been abandoned by a man. Esther scowled, apparently furious, but Penny knew her mom had to be relieved.

"This is beautiful stationery," said Penny, fingering the sheet. "Feel the bond. The embossed leaf. We should order a box."

Then her legs—her livelihood, her strength—trembled and weakened. She slid to the floor, the yards of crinoline and tulle of her gown billowing and burying her, providing a safe tent where she could have some privacy.

"She fainted!" Vita screamed in perfect pitch, well trained by her job as a (basic cable) soap actress. "Call an ambulance!"

"She's just crying," said Esther coolly.

"She's hysterical!" boomed Vita.

But Penny wasn't crying. She was laughing (hysterically) at the comedy of it all. The Bridal Barbie gown. Two hundred fancy white people waiting in the ballroom. The $75,000 of her mom's money gone to a wedding that wouldn't happen. It *was* funny, she thought. In a tragic, soul-annihilating kind of way.

Penny slowly gathered her wits and skirts. "As soon as my legs start working again, I'm going to get off the floor and sit on that couch," she said. "I'd like a cocktail. After that, I'm open to suggestions."

Chapter 2

"Penny, stay right where you are," said Esther. To Morris, she said, "You. Come with me."

Esther yanked Morris out of the charmless bridal prep room. Shutting the door behind her, she pulled the disheveled young man a few yards down the hallway so Penny couldn't overhear their conversation.

"Where is he?" she asked.

"I don't know," replied Morris.

Up to her diamond earrings with lividity, Esther would have liked to spit (but just couldn't). "You do his dirty work," she said, disgusted.

Morris said, "I'm just the messenger."

"Is your mother living?"

"My mother?" he asked.

"I'm going to call her, and tell her how you lowered yourself today," said Esther. Although Morris outweighed her by forty pounds (all of it male muscle), Esther matched his height. She bore into his blue eyes, as only a mother could, telegraphing the maternal manipulation trifecta: "Guilt . . . shame . . . disappointment . . . guilt . . . shame . . ."

"Stop," said Morris, blocking his eyes with his arm. "Okay, okay, he's in his room upstairs. I left him five minutes ago."

"Get out of my way," said Esther, maneuvering around the big lug in the narrow hallway.

"You're not really going to call my mother, are you?"

Esther left him to wonder. She plowed down the corridor, hurried past the open ballroom doors, and clicked across the marble lobby floor to the main elevator banks of New Jersey's swankiest hotel. An express car swished open and she punched the button for the twelfth floor. The wedding party had secured several suites there for the weekend.

Esther was alone in the elevator. In her short ride, a red rage rose in her body like mercury in a hot thermometer. She'd felt such intensity of anger only once before, the day her husband Russell Bracket announced he was leaving her for Penny's British au pair. Esther flashed back to that day, that minute, in the pong room of their mansion on Overlook Lane. Russell was expertly bouncing a hollow ball on a green paddle when he exclaimed, "I've fallen in love with Jemima!" like she should be happy for him about it.

Ping. The elevator doors opened. Esther strode toward the hotel's bridal suite. She knew the number, having sent a bottle of Dom Perignon there an hour ago. As she marched, her eyes flitted across door numbers and the pink toile wallpaper depicting scenes of bucolic life, children and their pets, apple trees. She was so focused, Esther didn't notice the large empty laundry cart in the hallway until she'd crashed into it.

She scanned the hallway for a hotel housekeeper. Seeing no one, she proceeded to Room 1212 and knocked on the door. Amazingly, it opened. The bastard hadn't yet fled. In fact, Bram Shiraz, twenty-five, stood right in front of Esther in the open doorway, guileless, in jeans, a black T-shirt, bare feet. She detected a ripple of disappointment in his eyes when he saw her. Had he hoped his visitor would be Penny? Did he really think her daughter would come up here to grovel?

Bram's expression quickly returned to his usual casual inscrutability, the placid blankness only handsome men could achieve. Esther knew that look well, from her former husband Russell. She'd been tricked by it, just as Penny had been suckered by Bram's mink hair, his round brown eyes and lanky build, foolishly believing this man was as sweet and soulful as he looked. Bram didn't deserve his physical gifts, thought Esther. He should be a hideous hunchback.

A half-packed suitcase was on the bed behind him.

Esther opened her mouth and a laryngeal squeak wobbled out.

Bram didn't wait for more. He returned to the bed and resumed packing as if she weren't hovering in the doorway, wishing him ugly. The gall of him! Each of his movements filled her with revulsion. At least now, with the wedding off, she wouldn't have to see him ever again. She should thank him for what he'd done.

Without look up from his toils, he said smugly, "You don't have to thank me."

As if he'd ended the wedding because she was opposed to it! As if he'd do anything selfless to save his life.

"You got what you wanted," said Bram. "Why are you here?"

Esther couldn't say why she'd felt compelled to storm up to his room. Honestly, she hadn't expected to find and confront him. She'd spent her entire adult life (early and enduring) avoiding tense situations. Now that she was in the vortex of one, she was at a loss.

Churning mentally for a tart and cutting reply, Esther's

eyes shifted left and landed on the room's dining table. An ice bucket with the champagne she'd ordered for the bride and groom was upon it.

Bram closed the suitcase. He sat on the bed next to it to slip on his socks and sneakers. "I know you blame me for Penny's injuries," he said. "They were accidents."

"How does someone accidentally dislocate her jaw?" she asked, finding words finally, plus the gumption to enter the room and close the door behind her. She moseyed toward the dining table, her slender fingers gripping the bottleneck. It was slippery with condensation, but she held tight.

He said, "I don't have to explain what happened. To *you*." He might as well have said "to *ewwww*."

Then he shrugged as if they were discussing the price of milk. That noncommittal rise and fall of his shoulders was, in her mind, as much of an admission as she could hope to get. Anger peaking, Esther went with it.

She made for the bed. Bram met her eyes and she saw the guilt inside. With the mighty force of middle-aged rage, Esther swung the bottle at his casually handsome head.

Chapter 3

With Vita's help, Penny crawled onto the damask couch in the blessedly private bridal chamber. Another knock on the door.

"It's Bram, come to tell me this is some kind of pre-wedding prank," said Penny. "He's got such an unusual sense of humor."

The erstwhile maiden of honor opened the door. Ms. Wistlestop pushed her way inside.

"Slight delay," said the wedding planner from inside her mist of perfume. "Everything's fine. Don't panic. We're waiting for the groom. And the best man, and . . . where's Mrs. Bracket? She should be here. We're five minutes behind schedule already."

Penny and Vita stared at the petite (yet plump) woman, a tempest in a teacup, with her strands of pearls, peach taffeta party dress, dyed-to-match satin pumps, nude hose, and whipped confection of a hairdo. Clearly, Esther, wherever she'd gone off to, had not yet informed Ms. Wistlestop of the change in plans.

"Girls!" snapped Mrs. Wistlestop. "Are you with me? We have an emergent situation."

"I though we weren't going to panic," said Penny. Over the last six months, she'd spent hours with Ms. Wistlestop sorting out the details. Napkin holders. Tablecloth tassels. Looking at the squat woman now, her face pinched, Penny marveled at the waste of time and distortion of perspective. How small things—petite Ms. Wistlestop and her checklists—had loomed large and formidable. But big things—her life—had been reduced to planning a five-hour event. Which was, as of six minutes ago, a nonstarter.

"We're not panicking!" said Ms. Wistlestop. "This is the best day in your life, what you've been dreaming about since you were a little girl in pigtails."

"If I did have girlish fantasies," said Penny, catching her ghostly reflection in the vanity mirror, "they sure didn't look like this." To Vita, she added, "Show her the note."

Vita handed Ms. Wistlestop what would be the last in their encyclopedia-high pile of wedding correspondences. The planner read Bram's decision wordlessly. She folded it neatly and handed it back to Vita.

Ms. Wistlestop reached into her pink purse and produced a walkie-talkie. Into it, she droned, "Attention wedding staff: We've got a Code Red situation here. I repeat: Code Red! Kitchen staff: Do *not* open the caviar." She released the talk button and fished in her purse for her PDA. "Give me a second to find the Jiltage Checklist," she said. "I need to speak to your mother about recoverable expenses."

"She's got to be around here somewhere," said Penny. "I wonder why I'm not freaking."

"Some jilted brides go numb," said Ms. Wistlespot. "Some go to the emergency room."

"What about the jilted grooms?" asked Penny.

"Never had one," said the planner. "Okay, here we are. First item on the list: inform guests. Most brides ask someone else to do it. They're too upset or embarrassed about being seen in the wedding gown if they're not getting married."

"It would have been embarrassing then, too," said Penny.

"Not a recoverable expense as far as the Plaza is concerned," said the planner, pointing at the gown. "I recommend trying to sell it on Ebay."

"I'll do it," said Penny.

"Just don't post a photo," suggested Vita.

"I meant I'll tell the guests," said Penny.

"I volunteer myself," said the planner. "I've done it dozens of times. I'm good. Very good."

Vita straightened her back and, with an earnest expression, said, "As maiden of honor, the responsibility falls on me. I'll show the appropriate pathos. I'll cry even." Seeing Penny's smirk, Vita said, "You can't blame me for trying."

Her friend was an opportunist actress, always searching for a signature role, the breakout part that would make her famous.

Penny said, "And now, appearing in the aisle, Vita Trivoli as 'The Runover Bride.' "

"I'll make you proud," said Vita.

Bram should do it, thought Penny.

"Is the food a recoverable expense?" she asked Ms. Wistlestop.

The planner frowned gravely. "Some of it," she said. Into her walkie-talkie she barked, "Attention kitchen staff: Do *not* shave the truffles."

"Well, let's get this over with," said Penny, hiking up the skirts.

"What are you going to say?" asked Vita, following her down the corridor toward the ballroom. "We should take two minutes and work out a script."

"I'll improvise," said Penny. "I'm still numb. I should feel . . . something. Something bad."

"And you think going out there in front of the guests will turn the switch? You'll willfully torture yourself to access the pain you're not yet experiencing? Hmmm," mulled Vita. "Not such a bad idea. An agony jolt. A cattle prod of degradation. It could work."

Cattle prod? Jolt? Penny didn't like the sound of that. "Maybe I should take a minute," she said, dragging her heels, literally.

"Too late," said Ms. Wistlestop.

The three women had reached the open ballroom door. Two hundred heads swiveled toward them. The guests sat in cushioned folding chairs that had been arranged in rows on either side of an aisle. The chairs were to have been rearranged around tables for dinner and dancing during the outdoor, poolside cocktail hour after the ceremony. At the end of each row of chairs stood a Hellenic vase with a spray of white roses. Connecting the vases, white satin ribbons and bows. Penny looked up the aisle at the rose-strewn altar. It seemed miles away.

"I'll come with you," said Vita.

Penny shook her head. "Get your car and wait for me out front. I'll say my thing, and then we'll make a break for my mom's house."

"Done," said Vita, who then dashed into the hotel lobby.

Penny said, "Give me a push."

Ms. Wistlestop nudged her with the force of a flea.

"Harder."

The planner proceeded to shove Penny with her shoulder like a linebacker. She stumbled four feet down the aisle. Immediately, the photographer and videographer pounced on her.

Penny frantically made the "cut" gesture and they backed off. She was fleetingly amused that her wedding album would consist of five shots of her slicing her throat with her index finger. She wondered if the photographer and videographer fees were recoverable.

Marching inelegantly up the aisle, she heard the murmurs increase in volume with each step. Her heart thudding heavily, she kept her eyes on the altar, and the rabbi who sat up there on a folding chair.

Once she reached the matrimonial center stage, Penny smiled at the confused rabbi and started to sweat. A trickle down her temple. A rivulet down her back. She drew a deep breath (that made her gag from the overwhelming rose scent) and smiled at her guests. She had appeared before audiences hundreds of times. She'd danced for thousands on Broadway, in some very skimpy chorus line costumes. But this performance (a veritable show stopper) was the first time she'd felt exposed.

The murmuring—which had grown beyond the level of politeness—stopped. Penny coughed into the (illegitimately) pregnant pause, wishing she'd let Vita do this.

She removed the microphone from its stand, held it up to her lips and said, "Hello, Cleveland!"

Silence. Not even crickets.

Penny cleared her throat, amplified. "I want to thank you all for coming," she said. "About five minutes ago, my fiancé, Bram Shiraz, had an epiphany. A bona fide 'Ah-ha!' moment. He realized that marriage is really about ownership. It's designed to treat the woman like a piece of property. Bram is far too enlightened to endorse an inherently sexist institution by participating in a wedding. Any wedding. In this case, his own. I'm Penny Bracket, the bride, for those of you who don't know me. But that's obvious. I'm the only one wearing a big, puffy white gown that weighs approximately five thousand pounds."

A wave of concerned murmurs rolled across the rows. "No, look, it's okay. Really," she assured them. "It's fine. I'm grateful that Bram made a political stand instead of just plain old ditching me. That would have been *harsh*. That might've made a lesser woman *upset*. She might want to throw something, or break something. Or tear something apart."

Rip. A few old ladies in the front gasped. Penny looked down. In the hand not holding the microphone, she was clutching a white ruffle. Unwittingly, she'd torn it from the bodice of her dress.

"Who likes lace?" she asked. "Anyone? And what about princess sleeves? Is there anyone breathing who genuinely admires Cinderella poof balls?" Penny grasped the top of her right sleeve and tore it off. She put the microphone back on the stand and tore off the left. She flung both into the crowd.

"What about pearl buttons? Anyone like these tiny, pain in the ass buttons?" She put both hands on either side of her sweetheart neckline and tugged, sending two dozen speeding pearl bullets into the crowd.

"How about satin bows?" *Rip*.

"And a tulle bustle?" *Strip*.

Penny yanked and tugged and pulled with the strength of ten jilted brides. She laughed and panted as she freed herself of her fluffy burden, the people in the ballroom forgotten, the rabbi forgotten. Bram *not* forgotten. In her mind, he lay in a bed somewhere, sleeping like an innocent babe while she wrestled this albino alligator of a dress to the ground. She had it by the throat, finally, and flogged it against the altar stage, pummeling the hell out of it until it was still, a dead lace thing.

Penny stumbled to her feet. Triumphant, she stared down at the corpse of a bridal gown. Beaming, she looked up, expecting applause for her victory.

Instead, she saw the (frankly) terrified faces of the old ladies in the front rows. And the leering grins of their doddering husbands.

She said, "Please sign the guest book at your leisure. The cocktail hour will start in a few minutes by the hotel pool, so help yourself to hors d'oeuvres."

She stepped off the altar. Wearing only her (something) blue bra and panty set, (something) new silver sandals, (something) old pearl choker, and (something) borrowed diamond bracelet, Penny strode back down the aisle and out of the ballroom.

Chapter 4

B ram was not dead, Esther realized with relief when she poked him in the ribs with her index finger. He was just unconscious. Knocked out cold. Esther liked him much better this way, sprawled and silent, his mouth hanging open like an inbred hillbilly.

She was astounded she'd acted spontaneously. One could say *violently*. She couldn't remember the last time—or any time—that she'd given in to impulse. She'd had dark thoughts, frequently, but until ten seconds ago she hadn't acted on them.

It felt good, she realized, to do what she wanted when it was bad.

But now she was in a spot. She squinted at Bram's motionless form and wondered, *What to do with you?* With a sudden blast of fear, she realized that other wedding guests—Bram's family, for instance—might come looking for the wayward groom, too.

Esther cracked the door. The hallway was empty, except (she had to squelch a peep of joy) for the large laundry cart she'd bumped into on her way in. She pulled the wheeled canvas cart into the room.

It was certainly big enough, she thought. First things first. She chucked Bram's suitcase into the cart (she couldn't very well leave it behind; people would wonder why he hadn't taken it with him). Then she wheeled the carrier flush against the bed, and rolled Bram's unconscious body into it on top of the suitcase. She stripped the bedspread and used it to cover him up.

Smoothing down her mussed hair and straightening her clothing, Esther checked the hallway again. All clear. She pushed the cart in front of her out of the room fairly easily. She glanced back and saw that the cart had left tracks in the plush carpeting. Quickly, she wiped them gone with her feet. She used the tip of the bedspread to wipe the door handle on both sides. Then she closed it.

Esther pushed her cargo toward the end of the corridor where she'd find the service elevator. She knew the hotel layout well. She'd inspected the premises thoroughly when choosing the venue, personally vetting every reserved suite for the wedding party and out-of-town guests.

She suspected the elevator had a security camera in the control panel. The only way she would avoid being taped was to wheel the cart into the elevator while she crawled in alongside it. The cart itself would block her. On tape, it would appear that the cart had been pushed into the elevator by someone who'd decided, for whatever reason, not to ride along with it.

Checking again for witnesses, Esther got on her hands and knees. Moving slowly (it took *forever*), she crawled and pulled the cart into the elevator.

Once inside, she realized she would still need to push the button to take her down to the hotel's subterranean parking lot. She was now on the far side of the cart, away from the doors and the panel. So she pushed the cart in a circle, crawling along the outside. On the tape, it would seem like the cart had spun, demonically, by itself. When she was directly beneath the control panel, she punched the button with the G on it.

If Esther had a crisis of consciousness about clocking Bram (not bloody likely), she would have been soothed by the Fates, who were clearly on her side: The elevator descended fourteen flights to the garage without stopping once.

When the doors opened, Esther crawled out of the elevator, then reached back inside to pull the cart out. Right over the elevator door, she spotted the one and only security camera. She easily unplugged it, and wheeled the cart at a good clip toward her red Volvo Cross Country wagon. Her heels echoed in the cavernous garage as she rolled along.

Though forty-five, Esther was tall (nearly six feet) and strong of spine and shin. She had an abundance of leisure time, and spent much of it at the Equilux Gym annexed to the famous Short Hares Mall. Antisocial by nature, she avoided the popular Pilates core strengthening classes, and stuck to the blissful solitude and monotony of cardio and free weight training. One wouldn't think by looking at lithe Esther in her sleek gray suit and diamond jewelry that she could bench-press 150 pounds. But she could.

While opening the wagon's hatch door, Esther estimated Bram's weight to be 170. Within her dead lift range. If she could put the lip of the cart against the rear bumper, she'd create a lever, make the job easier. She arranged the cart just so, and heaved from the bottom, tipping it and its contents into her wagon. The cart landed upside down, conveniently hiding Bram, the bedspread, and the suitcase underneath.

Esther hopped into the driver's seat and gunned it out of the garage. She took the first right onto the highway on two wheels. Worried about being pulled over, she slowed to a safe speed. She was only a few minutes from her mansion on Overlook Lane. With one hand on the wheel, she called the house on her cell.

"Bracket residence," answered Natasha Molotov, thirty-six, born and raised in communist Moscow, the family's longtime live-in house manager/babysitter.

"Thank God you're there," said Esther. "In two minutes I'm pulling up to the kitchen door."

"Why are you not at wedding?" asked Natasha.

"Why aren't *you* at the wedding?" said Esther.

"I couldn't watch," said Natasha.

"Listen closely: Bram called it off. He sent Penny a chicken-shit note. I found him in his hotel room and . . . overreacted a tiny bit."

"I see you coming."

The skid of tires on pavement. Esther tore up the driveway and slammed on the breaks at the top. Natasha was standing outside the kitchen door, the phone still pressed to her cheek, the cleavage-focal cocktail dress clinging to her robust curves.

Esther jerked the Volvo into park and jumped out of the driver's seat. She opened the hatch door and stood back. Natasha joined her boss at the rear of the car, teetering in her five-inch Candie's wedgies.

"We don't have enough laundry? You need to bring more home?" asked Natasha, seeing the canvas cart in the wagon.

Esther pulled the cart out. It landed upright in the driveway. Then she yanked away the bedspread, revealing Bram, an unconscious mound. Natasha poked at his leg with her long, lacquered fingernail. He didn't react. Which meant a lot. That fingernail was sharp.

"We should take him to the hospital, shouldn't we?" asked Esther.

"Why?" asked Natasha. "Is he sick?"

"Just knocked out."

Lazily, as if drugged, Bram's head rolled to the side, his eyelids flickering. He moaned.

Natasha screamed.

Esther did, too. The ladies in their formal outfits clutched each other. Their shrieks must have been too much for Bram's bashed brain. His eyes closed. He snored.

"Let's get him inside," said Esther.

The two women put the bedspread and his suitcase back into the cart, and then rolled Bram on top of them. He grunted when he landed. The Russian wasn't nearly as buff as Esther, so the older woman did most of the pushing as they maneuvered the cart into the kitchen.

Esther said, "Upstairs."

They wheeled through the mansion's eat-in kitchen and into the vast front foyer with a domed ceiling some forty feet high. A three-story entrance, as real estate agents called it, the foyer was an impressive sight, a huge "wow" factor for visitors (not that Esther had many). The prospect of hauling the laundry cart up all those stairs made her arms ache.

"You know the place I'm thinking?" she asked Natasha.

"How can we get him three flights up stairs?" asked the Russian.

"One step at a time," said Esther.

And so they did. The two women, in their heels, pulled the cart up, the wheels bouncing and crashing over each hump.

"Thank God for adrenaline," said Esther, the panic fuel giving her a boost as they reached the second floor landing.

Groggily, Bram said, "Wassahmm."

The women, surprised by the unexpected sound, let go. The cart bounced down the stairs, Bram rattling like a toy inside. It wheeled across the foyer floor and crashed against the mansion's front door.

"Shit!" yelled Natasha. "My shoe broke."

Indeed, one of her wedgies had lost its cork.

They retrieved the cart and started again, pulling the cart upstairs, Natasha (one bare foot) pulling, Esther pushing.

Midway up the second flight, Bram Shiraz appeared to be regaining consciousness.

"Last step," wheezed Natasha as they dragged the cart onto the top floor's dark and dusty landing.

Inside his cradle, Bram groped at the sides of the cart, trying feebly to lift himself out of it. Eyes slowly sharpening, he looked at Esther and slurred, "I knew you'd try to kill me! You're a man-hating, ball-breaking bitch."

"Here," said Natasha, removing her other shoe.

Esther said, "Thank you," and slammed the wedge onto Bram's noggin.

With a clunk, Bram collapsed into the cart, once again asleep.

"It *does* get easier each time," said Esther.

"Which door?" asked Natasha.

"Third on the left. It's locked, though. We'll have to find a key."

"I have master key in kitchen," said Natasha, who padded back down to get it.

Left alone with her unconscious once-and-never son-in-law, Esther leaned her hip on the laundry cart, remembering the last time she'd been in the playroom, the one part of the house she planned to demolish after Russell left. She never got around to it, though, due to the all-consuming events that followed his departure. Only now, she was grateful for her inaction. The playroom was the perfect place to stow Bram until . . . until she figured out what to do with him.

Esther studied the young man's face, and couldn't help admiring his thick, curled, dark lashes. Not only was he good-looking, Bram came from a wealthy New York City family. He was well-educated, had good manners, an impressive job. But none of that mattered. Esther knew what he really was, the beast that lived under his unblemished skin. She'd been suspicious since the day she was introduced to him. When Penny had her first "accident," Esther's suspicion turned to certainty.

Natasha—who'd always distrusted Bram, too; then again, she distrusted everyone—returned, breathing labored, with the master key. Esther slipped it into the dead bolt and released the lock. She pushed the door in and, recoiling from the stuffy pungence of disuse, turned on the lights.

"Roll him in," she said.

Natasha pushed the cart into the middle of the playroom.

"Check the toilet and sink," said Esther, pointing toward the windowless bathroom in the rear. While she shoved Bram to the side to access his suitcase, Esther heard a sputter and then running water, a flush and gurgle.

"It works," said Natasha.

"Help me get the suitcase," said Esther.

They hauled the luggage out of the cart. Esther carried it out of the playroom. She turned the light off and locked the door from the outside. "I have to go back to the hotel," she said. "I'll explain everything in detail later. Don't let him out. Penny can't know about this."

While she spoke, Esther unlocked the next door over and shoved the suitcase inside. Natasha said, "He deserves this?"

"You have to ask?"

Esther jogged down the stairs, dashed through the foyer and kitchen, out the door and into the Volvo. She checked her watch. Only twenty minutes had passed since she hit Bram over the head.

Her story would be that she'd gone searching for him and

had roamed all over the hotel. She'd even gotten in her car to circle the environs.

Esther steered the car out of the driveway and toward the Short Hares Plaza. Along the way, she replayed the events of the last half hour.

At the first traffic light she slammed on the brakes.

"Oh, no," she said to herself. "The bottle!"

Chapter 5

As Penny slipped into the passenger seat of Vita's lime green VW bug, her friend whistled at her blue bra and panty set.

"So," she asked, "how'd it go?"

"Very well," said Penny. "A bit drafty in there."

"Nudity," said the soap actress, nodding. "See, I would have tried to win over the audience with *empathy*. But I guess giving them cheap thrills work, too."

"Nothing cheap about this wedding," said Penny.

"One day you'll look back on this and it will all seem funny."

"Just drive."

The women cruised away from the Plaza. Penny busied herself by trying to access sadness. But all she felt at the moment was the lingering exertion of her melee at the altar, and ambivalent modesty when drivers in other cars noticed that she was in her underthings.

"Did you see the look on your mom's face when she read Bram's note?" asked Vita.

Penny said, "Don't remind me."

"I'd never seen a chink in her 'Lady of Short Hares' armor before. It was scary, like she's got this seething violence just underneath the placid Chanel surface. Makes you think about . . . you know."

"Can we stick to one Bracket family disaster at a time?" asked Penny. The VW was stuffy. She opened her window. The early evening blew across her exposed shoulders, and she felt the slightest chill. Not from the June air, though. The trace of frost ran deep in Penny, down to her bones. It got colder the closer they got to the mansion on Overlook Lane. Home. She closed her eyes.

"Whoa!" yelled Vita, the VW swerving sharply to the right.

"What?" asked Penny, lids jerking open.

"Some idiot just ran a stop sign and almost hit me!"

"That's New Jersey for you," said Penny cynically. "Highest car insurance rates in the country for a reason."

Vita pulled into the mansion's circular driveway. As they came to a stop, the car listed slightly. The driveway wasn't level. The tilt felt like home.

Natasha Molotov opened the mansion's front doors, looking anxious and suspicious—her default facial settings. Realizing the VW contained Penny and Vita, Natasha rushed down the mansion's steps in her bare feet, then onto the driveway, jumping like a cat when she hit hot pavement, and finally hopping back onto the bottom step where she waited for Penny with lush, open arms. In fifteen years of living with (or coming home to) Natasha, Penny hadn't seen her without obscenely high heels.

"You're a lot shorter than I realized," said Penny, who was five-ten herself.

"Come to Natasha," said the former Soviet comrade.

The warmth of her embrace hit Penny squarely in the soft

spot. Tears gathered, finally. She wondered if anyone else in the world could make her cry like Natasha.

"Oh, great," said Penny. "A hug from you and I start crying."

"Next time, I slap you instead."

"What's with the bare feet?"

The Russian's back muscles tensed. "What's with underwear?"

Penny broke the hug and glanced down at her body. "Since the wedding was cancelled, I decided to do a striptease for the guests instead. Some of them came all the way from Canada. They deserved a show."

"Tell me, from beginning of story to now," said Natasha. "Are you hungry? You can eat and talk."

The mention of food made Penny's stomach cartwheel. "No, thanks," she said, squeezing her abs.

"I could eat," said Vita, who despite being mini, could chow a Sumo wrestler under the table.

Natasha ignored her. "If you won't have snack, you should take soak. In your mother's tub."

Calling Esther's twelve-jet, temperature-controlled, marble-rimmed, two-seater Jacuzzi a "tub" was like saying Barney's was a "store."

"Brilliant," said Penny, already feeling the jets. "With the Parisian bath salts?"

"I won't tell your mother."

Penny allowed Natasha to guide her into the mansion, relieved to relinquish control of her movements to someone else. "What did Mom say?" she asked.

"I haven't heard from her. Or seen her," said Natasha with unnecessary vehemence.

"So how did you know the wedding was off?" asked Penny. "And why weren't you there?"

"I was coming when your mother called," said Natasha.

"You just said she didn't call."

"I forgot," said Natasha. "Very short conversation. Two seconds. She said, 'The wedding is off. Stay home. Goodbye.' So short, it doesn't count as real phone call."

Upon entering the house, Vita veered right, toward the mansion's state-of-the-art chef's kitchen with two Sub-Zero refrigerators, six-burner Viking stove, Italian tile, copper cookware, and a dishwasher that not only cleaned, sterilized, dried, and buffed your plates and glasses, it played music. Natasha always said, "For what dishwasher cost, it should have sex with you, too."

Penny and Natasha took the stairs up one flight. The mansion's second floor had seven rooms: Esther's master bed and bath suite (including a walk-in closet big enough to drive-in); Penny's room with a smaller bath, Natasha's bedroom (also with private toilet); Esther's office cum sewing room (where she'd never sewed a stitch, but had a collection of ten antique machines, one dating back to the nineteenth century); a library that Esther had converted into a display room for her five dozen original Queen Anne armchairs, a music room (where Penny took piano lessons for six years, despite not being able to play a note; also where Esther housed her collection of antique violins, despite the fact that she couldn't hold a bow); and last, what Penny grew up thinking of as the genie room, where Esther displayed—on the floor, walls, and ceiling—her two dozen turn-of-the-century Iranian medallion-patterned, hand-stitched silk and wool oriental rugs.

"Isn't this yours?" asked Penny, finding pieces of a broken wedgie on the stairs.

"How'd that get there?" asked Natasha, seemingly perplexed. The Russian took the shoe parts and put them under her arm.

"Nice dress, by the way," said Penny. "Sorry about that split."

"What split?" asked Natasha.

"The seam. On the side, there."

"Motherfucker shit!" said Natasha, examining the tear. She then launched into a Cyrillic screed that ended with (in English), "She'll pay for this."

"Who?"

"No one," said Natasha. "Dry cleaner."

"Isn't it brand new?"

"I dry clean before I wear."

"I must be going crazy," said Penny as they rounded the railing and went left, toward the master suite. "I swear I can smell Bram's cologne."

Natasha said, "I smell nothing."

"It's obvious," insisted Penny, sniffing. "He used way too much of it."

"There is no smell," insisted Natasha as she tugged Penny down the hall and into Esther's airplane-hangar-like bedroom, passed the king-size bed, the double closet doors, the ample sitting area, the pillow-piled lounges, the beveled mirrored bureaus and mahogany dressers, and into the bathroom where she turned on the Jacuzzi faucets, all three of them, full-blast. Natasha spooned in jasmine salts, and the room filled with scented steam.

Penny removed her bra and panties and slid into the rising foamy water. Natasha flicked a switch on the Jacuzzi's console to dim the lights. She flicked another switch and her mom's *Midnight in the Rain Forest* CD started playing. The soft plop of droplets on treetops, the caw of a toucan, the peeping lemurs.

As the tub filled, Penny let herself slide off the bench seat to submerge. She pulled the pins out of her dark hair and shook it loose, the water washing away the stiff hair spray and gel.

She scrubbed her face clean of the wedding war paint. Her lungs starting to compress, she surfaced to breathe.

"Hey," said Vita, on the edge of the tub.

Penny, startled, instinctively cupped her breasts.

"Like I haven't seen those before," said Vita. "Like I'd ever forget what they look like. How many skinny dancers have big, round porn star jugs like yours?"

Vita's jugs were also big and round, surgically so. On her Girl Entertainment Television (the GET channel) soap, *The House of Blusher*, Vita's character, Cherry Bomb, decided to get herself implants to ensnare her love interest, a podiatrist with a fetish for softball-size boobs. Vita was informed by her director that she could either stuff her bra (and thereby restrict Cherry's usual smutty, titty wardrobe), or get her own implants, which the show's producer (who Vita was humping at the time) agreed to pay for. Cherry's popularity grew along with her cup size. Vita decided to get a new boyfriend to go with her big bumps. She proceeded to dump her producer for the actor playing the doctor fetishist, only to be dumped in turn when he realized he (the actor, not the podiatrist) was actually an ass man. A *man's* ass man.

Penny reached for the basket of shampoos, conditioners and finishing rinses on the Jacuzzi shelf. "I might be losing it," she said.

"Might be?" asked Vita, and bit into the sandwich she'd brought up with her.

"I can feel Bram's presence. Palpably. Like he's nearby."

"Lingering shock."

"A few weeks ago I had a nightmare about him bolting," said Penny. "Every bride probably has that dream at least once along the way. Don't you think?"

"Definitely," said Vita. "I'd never stop dreaming about it. Except I'd be the one bolting."

"I still can't believe it."

"While you process," said Vita "let's talk Morris Nova. I'd do him."

"I'm sure you could," said Penny. "But don't you get tired—of *doing*?"

Vita chewed on that (along with her sandwich). "But *doing* is what I . . . do."

"Haven't you done enough?"

"I'm twenty-three years old!" said Vita. "I've only just begun. And I'd like to point out, again, the irony: that I grew up in a home with sickeningly, blissfully happy parents, and I have no interest in getting married. Whereas you've been on a husband hunt since college, and your parents weren't exactly—"

"My parents *were* happy," protested Penny. "For five minutes."

"You should tell your mother the truth," said Vita. "About your injuries."

"Can you imagine that conversation?" Penny snorted at the very notion. "I won't have to now. It's not like Bram will ever step foot in this house again."

"If he did, your mother would slice his dick off."

"She'll need a big knife," said Penny.

"Where is she anyway?" asked Vita. "One would think the jilted bride's mother would cleave to her daughter's side at her time of greatest need."

"My mom doesn't cleave," said Penny. "She must still be at the hotel dealing with Wistlestop. I'll call her cell." She reached for the tubside phone. Hitting the Talk button, putting the unit to her ear, Penny heard that the line was already engaged.

"—can smell him," she heard Natasha say.

"He does *reek*," said her mom. "And I'll pay for your dress. Just relax, okay? Relax! Just calm the fuck down!"

"Do I feed him?" asked Natasha.

"Throw scraps of garbage at him," said Esther.

"Hello?" Penny interjected. "Mom? Is that you?"

"Penny?" asked her mother after gulping.

"Throw scraps at who?"

Natasha said quickly, "A stray dog at the kitchen door. Esther wants to feed it so he won't starve to death on the property and be picked apart by horrible vultures."

"Imagine the awfulness of *that*," said Esther. A real threat: Essex County, due to the explosive deer population, was overrun with turkey vultures.

"You're arguing about a stray dog on my botched wedding day," said Penny.

Natasha said, "I hang up." *Click.*

Down to two on the line. "Mom? Where are you?" asked Penny.

"Still at the hotel. I've got some loose ends." With her rarely issued soft voice, Esther added, "Look, even though I had my doubts about Bram, I'm terribly sorry you have to go through this. And I'm sorry I'm not home with you now. I'll get there as soon as possible."

Penny's eyes welled again. Was there any substitute for mother love? she wondered. At any age? However stilted? She remembered reading once that a woman without a mother or a daughter was alone in the world.

"Hurry," she said.

Chapter 6

Esther snapped her cell shut. "Whew," she said to herself out loud.

The near miss on the phone did force the issue. She'd kidnapped her daughter's fiancé, and Penny probably wouldn't approve. In the three seconds between deciding to bash him and actually doing it, Esther hadn't thought through the aftermath. She nabbed him. Now what would she do with him?

And how would she make sure no one—especially Penny—found out? She'd have to get Penny out of the mansion. Encourage her to go back to her apartment in the city. But first on the agenda: bottle retrieval. Her prints on the Dom were the only proof she'd been in Bram's hotel room. She knew that glass was the optimal surface for collecting fingertip oils (Esther was vaguely repulsed that she *had* fingertip oils, let alone left a drizzle of them wherever she went). Plus, bits of skin, hair, and blood (yuck) might also be found on the bottle. If so, Bram's disappearance wouldn't be written off as the flight of a wayward bridegroom.

She was back at the Plaza, having left her car with the valet, and keeping her head low to avoid any of her aimlessly milling wedding guests. She'd screened two calls from Ms. Wistlestop in the last few minutes. Esther would take care of that business in good time, immediately after she'd covered up her crime.

"First things first," she sang to herself as the elevator lifted her to twelve.

Striding down the hallway, she searched her clutch for Penny's room key card. Her daughter gave her the plastic rectangle to hold until after the reception since pockets were the one thing Penny's voluminous gown lacked. Esther slipped the card into the slot. The green light signaled the lock was disengaged. She turned the knob and started to push . . . but the door swung open, pulled fast and hard from the inside, propelling Esther into the room, where she stumbled on the lip of the too thick carpeting and crashed, arms flailing, into a human body. A male body, tall, barrel-chested, in a black tux. Her nose against the knot of his bow tie, she couldn't see his face.

He said, "Esther Bracket?"

She dared to look. "Keith Shiraz," she said. "Hello."

Bram's widowed father. The big man from New York who'd paid for the floor of suites at the hotel. She met him for the first time last night at the rehearsal dinner, but they'd hardly spoken. He'd introduced himself and said, "When my son first told me he was engaged to a girl from New Jersey, I had only one question for him."

"What might that be?" Esther gamely asked.

He grinned. "What exit?"

After just those two words, Esther reached her limit of Keith Shiraz, but had only begun to swallow martinis. When the time came, she claimed to be too emotional to toast the bride and groom. Keith, however, wasn't one to pass on ceremony. He stood up, wiped the corners of his eyes and said he'd always dreamed his son would share his life with a good woman, just as he'd shared his with Bram's beloved departed mother, Alice, God rest her soul.

When Keith evoked God, Esther felt compelled to pray. *Oh, Lord,* she asked silently. *If you are merciful, send me another martini.*

Now, a day later, in the bridal suite doorway, a dry-eyed Keith Shiraz, asked, "What are you doing here?"

She replied sharply, "Looking for your son."

"Me, too," said Keith. "How'd you get a room key?" He pointed at her hand, the card between her fingers.

"My daughter gave it to me," she said.

"He's not here," said Keith.

"May I come in?" she asked.

He stepped aside, and Esther entered the bridal suite. She quickly scanned the room for the bottle, which, she imagined, was covered in blood with clinging clumps of scalp and hair.

Her eyes swept the floor. The bed, the table, the dresser. She tried to recall what she'd done with the bottle when she pulled Bram's dead (yet alive) weight into the laundry cart. Her memory was blurry. She felt a flutter of panic in her stomach.

And then she caught the wink of green glass underneath the night table to the right of the bed. Her fingers itched to bend down, snatch the Dom, and get the hell out of the hotel. Esther felt Keith's eyes on her back, though. She forced herself to smile at him placidly.

She said, "Bram clearly left the hotel. You should go search for him—out there." She cocked her head toward the window.

"I want to apologize on Bram's behalf," he said. "As soon as I find him, I'll make sure he apologizes to you and Penny himself. This is a disaster. My parents flew up from Florida. They're in their eighties, in poor health. This is probably the last trip they'll ever make, and they wanted it to be full of love and joy. They're devastated."

"You should go to them," said Esther, her gray eyes shining with sympathy. One of them, anyway. The other was locked on the green bottle.

But he didn't. Keith plopped down on the bed and put his head in his hands. When he sat, he inadvertently nudged the bottle with the toe of his shoe. It rolled a few inches, clunking against the leg of the night table. The neck was sticking out, plainly visible. If Keith looked down, he'd see it.

Esther scurried to sit next to Keith on the bed, trying to kick the bottle out of sight. She said, "There, there," awkwardly patting him on the shoulder, which she couldn't help notice was thickly muscled under his tux jacket.

He said, "I thought you'd be angry."

"Oh, well, you know, anger doesn't help," she espoused, eyes glued on the still visible cork. If only she could just grab it and get out. She glanced at Keith. He was rubbing his eyes now. Esther reached forward with her hand.

Which Keith promptly seized, holding on with both of his. "Thank you, Esther," he said. "For being so kind." He kissed the back of her hand as if she were Queen of the Realm. The unexpected contact sent an electric charge from her knuckles to her toes.

Speechless, Esther froze.

He let go of her hand, which, in her petrified condition, remained aloft. Keith crinkled his brow and said, "I just don't understand it. Any of it."

She said, "I'm sure, in time, we'll come to under—"

"For instance, where's the bedspread?" he asked.

"The b—"

"And why is that champagne bottle on the floor?"

"I didn't notice any bottle," she said.

"You just kicked it," he said. "You've been staring at it."

"Ohhhhh," she chirped. "You mean *that* champagne bottle."

Esther bent down and picked it up. Her back to Keith, she quickly inspected the glass, relieved to see that it was clean of hair, scalp, and blood. She held it up triumphantly, running her hands up and down the length of it, smearing old fingerprints and making new, explicable ones.

Her mission accomplished, she stood up, replaced the bottle in the ice bucket, and said, "That goes there. Good. So then"—she clapped her hands—"I'll let you get back to your sick, elderly parents . . ."

"What about the missing bedspread?" Keith asked.

"Why does this bother you? Do you suspect"—mocking laughter—"foul play?"

"It's just strange," he said. "Unexplained. Makes me wonder."

"Maybe Bram spilled a drink on it and the maid took it away."

"Possible," he said, getting up and walking toward her, which sent that electric current zinging along her spine.

"You should call housekeeping," she said.

"What about this?" he asked, lifting the bottle out of the bucket. "Dom Perignon on the floor? Makes no sense."

"Perhaps someone tried to steal it, but was interrupted, dropped the bottle and ran?"

"How would a thief get in here? There are only two key cards. You've got one, and Bram gave me the other."

"You didn't give it to anyone to hold? Does your date carry a purse?"

"I'm not with a date," he stated.

So the broad-shouldered, knuckle-kissing widower didn't have a girlfriend. Esther tried to remember when his wife died. Penny must have told her. A couple of years ago? The death had been grisly, prolonged—cancer or some other horrible disease. Her own husband, Russell, had died swiftly, in one fell swoop, one could say. Which was better for everyone.

"I'm going to give the bedspread and bottle mysteries some serious thought," she said. "And I'll get back to you with any bright ideas."

"I think something went on here," insisted Keith.

"Something did," said Esther, losing her patience with his suspicions (even though they were right on the money). "Your son destroyed my daughter's wedding day. He acted like a coward. He probably stole that bedspread when he sneaked out of here like a criminal. Like a thief in the night."

"Oh, God, Esther," moaned Keith, shaking his head, which sat atop a nicely muscled neck. "Bram messed up today. Badly. But you can understand why I'm worried about him. He's my only son."

A father's love. A luxury Bram surely took for granted, thought Esther. Penny never got to experience the protective, unconditional love of her father. If she had, maybe Penny would have made a better choice in a fiancé. Perhaps, if she herself hadn't had such a nasty piece of work for a father, she wouldn't have chosen to marry Russell. Bad fathers and bad choices all around.

Keith, on the other hand, seemed genuinely concerned for his son. He would have been a wonderful father figure for Penny, Esther thought with sudden, savage sadness.

"I'm sure Bram is safe," said Esther. "Wherever he is."

"It's just bizarre that he's gone," said Keith, his enormous gray eyes—much like her own—pleading for another hit of reassurance.

"I bet you'll hear from him by tomorrow," said Esther.

Chapter 7

Clean and clear-headed, Penny drained the tub and rummaged in her own bedroom for wearable clothes. Her closet was full of high school stuff. She grabbed an old pair of (by today's standards, ridiculously high-waisted) Levi's and a bright orange tank. The jeans, much to her relief, fit well. The tangerine T-shirt brought out the rust in her long chestnut hair. The old, worn cotton made her feel cozy and safe. She was glad to be home.

"Amazing what a hot bath can do to shift one's perspective," she said to Vita.

"Over Bram already?"

"And it's not even seven o'clock."

Vita decided to change out of her magenta creation, and put on a pair of purple track pants and an old blue T-shirt that read, NOT AS EXPENSIVE AS I LOOK.

"I can't believe this fits you," said Vita, tugging on the T's tiny neck hole. "It should say, 'Not as Expansive as I Look.'"

"I haven't worn that since seventh grade," said Penny. "And even then it was tight."

"Your mom's a keeper?"

"I should show you the basement archives. Drawings from kindergarten. Spelling quizzes from second grade."

"Where did you go to school?" asked Vita.

"The Short Hares Institute of Technology. Private, of course." Rummaging in her dresser, she said, "Here's an old school T."

Penny held up the shirt with her alma mater's insignia.

Vita said, "S.H.I.T.?"

"It was a crappy school," said Penny.

The two women, comfortably dressed, headed downstairs to the kitchen. Despite the mansion's twenty-odd comfortable rooms, everyone always seemed to end up on stools around the kitchen counter. On the second floor landing, Penny sniffed the air carefully, detecting lingering traces of Bram.

"Do you smell that?" she asked Vita.

Her friend crinkled her dainty nostrils. "Mustard?"

In the kitchen, on the first floor, Natasha was waiting for them with a knife. She was fixing sandwiches—sourdough toast with Dijon mustard, prosciutto, and provolone.

"Your favorite," said Natasha.

"This is heaven, thanks," said Penny, taking a bite. "Did you feed the dog?"

"What dog?"

"The stray. The one you told Mom about."

"Oh, *that* dog," said Natasha. "I threw it hard-boiled egg."

"It'll be back," warned Vita. "Feed a dog and make a friend for life."

Bong. Door bell. Penny shook her head knowingly and said to Vita, "Amy and Nicole, has to be. I bet they've come trolling for the gory details of my humiliation."

"What're friends for?" asked Vita.

Padding through the kitchen and into the three-story entryway, Penny opened the mansion's twelve-panel front door, fully expecting to be surrounded by ten friends offering sympathy and promises to murderlize the bastard.

Instead, she found a tiny teapot of a woman.

"Ms. Wistlestop!" exclaimed Penny. Two white vans were parked in the driveway behind the planner.

"Penny, hello," said Ms. Wistlestop. "Sorry to come by unannounced. I tried to reach your mother on her cell half a dozen times."

"She's at the Plaza."

"I didn't see her," said Ms. Wistlestop. "And I couldn't wait. I took it upon myself to salvage what I could and bring it to you immediately. Everything else has been sent to local charities and shelters."

"Salvage what?" asked Penny. Her romantic life? Her dreams of a happy future?

"Nonrecoverables. The food. Flowers. The ice sculpture," she said. "Plus, there's a vanload full of wedding gifts."

Penny blinked. "We didn't order an ice sculpture."

"It's a surprise gift from the father of the groom."

Three men jumped out of the back of the van and struggled to unload the two-foot-high, three-foot-wide, bulky, slippery sculpture.

The ice had been cut into two interlocking hearts. Like the Olympic rings. But only two. And heart-shaped. Had the wedding gone the other way, Penny knew she would have adored the gift. The simple message of love, of conjoined lives and passions. She smiled, imagining Keith unveiling the sculpture with a flourish. The oohs and ahhs. She and Bram embracing Keith, kissing each other. How the ice hearts would have warmed the real ones beating in their chests.

One of the men asked, "Where do you want it?"

Penny said, "Just drop it over my head, thanks."

Ms. Wistlestop scrolled through her BlackBerry. "As for

the food, we are delivering eighty servings of prime rib, seventy servings of grilled salmon, fifty roast half chickens, thirty pounds of shrimp cocktail—"

"Let me see," said Natasha, emerging from the kitchen to handle this, to Penny's eternal gratitude. The Russian took control, perusing the list of items, calculating in her head where they would go. "We have large storage freezer in basement. And upstairs refrigerators can take some. Have men drive around to kitchen door."

But the men were busy unloading the next bombshell. The wedding cake stood three tiers high on a rolling cart. The frosting—white chocolate—was iced to resemble three woven baskets, stacked on top of each other, each strewn with purple, pink, and blue flowers with green twisting sugar-spun vines.

Penny said, "I can polish that off by midnight."

Vita, who'd just arrived from the kitchen, said, "I call the bottom tier."

Natasha tsked and said, "I take the cake."

"How true," declared Penny. "And I know the perfect spot for the ice sculpture. If you'll follow me."

The three men turned the cake trolley over to Natasha. They grunted obscenely to lift the ice sculpture onto a dolly. Then they pushed it along as Penny led them through the marbled entrance, past the pong room with its three tables for round robin tournaments, the solarium with its garden views, the formal dining room that sat twenty, the living room Penny hadn't spent ten minutes in, the home gym that her mom rarely used since she had a trainer at Equilux, and the show room—a long galley that contained Esther's collection of Colonial folk art chess and checker sets.

At a set of French doors that opened onto a patio, Penny directed the men to follow her. She walked down the bluestone path, among the immaculate gardens that, at this time of year, were bursting with peonies and azaleas, to the right of the all-weather cabana, and down a short set of flagstone steps to the kidney-shaped swimming pool.

Penny said, "Right here, fellas." She stood at the pool's edge.

The men placed the slippery love links next to her, and promptly left her alone with it. Penny ran her hands along the frozen curves and swells, her palms tingling with cold wet. She closed her eyes and let her fingers glide over the surface of the ice, thought of Bram's sculpted body, the thousands of times they'd had sex in the two years they'd been together. She'd done all she could to please him. He'd had countless orgasms—huge, spattering, hit the dartboard across the room eruptions. She'd made him gasp and clutch at the sheets like he'd die if she stopped—or kept going. Yet despite ample evidence to the contrary, she had never been able to shake the feeling that he wasn't satisfied.

Penny kissed the hearts, both of them, her lips sliding on the surface. Then she pushed the sculpture into the pool. She thought it would bob and crackle, like an ice cube in a glass. But the hearts plunged straight to the bottom.

Chapter 8

*S*plash.

Bram Shiraz jolted awake. He'd been dreaming about falling off a cliff into a river. But no, he realized with relief, he wasn't drowning.

His head, however, churned like a tide pool. Groping along his skull for the tender spot, his fingers located a bump the size of an egg. Vision fuzzy, he blinked at the white canvas walls close around him. He tried to move, but a bedspread was tangled around his legs. In the struggle to free himself, the cart tipped over, spilling him onto a carpeted floor.

Bram looked around and tried to figure out where he was. The room was dim. The only light filtered through a rectangular skylight on the ceiling. A beam shone through it, right over the cart, like a spotlight. He stood too quickly, not realizing that a sudden change in altitude would throw him off balance. Falling, he landed with a thud next to the cart, rolled onto his back and lay flat in the middle of the room.

The last thing he remembered was packing his suitcase in the bridal suite at the hotel.

Was it still his wedding day? Penny's face popped into this foggy consciousness, the red lips and dimples he'd loved to trace with his tongue. The brown hair that tickled his chest when she straddled him in bed. Her wide dark eyes always alert, gauging his reactions, scrutinizing him, constantly taking measure.

Groaning, Bram rolled onto his stomach and pulled himself up on all fours. When he was in ninth grade, he'd been walloped with a line drive in the forehead. He'd felt that same wooziness then. He knew he'd been hit, but he wasn't sure with what, or by whom. Nor did he have a clue where he was.

Despite those significant unknowns, Bram was aware of who he was—and what he'd done earlier today (yesterday? last week?). He staggered under the crushing weight of guilt, that pain worse than the havoc in his head. Bracing for a dizzy spell, he pushed himself to his feet. He walked to the nearest wall. He flicked on the light switch.

He could see, although the brightness hurt. The room was square and windowless (except for the aforementioned skylight), the ceiling at least fourteen feet high. The floor was carpeted. Like the walls, the carpet was a peaceful shade of lavender. Waist-high bookshelves were lined up against two walls. They were full of toys, picture books, and old video clamshell boxes. He bent down to read the titles (his brain sloshing inside his skull): *Cinderella*, *Snow White*, *The Little Mermaid*. On one wall, a hanging corkboard was covered with Magic Marker drawings. Princesses, unicorns, cats, dogs, witches, castles. A thirty-two-inch TV sat on a black metal stand (no cable or antenna). Underneath it, a VCR. A pink velour-covered couch, kid size, was positioned in front of the TV. Other furniture: a little table, white, with two white chairs tucked neatly underneath. An old-fashioned school desk. Bram lifted the top and found a hundred or so broken and half-chewed crayons, a bottle of Elmer's stuck in a hard white blob of dried glue, a pad of colored construction paper.

He closed the desk, frowning. He looked up and was startled by his own reflection in an oversized horizontal rectangular mirror that dominated the room's northern wall.

"I look like shit," he said to himself.

He guessed, based on what he was wearing—the same jeans and T-shirt he wore while packing—that he hadn't lost much time. His hair was disheveled, but clean. He seemed generally intact and unmolested, except for the contusion on his head. Walking up to the mirror, he parted his hair to examine the bump. He thought he could see it throb and pulse, as if the egg were about to hatch.

Flinching with disgust (flashing to the scene in *Alien*), he turned his back on the mirror. From that spot, he noticed that the room had two doors. One was slightly open. He investigated and found a small bathroom with a narrow stall shower, a low toilet and small sink.

Bram checked the other door. Bolted shut. He used his considerable strength to try to force it open. No good. Slamming his shoulder against it agonized his reeling head.

Taking a seat on the kiddie couch, his long legs sprawled in front, Bram decided to rest. The surrealism of the situation made him doubt, briefly, that he was actually awake—or fully conscious. He could be having a stress- and guilt-induced hallucinatory episode. He closed his eyes and drifted.

Clunk. The unmistakable metal-on-metal sound of a dead bolt unlocking. Bram tried to scramble to his feet but stumbled and fell. From the floor, he watched the door open. A tray of food was pushed on the carpeting into the room. He crawled toward the door, arm outstretched to catch it before it closed.

But the door slammed shut. With a metallic click, the dead bolt slid home.

Forcing himself to his feet, Bram banged on the door. "Let me out of here!" he yelled. "What the fuck is going on?"

Getting no response, he stopped. The pounding and yelling hurt his head.

His sneaker grazed the tray on the floor. Looking down, he saw a plate of prime rib with sauce au jus, wild rice, and steamed broccoli drizzled with Hollandaise. A second plate contained grilled salmon, a ramekin of dill sauce, couscous with raisins and pine nuts, plus a ragout of zucchini and yellow squash. Yet another dish had half a garlic-and-rosemary roast chicken, potato au gratin, and a marinated artichoke heart.

He recognized the menu and laughed at just how demented this dream was.

"What's so funny?"

The question came through speakers, there, bolted high on the mirrored wall. He thought it was an older woman speaking, but the voice was too scratchy and distorted to be sure.

"Who are you?" he asked.

The low hum of the speakers fell flat.

He walked up to the mirror and peered into it. Was it a two-way? He couldn't see anything in the glass but this own bloodshot eyes, but he knew he was being watched. He could feel it.

This is not a dream, he realized. He was now willing to accept this bizarre reality: For reasons that, at present, remained unclear, he'd been kidnapped and locked up in a little girl's playroom. Was he to be a sex slave? A medical test subject? Ransom bait?

Whoever had done this, he or she didn't intend to starve him. "That's one good thing," Bram said to himself. First, he would build up his strength—physically and mentally. Then he'd devise and execute an escape. Once he fought his way free, he'd take revenge on his captor(s).

In a twisted way, he was glad for this unexpected turn of events. Planning his flight would focus his thoughts, occupy his mind. Otherwise, he'd be alone with his guilt and regret, thinking about Penny and what he'd done to her.

Bram lifted the tray and put it on the tiny table. He sat on one of the chairs (having to position his knees on either side of the table) and fortified himself.

Chapter 9

Natasha and Esther watched Bram in the playroom. They were seated at the console in the aptly named control room next door. The two rooms shared the mirrored wall. It was a two-way. The women in the control room could watch him as if the mirror were a plain glass window. Bram, in the playroom mirror, could see only himself.

"He is very pretty eater," asked Natasha. "Napkin on lap. Mouth closed when chewing."

Esther, still holding her purse, having rushed up to the playroom as soon as she returned from the hotel, said, "His father might be a problem."

Natasha had already told Esther about Ms. Wistlestop's visit, and the challenge of finding storage for all the food. "The gifts are in front hallway," said Natasha.

"I noticed," said Esther. "You'd have to be blind not to."

"They send another van later with flowers."

Esther said, "Where's Penny?"

"She went to bed."

"It's eight o'clock."

"I give her Valium."

"Did she ask for it?"

Natasha glared and said, "She wanted two. I give her one. Vita took pill, too, and went back to hotel."

"So we've got all night to deal with *him*," said Esther, rubbing her palms together.

"Torture?" asked Natasha, pencil eyebrows rising.

"I wouldn't know where to begin," said Esther regretfully.

"Back in Russia, KGB tortured many of my family and friends. Electrocution, starvation, plucking hair one by one until entire body is bald—"

"We pay to have that done in America," said Esther.

"Prisoners forced to sit in huge vat of hot mud, rubbed with salt until layer of skin is peeled off, strapped to table and smeared with seaweed and silt from the Volga . . ."

"Again, was the gulag a prison—or a spa?" asked Esther.

"I have uncle—he wrote anti-Soviet underground newspaper—he was captured and taken to gulag. They put him in cold, dark room, forced him to drink gallon of water. They refuse to take him to bathroom, and then beat him when he pissed all over himself."

"Lovely," said Esther as she nodded absently, watching Bram eat, the polite fork switching as he carved his meat, the decorous napkin dabbing. "Twenty thousand dollars worth of catering," she lamented.

"You want him to write check?" asked Natasha.

Esther scoffed. "I don't care about the money. But I will make Bram pay. Oh, yes. He will pay."

Flicking the Speaker On switch atop the control room's console, Esther spoke into the microphone. "Good evening, Bram. This is Esther Bracket."

As the two women watched, Bram jumped to standing, the child-size chair falling over behind him. "Esther?" He seemed confused, and then a light went on behind his eyes. "It was *you*! You came to my hotel room and hit me with a champagne bottle!"

She continued, "Welcome to my home. You are currently in a locked room that was built for maximum security, with an escape-proof door, no windows, no wall vents, and twenty-four-hour surveillance equipment. You can't get out so don't bother trying."

"You're insane!" he shouted.

"Since you destroyed my daughter's wedding, I think it's only fair that you take responsibility for some of the fallout."

"You crazy bitch!" He'd approached the mirror, yelling into it, nostrils flaring, his face red. But Bram stood three feet to the left of where the women sat, and the sight of him raging into space, made them giggle.

"If you don't speak to me with the proper respect," said Esther into the microphone, winking at Natasha, "I'll sign off, then."

"Wait!" he said. "How's Penny?"

"Like you give a shit," said Esther. "Don't ask about her, don't think of her, don't mention her name."

Bram hung his head, nodded to himself, and returned to the chair. He uprighted it and sat down, his legs bent sharply, arms folded across his chest. He was listening.

Esther said, "As I was saying, since you've forced me to eat the cost of the wedding, I'm going to force you to eat the wedding itself."

"Eat the . . ."

"Two hundred servings of prime rib, salmon, and chicken are chilling in my kitchen fridges and my basement freezer. And their side dishes. Not to mention the thirty pounds of shrimp on ice in the guest bathtub."

"Make that twenty-eight pounds," whispered Natasha, patting her belly. "I like shrimp."

Into the microphone, Esther said, "I'm not letting you leave until you've eaten every last bite of it. Every grain of wild rice. Every slice of steak. Every blooming bliss potato."

Bram said, "You want to force-feed me to death."

"I didn't say 'to death,' but we can hope." Natasha stifled a laugh. Esther shushed her and added, "And I want you to write return shipping labels for every wedding gift. I've got a wall of wrapped presents in my foyer. They've all got to go back."

"Anything else?" he asked.

Esther turned off the Talk button to consider.

Natasha suggested, "He should do it all—*naked.*"

"He's my daughter's fiancé. That would be disgusting."

"If you say so," groused Natasha.

Esther turned the microphone back on. "I want you to write a personal letter to the wedding guests. Apologize for your pathetic cowardice, claim full responsibility for destroying their weekend, and beg forgiveness for crushing the dreams of an innocent girl. You hate yourself, you're ashamed, etcetera, etcetera."

Natasha whispered, "Nice."

"And then I can leave?" he asked.

"If your stomach doesn't explode—although that'd be one mess I'd happily clean up—I'll consider letting you go," said Esther.

Shaking his head, Bram said, "I knew you were capable of something this twisted."

"I didn't!" said Esther. "It's a fascinating course of discovery, isn't it, what we learn about ourselves as we get older?"

"Fascinating," grumbled Bram.

"When you finish your dinner—clean your plates!—write a letter to your father. Tell him you're okay, you don't want to be contacted. That you need some time for yourself and you'll get in touch when you're ready," said Esther. "Supplies in the desk behind you. You're such a selfish lout, Keith probably expects you to hide like a rat in a hole anyway."

Esther switched off the microphone.

"If he's not going to be naked," said Natasha, "what about clothes? He can't wear the same thing day after day."

Esther stroked her chin. "You're right. They'll get tight before long, too. Hmmm. Let's have a look in his suitcase. See what he's got."

They swiveled their desk chairs away from the console. Bram's suitcase lay on its side on the floor. Standard carry-on size with a silver shell, the luggage's combination lock wasn't snapped closed. Esther pushed the top release button and the kit sprang open.

"He is very pretty packer," said Natasha.

Bram's clothing was folded neatly, his small toiletry case clean and organized in the top zipper compartment. Esther rifled through his belongings. He'd packed only enough for a day or two. Wherever he thought he was going, he didn't plan to stay for long. Or maybe he was going to buy new things when he arrived. As she rummaged, Esther's hand touched something hard and sharp-edged. She pushed aside his shorts and socks to see what it was.

"Now that's surprising," she said as the two women stared at a framed eight-by-ten photo of Penny. Her daughter stood on a forest trail, her brown hair in a sloppy ponytail, a flannel shirt tied around her waist, khaki shorts, a tank top, boots, and wool socks. She held a walking stick and beamed at the camera.

"Beautiful," said Natasha.

Esther agreed. Penny looked radiant—never more so than in this photograph.

"He leaves her, but brings her photo with him?" Esther was

confounded and a bit shaken by the discovery. Judging from the look Penny bestowed on the photographer (who Esther assumed had to be Bram), her daughter was genuinely in love with him. Whatever their relationship had become, it'd been good once. For at least the time it took to set up and take this shot, on this particular day.

Esther propped up the frame on the console, instantly and vastly improving the room's decor.

Chapter 10

W hen Penny woke up in the morning, her top and bottom eyelids had fused during the thirteen hours of dreamless sleep. Not wanting to tear them apart just yet, she snuggled into her pillow. The comforting scent of clean linen lulled her back into slumber.

And then she remembered.

Penny whimpered. She was supposed to be waking up in the bridal suite at the Plaza with Bram pressed to her cheek, not her childhood pillow. She promptly flung it across the room, accidentally hitting her framed poster of Bon Jovi, knocking it off the wall, wincing at the crash.

"Sorry, Jon," she mumbled.

An image sprang from nowhere into her head, of Bram in khaki shorts, wool socks, hiking boots, a flannel shirt tied around his waist. That great day, about a year ago, when they decided to go urban hiking in Central Park with Bram's new digital camera. Giggling in their matchy-matchy outfits, they trudged around the park and made a picnic in the Sheep Meadow. Instead of throwing away the leftovers, they tossed pieces of crust and Oreo at a few squirrels as they walked into the trees. Before long she and Bram were surrounded by rodents, inching closer and closer. A brash gray squirrel climbed on Penny's boot. They had the photos to prove it. He said the siege reminded him of an early scene from Hitchcock's *The Squirrels*. She suggested it'd make ominous footage for the grisly Fox television documentary called *When Critters Attack*.

Bram proposed that afternoon. "I want to make you happy," he said, which was just one more thing they had in common.

Squirrels were ruined for her now. Next time she saw one, she'd throw a rock at it.

Next time she saw Bram, she'd throw a rock at him. The three-point-one carat kind. Better yet, she'd mail it. He'd be furious she could be that careless. Twisting her engagement ring, Penny decided that, for now, she'd wear it. Just so she knew where to find it when the right moment came to give it back.

She kicked her way out of bed. In her cotton tank and boxers, she padded down the sweeping staircase, through the mansion domed entrance. Massive bouquets of white roses in huge vases were pushed up against the foyer walls. The smell was divine.

And the look? "Funeral parlor," Penny said to herself.

She went straight for the kitchen. " Morning, Natasha," she said, dragging herself onto a stool at the marble-topped breakfast island with its own sink, fridge, trash compactor, and garbage disposal.

Natasha was piling plates on a tray. Penny checked off every item on her wedding menu as she counted the plates. Five, including one with a wedge of wedding cake that would choke a horse.

Penny asked, "Who's got the big appetite?"

The Russian shrugged and said, "Is for that dog. The stray."

The hillock of food was the size of a dog. A Great Dane. "Is this a very large animal?"

"Average," said Natasha.

"Since when do you care about strays?"

"I sympathize with helpless, starved animals. Who could resist sad begging eyes and whimpering?"

"I'm surprised to hear this," said Penny, "since you always took Mom's side whenever I asked for a pet." She took the cake plate off the tray. "A fork, please."

Natasha handed it over. "I was neutral," she said.

"I think you referred to dogs as 'mangy mongrels.'"

"I love mangy mongrel. There is no cuter dog than mangy mongrel." Natasha sliced a new hunk of cake and added, "Your Russian accent is very bad shit."

"Let's do it."

"What?"

"Feed the dog. I want to get a look at him. Her."

"No!" said Natasha, way too vehemently. "He is shy. He won't come for you. Only me. And I take food to our secret place."

Penny asked, "You and the dog rendezvous?"

"You have problem?"

"None. Except for being abandoned on my wedding day, but that's a separate issue."

Hefting the tray off the counter, Natasha let Penny open the kitchen door for her. Then the Russian dashed off with the tray, running into the backyard, toward the woods.

Penny went back to her wedding cake. When she finished her slice, she searched the fridge for more delights and found a tin of Beluga caviar. Her mouth watering, she got a spoon and scooped out a round mouthful. The black eggs popped under her teeth, spraying briny juice against her tongue. A taste explosion. She was on her fourth spoonful (and feeling so much better) when the front door bonged. Setting the spoon on the counter, Penny jogged back through the kitchen, and into the mansion foyer.

It's Bram, she thought. *It's not Bram. He wouldn't dare. He might. He changed his mind. He's in Fiji. He loves me. He hates me.*

Penny wiped her face clean of expression and opened the door.

Morris Nova gasped loudly when he saw her. "Jesus Christ, Penny, are you all right?"

"I'm fine," she said. "And you?"

"Your eyes," he said. "They're puffy. You've been crying."

"I've been sleeping," she said. "Are you acting as Bram's messenger boy again?"

Morris shook his head. Penny struggled against her disappointment. She invited him in.

"You grew up here?" he asked. "Not too shabby." Morris was bug-eyed at the grandeur, the opulence. "All these flowers were from the wedding?" He sniffed a rose from one of the fifty vases, plucked free a single bloom and smiled dreamily, longingly, at her.

Oh, no, she thought.

"Morris, listen carefully," said Penny. "I want details. The whole scene. Every word spoken. I don't expect a dramatic reenactment, but if you could try to do inflections, I'd appreciate it."

Morris hesitated, stared down at the rose in his fist, as if he might eat it. "We were in his hotel room," he said slowly. "Five minutes before I came to you."

"Did he write the note in front of you?" she asked. Morris nodded. "Was he crying when he wrote it? Bent over the table, tears spotting his sleeve? Pausing to sob on the bed? And, also, what was he wearing?"

"Normal clothes," he said.

Useless, thought Penny. "Not the tux?"

"I said something like, 'Dude, it's black tie, not blue jean.' " He laughed. She didn't.

"And he wrote the note where?" she asked.

"On the desk in the room."

"Crying?"

"Sorry."

"Then what?" she asked.

"He put the paper in an envelope and asked me to take it to you right away."

"In his words."

" 'Take it to Penny right away.' "

"He said my name?"

"Is that important?" asked Morris.

"Go on," she said.

"I refused. He said, 'If you don't give her the note, she'll be left hanging.' "

"And *then* he fell on the bed and sobbed?" she asked.

"He started packing. I left. And that's it."

She said, "Where did he go?"

Morris's baby blues got misty, as if *he* might start crying. He cleared his throat and tilted his head. He opened and closed his mouth like he was making sure it still worked.

Penny thought, *Here it comes*.

"You do realize," Morris said, "that however bad this seems now, it could be good for you in the end. Bram closed a door. I can open a window."

Penny said firmly, "The window is closed. And locked."

"We can break the window," he suggested, taking a few steps toward her.

"Stop right there," said a voice behind them.

Morris and Penny turned to see Natasha clomping down the stairs in her Candies. She was an imposing figure, Penny thought, and understood why Morris started backing toward the door.

"I was just leaving," he said to the advancing Russian. To Penny, he said, "Call me!"

Natasha clomped to Penny's side. "Your mother went out early. She will come back soon."

"I thought you were outside. You left through the kitchen door and somehow you appear upstairs?"

"I take back stairs," said Natasha indignantly. "I needed something in my room."

Penny said, "What did you need?"

"I have personal matter," said Natasha.

"What?"

"In Moscow, KGB cut out tongue for asking too many questions. And then they serve raw back to you with mustard. My cousin, he ate his own tongue—and pinkie."

"Wonder what crime warranted the pinkie punishment," said Penny.

"Sticking nose in where it doesn't belong," said Natasha.

"You'd think they'd take the nose for that."

Natasha clucked her (intact) tongue and went back to the kitchen.

Chapter 11

Esther Bracket skulked by the concierge desk at the Plaza as stealthily as a five-foot-ten-inch blonde in a black Jil Sander pantsuit and black movie star glasses could. Every few minutes an acquaintance, hotel employee, complete stranger, came over to offer his or her condolences. A cancelled wedding was like a death. In all black, Esther appeared to be in mourning.

The concierge had been occupied with the same doddering crone for ten minutes. Esther checked her watch, knowing Penny had to be awake by now. It would only take ten seconds to slip the letter from Bram to Keith on the desk, but she couldn't do it with the concierge standing right there.

"Take your break already," she said to herself.

The wait was interminable. She pretended to read the hotel brochure—which used the word "elegant" five times in the first paragraph—when, finally, the concierge vacated his post. Esther removed the letter—written on a piece of yellow construction paper—from her tote. Slyly, she backed up to the front desk until she felt it behind her. The she dropped the letter over her shoulder.

Walking briskly forward (away!), she looked over her shoulder to double check that the letter had been safely (and anonymously) left on the desk for the concierge to find upon his return.

"Drat," she said, seeing that the yellow paper had *not* landed on the desk, but lay on the floor in front of it. And the concierge had returned. Esther resigned herself to waiting. Again. She plopped down on a velvet-upholstered couch and stared at the letter, her nerves alert. Someone would see it and realized it was meant for a hotel guest, give it to the concierge. Half a dozen people approached the desk. But none saw the letter, or bent down to pick it up.

"It's bright freaking yellow!" she whispered to herself. How myopic were these hotel guests? She pitied their self-absorption, the tunnel vision, the dumbfounding lack of observational skills.

"Esther Bracket?" said a male voice behind her. "Is that you?"

Grimacing, Esther turned toward him. Keith Shiraz was smiling down at her. "Hello," she said.

"You look mysterious today," he said. "All in black. Like you're about to pull off a caper."

"Don't be ridiculous!" she said, her voice three octaves higher than normal.

Keith didn't seem to notice. "What brings you here?"

"More wedding loose ends," she lied.

"My parents are on their way back to Florida," he said. "My other guests have also left. I'm the last Shiraz here. And I hate to eat alone." He pointed toward the open double doors of Coq et Boule, the hotel's two-star restaurant.

"I recommend the crêpes suzette," she said.

"Please join me," he said, not willing or able to take a hint.

Esther stood and said, "I really need to get home to my daughter."

"Give her my love," Keith said, clearly disappointed. He cx-
cused himself with a quaint little bow. Esther exhaled gustily.
She couldn't loiter now. Without daring to look for the yellow
paper, she hastened to the exit.

"Wait! Stop right there," shouted Keith from across the lobby.
She froze. Bracing herself, Esther turned around.

Keith dashed over to her, waving the yellow construction
paper.

"Look at this!" he said, shoving the letter under her nose.

His encroachment, the waxy scent of crayon, the tension
of waiting and lack of sleep, all combined to make Esther's
head swirl suddenly. She put her hand on Keith's forearm to
prevent sway.

He put his hand over hers—Esther couldn't help noticing
how soft his palm was, despite its heaviness—and asked, "Are
you okay?"

"Just tired," she said.

"You need something to eat," Keith announced, and walked
her into the sunny lilac and lime colored dining room of Coq
et Boule.

Holding her by the upper arm, his knuckles dangerously
close to the side of her breast, Keith deposited her in a cushioned chair at a table for two by a picture window that overlooked a glorious, shimmering, seemingly endless stretch of
black highway.

A young waiter came over. Without looking at a menu,
Keith ordered, "Two strawberry and chocolate crêpes, a large
pot of hot coffee, two Ojs, side of bacon, ham, sausage." Turning to Esther, he asked, "You like meat?"

"I suppose."

To the waiter, she said, "Make it two sides of bacon."

That business concluded, Keith said, "Let's take a look at
this," and picked up the folded construction paper.

Esther lurched forward. Not for a better view. The chair behind her had knocked into hers.

She turned, and saw that a large man had taken a seat behind her at the next table. He was adjusting his chair, and himself, without any consideration for those around him. Finally, he seemed to settle down.

Esther smiled at Keith. She was about to speak when her chair was knocked again from behind, causing her to rattle the silverware.

Keith said, "Hello over there, sir. You're bothering my friend."

The man ignored him. Keith repeated his complaint, and the man said, "I heard you the first time."

She watched Keith's gray eyes darken to coal. He said, "Pardon me, Esther," and walked over to the chair bumper. Leaning down, Keith whispered in his ear. Esther tried to hear what he said, but couldn't make out a word. The diner, however, understood perfectly. His face drooped, skin blanched. His lip trembled, his chin quivered. While Keith sat back down in his chair, the man ran out of the restaurant like his ass was on fire.

"What did you say to him?" asked Esther .

Keith shrugged. "I told him his fly was unzipped."

"And that made him flee in apparent terror?"

"An unzipped fly can be very embarrassing."

"What business did you say you were in?" she asked. Esther was aware that Bram's family had money, but she wasn't sure of its source. Hopefully, it wasn't waste management.

"I own a car and limousine service, branches in Manhattan, Staten Island, and Newark," he said.

"How nice," she said, thinking, with trepidation, *He's connected.*

Keith unfolded the yellow construction paper again. "This was on the floor by the concierge desk! I'd recognize Bram's

handwriting anywhere. We exchange monthly letters, something we started when he was in college. We've talked about
switching to e-mail, but decided not to break tradition." Keith
paused. "I wonder if he left this for me yesterday, and it was
on the floor overnight."

Esther said, "It's possible."

He spread the paper flat on the table. He read it quickly, and
turned it around for Esther.

Dear Dad,

*I'll explain everything soon, but I need to be alone for a while.
I'll contact you when I'm ready. Don't try to find me.*

> *Sorry,*
> *Bram*

Esther had already read the letter, to vet its ambiguity. She
had approved of its brevity at the time. But now that she was
aware of their father and son weird-but-admirable pen pal
habit, she realized his letter should have been more personal,
heartfelt. She felt an unexpected sting of jealously. She and
Penny seldom exchanged meaningful words—on paper or
otherwise.

"You see? He's fine. All that worry for nothing," said Esther.

Keith reread the letter, folded it, and put it in his breast pocket.
He said, "Why on earth did he write in crayon on construction
paper? Has he gone into hiding at a nursery school? And why
brown? He hates brown. And yellow. Especially together. He
doesn't like colors that remind him of bodily functions."

Esther said, "He's a lawyer, not an interior decorator."

Keith laughed. When she didn't join in, he said, "You're not
serious."

Genuinely confused, Esther asked, "Did straight men start caring about design when I wasn't looking?" Granted, she hadn't been looking for twenty years.

"Bram isn't a lawyer!" said Keith. "He's a set designer and carpenter. On and off Broadway."

"He's an attorney," she insisted. "I remember Bram telling me he did contracts for the Newhouse family."

"He's a contractor at the Newhouse Theater at Lincoln Center," said Keith. "That's how Bram and Penny met. Bram built the sets for *Anything Goes*. Penny was a dancer in the chorus."

"I'm aware. I saw the show three times," she snipped.

"Their first date was to the opening night party."

"I knew that," she said. But she didn't. Esther tended to tune out whenever Penny talked about Bram—or any of her boyfriends over the years. Esther treated them uniformly with disinterest, which might have been interpreted (by the overly sensitive) as dislike. Penny stopped bringing her boyfriends home in high school. She stopped talking about them in college. Whenever Penny casually mentioned her romantic life, Esther abruptly changed the subject. If she didn't hear about her daughter's relationships, she could pretend they didn't exist. Bram, however, couldn't be ignored. Penny had been pushy about him.

"He dressed like a lawyer," said Esther. She remembered, at several dinners at her house, Bram had shown up in black or blue tailored suits.

"He was trying to make a good impression on you," said Keith.

He'd achieved the opposite. From the first dinner she'd hosted for the couple, Esther pegged Bram as a snotty Manhattan lawyer who condescended to tolerate her suburbanity. He hardly ever spoke, as if he were too lofty for her conversation. He pushed food around on his plate, as if he was above eating. Esther flashed to the abundant tray Natasha slipped into the playroom the night before. He'd cleaned those plates, she thought, smiling.

"Bram could never work in an office," said Keith. "He's a born builder. The summer he was twelve, he took apart some old Adirondack chairs we were replacing, and used the wood to build a tree house. I remember driving from the city to the East Hampton house on a Friday and finding Bram hammering the planks into a platform. He'd invented a rope and pulley system to haul the lumber into the tree. He did this without instruction. I was amazed. He continues to amaze me. Give him some tools and a pile of junk, and he'll build the Eiffel Tower."

Keith was beaming. How proud he was of his son. Esther wondered if Keith knew about the injuries Penny had sustained since she met Bram, the talented builder, so good with tools.

"Your wife is dead?" said Esther.

Keith blinked at the speedy shift in conversation. "She is. I understand your husband died in a terrible accident?"

"Some say 'terrible,' " she replied. "Others say 'lucky.' "

He let that one go. "So we're a widow and widower."

"My husband died on his way to signing our divorce papers. I prefer to think of myself as a divorcée."

"And when was this?" he asked.

"Fifteen years ago," she said. "And your wife's demise?"

"Just over two years ago," he said.

"Long, agonizing illness?"

"Heart attack," he corrected. "While shopping at the Pottery Barn in SoHo."

"How coincidental!" said Esther. "My husband was standing right outside a Pottery Barn at the Short Hares Mall when he . . . fell."

Their crêpes, coffee, and pork products arrived. Keith poured milk into his coffee and helped himself to sausages. "Look at those crêpes!" he exclaimed, smiling brightly at Esther, his eyes alive with the anticipated pleasure of breakfast.

Esther felt herself smiling, too. He was a good man, she thought. Full of fatherly love, appreciation for simple pleasures, self-assurance. Despite her feelings about certain members of his family, Esther liked Keith. But her like had limits. After all, she had his son locked in her attic.

"Are you heading back to the city today?" she asked, cutting into her crêpe.

He patted his breast pocket. "Now that I've heard from Bram, don't see any point in staying."

"I'm sure he'll contact you again soon."

"You say that like you know something," he said sharply.

"I'm just being positive," she stammered. "Seeing the upside. That's me! Ever optimistic!"

"I don't like the yellow paper and brown crayon," said Keith, chewing his bacon while he talked. "The missing bedspread. Champagne on the floor. It bothers me."

He pursed his lips and peered down at his plate. Esther noticed that he hadn't lost any of his hair, which was mink brown like Bram's, but with strands of silver at the temples. She calculated his age at around fifty; he looked closer to forty-five.

"Bram is a capable young man," said Keith, scooping up half a crêpe and eating it in a single bite.

"It's only natural for a parent to worry," said Esther.

"If he were in danger, he'd get out of it. He's resourceful."

"Not that he's in danger," said Esther.

"When he was eight, he got locked in an upstairs bathroom," said Keith. "He used manicure scissors to shred some towels, tied them together, and scaled down the facade of our town house on West Eighty-sixth Street. Alice—my wife—

answered the buzzer and found Bram on the stoop grinning like the Cheshire cat. I shouldn't worry about him. If he had the right tools—anything, a fork, a knife—Bram could escape from Alcatraz."

Esther swallowed. The bite of crêpe landed in her stomach like a rock.

On his food trays, Natasha had given Bram stainless steel knives, forks, and spoons.

Standing abruptly, she said, "I just remembered something I have to do. I'm sorry. I've got to go. Thanks for breakfast." She ran out of Coq et Boule, through the lobby, into her parked Volvo, and zoomed away, narrowly avoiding a collision with a green VW in the hotel driveway.

Chapter 12

Where is that dog? wondered Penny. She'd searched the grounds, the gardens, the woods, the surrounding blocks. Winding her way up the driveway to the mansion's front door, Penny theorized the dog might have choked on all that food Natasha put out, or cut itself biting into a china plate (why Natasha served an animal on china was a question she hadn't yet asked). The pooch might have been attacked in a melee with a rabid raccoon over the prime rib. No sign of the tray, either. Natasha's spot was indeed secret. Penny couldn't find it anywhere on the property's three acres.

She sat on the front steps and whistled one more time for the stray she'd already named Lester, even though she didn't know whether it was a male or female. The gender didn't matter. She'd name it Lester, and it would be her new best friend. She'd lavish attention upon it, and she'd be rewarded with the loyalty and affection of a dumb animal.

Of course, she'd need a cage. And a leash. And a collar. Plus whatever other kind of constraints one used to assure the continual devotion of a dog. It'd be bridled love perhaps—but love nonetheless.

While Penny whistled, Esther's red Volvo tore up the driveway and came to an abrupt stop. Right behind the Volvo, Vita's green VW bug followed, also skidding to a stop, missing the Volvo's bumper by inches.

Esther rocketed out of her wagon, patted Penny on the head, and said, "I'll be right back. I need to check on something."

"Mom, I want to adopt the dog," said Penny. "And I'm thinking of moving back home for a while."

"We'll talk in a second," said Esther as she dashed inside the house.

Vita was slower to exit her car. "I'm totally rattled," she said to Penny. Walking unsteadily, Vita sat next to the ex-bride on the steps.

"Am I unlovable?" asked Penny.

Vita ignored the question. "Remember yesterday, when we were driving over here after the not-ceremony, we almost got hit by a lunatic driver?"

"Vaguely," said Penny. Everything about yesterday was shadowy.

"The same car nearly hit me again, speeding out of the Plaza Hotel three minutes ago. So I followed the maniac. Nothing makes me as angry as aggressive drivers. I get so pissed off about other people's road rage."

"And this is interesting to me . . . why?" asked Penny, grinning.

"Here's why, you bitch," said Vita. "The car that nearly killed me—twice—just so happens to be your mother's." She was pointing at Esther's Volvo.

"Impossible," said Penny. "Mom was at the hotel yesterday when we drove over here."

"It was the same car, same driver," said Vita.

"Are you suggesting that my mom lied about her where-abouts yesterday?"

"Yes," declared Vita. "And you have to ask her about it."

Penny said, "No way."

"Then I'll ask her," said Vita, today in a red and white striped tube dress and black high-tops. "And you are lovable. Even when you're acting like a shit. My legs are shaking. Think Natasha is still feeling generous about the Valium?"

"Let's ask," said Penny.

They went inside, and Vita marveled at the wall of gifts in the entryway. "There must be a hundred boxes."

"One hundred and thirty-five," said Natasha, who had catalogued the incoming.

Vita asked, "Where's Mrs. Bracket?"

Natasha said, "She has stomach upset."

"Any sign of the dog?" asked Penny.

"Forget about dog," said Natasha.

"I'm going to catch it, and love it, and call it Lester."

Natasha insisted, "It's gone. Run away in woods. It could be in Newark by now."

Penny shook her head. "In Newark, stray dogs don't get prime rib. Unless it got hit by a car—which is entirely possible—it's coming back here. And I'll be waiting, with my cage and my leash and my collar." But first, she'd have to buy the stuff. "Vita!" she said.

"Penny!" replied her friend.

"We're going to the mall."

"Not until I have a talk with your mother about her driving."

"Give me your keys," demanded Penny, palm out.

"Calm down. I'll take you," said Vita. "You might want to put on some clothes first."

The mall would be packed on a Saturday morning, just how

she liked it. "I'm going," said Penny, taking the stairs three at a time. She made a left, went into her room, and threw on her high school jeans. The prospect of going to the Short Hares Mall—glass elevators, gold tiled floor, hundreds of A-list stores—gave her a greedy thrill, despite her family's unhappy history with the place. She'd get some retail therapy. Shop the pain away. She'd outfit her future canine pal, and then she'd outfit herself for her new life.

Her new life as a jiltee. Better that than a divorcée, she figured, having seen up close how that process sucked the vital fluid from a woman's marrow. Her mom had tried to train her to be wary of men and commitment. Penny rebelled, starting in eighth grade, saying yes to boys as often as she was asked. She kept her body in great shape to widen the dating pool. Added benefit: She'd turned the lifetime of gymnastics and dance classes into a career.

Saying yes to Bram's proposal might have been my ultimate act of rebellion, thought Penny as she dragged a brush through her hair. She wondered if all jilted brides felt equal parts humiliation, disappointment, rejection—and relief.

THUD. A plaster-shaking crash came from above. She looked at her ceiling.

Odd, she thought. The room above was a locked storage area. Had Mom gone up there?

Curious, Penny walked toward the second floor landing. She looked downstairs into the empty foyer. Vita and Natasha must have gone into the kitchen. She looked upstairs, toward the attic.

"Mom?" she called. "Are you up there?"

No response.

Penny hadn't been on the third floor in a decade. Her mom kept it unlit, unheated, unaired. The rooms were used to store Esther's subpar carpets, chairs, sewing machines, and chess sets. It was possible, she thought, that a raccoon had infiltrated the skylight in her old playroom and knocked over a pile of furniture.

"Hello? Anyone up there" she called, louder this time. Penny was answered with eerie silence. The thud was nothing, she decided. Penny made a mental note to tell Natasha that they might have a pest problem on the third floor. She walked a few steps downstairs.

THUD. This time she felt the vibration in her guts. *That was no raccoon,* she thought. It had to be bigger. Much bigger. Penny turned around and walked up to the third floor to investigate.

Chapter 13

Knees straddling the kiddie table, Bram hunched over his inventory list.

(3) six feet jump rope
(4) 2x3x1 bookshelf—nails reusable???
(1) tennis racket—strings reusable???
(1) table—legs detachable (check)
(2) chairs—legs detachable (check)

"If I had a hammer," Bram said to himself. He'd hammer in the morning; he'd hammer in the evening. All over Esther Bracket. Bram had been awake since the first ray of sunshine shone through the skylight. Hours of alone time were taking their toll. He'd been inside the prison for almost twenty-four hours (as far as he could tell), and he didn't intend to pass another day locked up.

He'd been milling around the room for about an hour when he went into the john. When he emerged, a fresh tray sat on the floor by the door. His eyes darted toward the mirror. Was he being monitored round the clock? Esther had to be working with a partner. The Russian, probably.

Bram put the tray on the table next to his inventory list. While he ate, he tried to estimate the height of the ceiling. If Bram had one failing—in terms of his carpentry skills—he was a poor judge of distance. Which was why, on the job, he wore a fifty-foot tape measure on his belt. He could picture it now, the silver square, hefty and compact, on his dresser at home where he'd left it.

"I miss you," he said aloud, thinking of his trusty pocket measure.

"Already?" someone said, making him drop his fork. "It's only been a few hours."

"Esther?" he asked. The PA system was ancient (he'd examined the speakers—they had to be at least twenty years old). Like yesterday, her voice was scratchy and nearly unrecognizable.

"Were you expecting someone else?"

"I can start writing address slips, if you'd like," he said, feigning amicability. "My schedule is more or less open at the moment."

"Why did you tell me you were a lawyer?"

Surprised, he said, "I didn't. You got that idea, somehow."

"You could have corrected me," she said. "If you had balls, you would have."

Bram (whose balls were well above average in size) said, "You're right. I'm sorry. I wanted to. I had a speech worked out. But I never got the chance."

"You had ample opportunity," she said. "All those dinners at my table."

"It would have been an awkward segue," he said. "My work, as a subject, never came up at those dinners. You and Penny talked about the house, news of people I don't know and never will. When Penny tried to include me, you did your best to cut me out. It wasn't fun, being the invisible boyfriend. I know you wished I'd go away and never come back. And now, you've locked me up in your home. I'm sure you see the irony."

If Esther saw it, she didn't say so.

Bram waited with his hands in his lap for her to speak. After a few minutes he resumed eating. The wedding catering was delicious. Especially the salmon. He could eat it all day. And he probably would.

Sensing she was still watching, he said, "This room. Penny's playroom, obviously. The speakers were installed when she was a toddler, I'm guessing. And you're sitting in an observation room, for spying on your child. I can't imagine why a toddler needed to be spied on. Unless she had some kind of problem."

"Penny's only problems have been a derelict father and loser fiancé. Both of whom are no longer factors," said Esther. And then, "Why did you empty that bookshelf?"

Shit! He'd meant to replace everything, make it look like he hadn't been fiddling. Standing abruptly, he knocked over the kiddie chair.

THUD. "Sorry," he said, and took two steps toward the pile of children's books on the floor. He picked up *Green Eggs and Ham* and said, "I made a vow last year to revisit the classics."

"You'd best not use the word 'vow,' " she warned. "So you and Penny must have thought it was hilarious, my mistaking you for a lawyer. I hope you had a good laugh at my expense."

"We didn't laugh," he said. "It wasn't funny."

"What's that you're drawing? Bring it over to the mirror."

Bram said, "Just doodles. Nothing." He tried to scramble back to the table to rip up his inventory list. In his haste, he tripped over the pile of books and hit the floor hard.

THUD. As he fell, Bram's jaw collided with the downed kiddie chair, making him see stars.

"Oh, God," he moaned. "I think I shattered my jaw." He cradled his mandible, talked through clenched teeth. Rolling on the floor in agony, he said, "Call a doctor! This is serious, Esther. If you have any heart at all, you'll take me to the hospital!"

Silence. Bram continued to writhe in agony, cupping his lower face protectively, moaning. He kept it up for as long as he could. Had to be ten minutes. And then he started to feel foolish.

"Okay, I'm back," said the voice. "What did I miss?"

She hadn't seen his performance? "I think I shattered my . . . never mind."

"I want the utensils."

His heart skipped. "What utensils?"

"Knife. Spoon. Fork. Put them by the door and go lock yourself in the bathroom. You can eat with your hands until I get plasticware. And if you try to rush the door, I'll shoot you."

"You don't have a gun," he scoffed.

"Everyone in New Jersey has a gun," she said matter-of-factly.

He believed her. Bram placed the knife, spoon, and fork by the door, and locked himself in the bathroom.

While she took his tools away, Bram checked the bathroom (again) for hidden cameras. Finding none, he squatted on the floor and reached behind the toilet. Hand touching his prize, he pulled out the wad of toilet paper. Peeling back the white squares, he smiled as he looked down at one knife, one fork, and one spoon.

He'd stolen them from last night's tray. By now those dirty plates had already been emptied into the dishwasher, no one the wiser about the utensils that hadn't been among them.

Chapter 14

The warbled "Mom?" from the stairs almost made Esther's heart arrest. Penny's voice was close. Too close. Esther rushed out of the control room (closing the door behind her) to find Penny on the third floor landing.

"What are you doing up here?" Penny asked, peering over Esther's shoulder.

"Nothing, just looking at some stuff in storage."

"I heard a thud. Two thuds," said Penny.

"Oh, that was me," said Esther, nodding energetically. "I knocked over a chair with my big hips. I'm so clumsy! Such a klutz! We all can't be as graceful as you are."

Penny squinted hard, and Esther knew her daughter wasn't convinced. "Are you feeling okay?" Penny asked.

"Tip top!" said Esther.

"I knew you'd be happy about what happened," said Penny. "But I didn't think you'd gloat."

"No! I'm not happy," said Esther. "It's horrible what Bram did to you. I'm so sorry, Penny."

"That came close to sincere," said Penny. "I want to talk about the dog."

"Dog? You mean Bram?" *Progress!* thought Esther.

"The stray. The one Natasha's been feeding since yesterday. I'm going to catch it, and keep it, and make it mine. And I'm moving back for a while," said Penny. "The dog and I are going to live here. Together." She glared with brazen defiance, a clear challenge. Her daughter's body had grown, thought Esther, but Penny's face, especially scrunched up petulantly, hadn't changed since she was six. If she lived to be a hundred and Penny seventy-eight, Esther knew she would always see Penny's baby face, her starfish hands.

She also knew that Penny's moving back might seem like a good idea *today,* but her daughter was certain to change her mind *tomorrow* (or next week). The girl was vulnerable. The appeal of home—of company, cooked meals, washed laundry, paid phone bills—seemed comforting. Esther had missed Penny since she moved to New York five years ago, but, as a parent, she had to encourage self-reliance, resilience. Plus, there was the niggling matter of Esther's imprisoned houseguest. No, Penny would have to go back to the city. And soon.

"Why don't we go downstairs, hash this out," said Esther, leading the way.

"Nothing to discuss," said Penny.

"What about your apartment?"

"I was going to give it up anyway, when I moved in with Bram." Penny's voice hitched at the mention of her fiancé's name.

What am I going to do with him? Esther asked herself for the hundredth time. Drive him into the Pine Barrens? Knock him on the head again and hope for amnesia?

Esther said, "I'm thrilled you want to come home! But you should take a few days to think about it. Why don't you and

Vita drive into the city? Go shopping. Have a few treatments. On me."

Penny puckered. "I thought you'd tell me to be self-reliant. Resilent."

On the second floor landing now, a full flight away from the danger zone, Esther said, "You should have told me Bram isn't a lawyer."

"Does it matter?" said Penny. "Lawyer, set designer, plumber. You'd hate him regardless."

"I have good reason!" said Esther.

"My injuries," said Penny. "What if I told you they were consensual?"

"You consented to being smacked around?"

Bong.

"It's Bram!" said Penny, eyes alive at the sound of the doorbell.

"It's not," said Esther, assuming another van from the Plaza had arrived.

"It could be," said Penny.

"Impossible," said Esther.

Penny skipped toward the door and said, resentfully, "You're always so negative."

Esther stopped herself from saying, *I am not!*

While Penny went down to get the front door, Esther dashed upstairs to get the utensils from Bram. It took only a minute. And then she rushed back to greet whomever had come calling.

A man. He had his arms around her daughter.

"Keith," said Esther, descending the stairs, sliding the utensils into her jacket pocket. "What brings you here?"

He stroked Penny's hair and looked up at Esther. She thought he drew breath when he saw her. Penny peeled herself off his chest, her eyes red and puffy. She'd been crying to him, taking comfort from her almost father-in-law. Esther trampled a spark of jealousy. Penny had always sought out the attention of men.

"Welcome," said Esther, traipsing downstairs, achieving *casual,* all the while praying Keith wouldn't ask for a tour of the house.

"Long time," he said to Esther with a grin. To Penny, he assured her, "I will find him. If I have to hire twenty investigators, spend a million dollars, we'll get to the bottom of this."

Keith squeezed Penny's shoulder. His lips, a pucker of encouragement. His eyes, the steel of confidence. His brow, the knit of concern. No wonder Penny balled in his sympathetic presence. He was good. Oh, yes. But she was better.

"What brings you, Keith?" she asked.

"I wanted to make sure you were okay," he said. "You left breakfast in such a hurry."

"I'm fine," she said.

"Breakfast?" asked Penny.

"I went to the hotel to take care of business, ran into Keith. I had to leave due to a sudden headache. It's gone now."

"Good," said Keith. He paused to take in the entryway, the wall of wedding gifts. The funeral flowers. "You have a beautiful home."

"Mom's an antiques collector. Rooms and rooms full of stuff. The finest collection of Queen Anne chairs in three states," said Penny.

"Really?" said Keith.

"Give him a tour," said Penny. "Along with the stuff on display, she's got a ton in storage on the third floor. Enough to fill another house, right, Mom?"

Esther gulped. "Yup."

"I'd love to see it," said Keith.

Esther opened her mouth, mind scrambling for an excuse,

when Vita banged open the door to the kitchen. It was the first time Esther had been glad to see her.

Vita said, "Esther Bracket. Ma'am, I've got a few questions for you. About your driving, ma'am."

What was this flake nattering about? "Pardon?" asked Esther, barely achieving polite.

"At approximately ten this morning you were observed leaving the Plaza Hotel, when you nearly crashed into a green VW bug—mine. I gave chase, although you didn't notice me— and followed you to your own home. Yesterday at approximate four in the afternoon, I was nearly run off this very street by a lunatic driver in a red Volvo."

"Couldn't have been me," said Esther. "I was at the Plaza."

Penny said, "Homocide dick?"

Vita said, "You like?"

"Too authoritarian."

"You'd prefer sweet-cheeked girl P.I.?"

"Who wouldn't?"

Vita turned back to Esther, licked her lips and asked, "Come on, honey. You can talk to me. I'll listen. I'll listen real close. Do any of your neighbors drive a cherry red Volvo wagon that looks exactly like yours?"

"Actually, yes, a few of them do," said Esther.

"You wouldn't be lying?" drawled oddball Vita, who was officially off Esther's Christmas list. "Mind if I knock on some doors? Make some new friends?"

"You can try," said Esther acidly. Her neighbors would lock their doors if they saw Vita coming.

"Any sign of the dog?" asked Penny.

Vita stopped licking her lips (thank God) and replied in her normal (although annoyingly nasal) tones. "Natasha and I called and whistled for twenty minutes."

"Where is Natasha?" asked Esther.

"She went out," replied Vita.

Keith, who'd been transfixed by Vita's tarty performance, asked, "Excuse me, Esther. But is that a fork in your pocket?"

"Or is she just glad to see you?" asked Penny.

That made Vita and her daughter giggle like idiots. Keith blushed handsomely. On such a rugged man, a splash of pink gave him an appealing soft touch.

Penny said, "We're going shopping."

"In the city?" asked Esther.

"The mall. You said it was on you." Turning toward their guest, Penny asked, "Will you come over for dinner tonight, Keith? Please?"

"I'd love to," he said, glancing at Esther, "but I don't want to intrude."

"He's leaving town, unfortunately," said Esther.

"I've changed my mind," he said. "New Jersey gets more interesting by the hour."

"No, no, this town is very dull," corrected Esther. "Bore-ring. You should get out of here while you still can. Go. I mean it."

Keith laughed. "Short Hares isn't so bad. Some of the locals are captivating," he said, this time looking right at her. Everyone saw.

Esther's panties felt damp suddenly. She thought that she might have lost bladder control (she'd been reading that such things happened). But then realized: She was attracted.

"What do you mean by 'captivating'?" she asked.

Penny cleared her throat. "I know when I'm not wanted," she said, and then she and Vita scurried out the door. Esther and Keith listened to the bug roar to life, the sound soon diminishing, and then all was silent—except for the loud crackle of tension along her shoulder blades.

"Do you hear something?" asked Keith.

"The crackle?" asked Esther.

"Pounding. Like a hammer. From upstairs," he said.

Esther gulped. She had to get him out of there. "Why don't I show you the grounds?" she asked, leading Keith out the front door, taking hold of his forearm as they walked.

He let her, falling into step at her side. Keith was probably five inches taller. Esther, at five-ten, wasn't used to feeling puny.

She led him past the pong room, dining room, the solarium, the gallery. Through the double doors into the backyard, down the flagstone path that skirted the house, veering off toward the pool and the gardens that Esther paid thousands of dollars each year to maintain. She did some of the planting and watering herself, but she had a professional do the grunt work. Esther did not grunt.

The garden had two main beds set against a stone wall. Along the property border, Esther's pride: Mammoth eight-foot-high azalea bushes, all grown into each other, were in full bloom. She'd had her gardener, Mr. Alonzo, trim them into a Greek key shape that, at eye level, looked like the outer wall of a maze.

She picked a pink flower and said, "I've got nosy neighbors."

"This is quite a trim bush," said Keith.

Which inexplicably made Esther blush. Vividly. Damn her capillaries.

"Your neighbors," he said. "What is it you don't want them to see?"

"I just like my privacy."

"It would be awful to feel like you're being watched," he agreed. "Like in those interrogation rooms, with the two-way mirrors."

"Yes," Esther croaked. "That would be awful."

Russell had insisted on building the playroom. Penny was

his precious child, he said. He wouldn't let anything bad happen to her "under his watch." Esther didn't, at the time, think he meant that literally. But this was in the early 1980s, at the height of child molestation hysteria. Several high profile media cases—a nursery school teacher in Summit, a camp counselor in Perth Amboy—dominated the New Jersey newspapers. Every day the *Star Ledger* published new accusations about babysitters, stepfathers, priests. The first wave of spy gear and nanny-cams appeared on the market. Russell bought into the hysteria, and the technology. He hired a contractor to soundproof the playroom, put in the PA system, and install the mirror. Esther couldn't argue the point. Safety had to come first. Russell demanded that Esther observe Penny with the au pair—the one he'd hand selected (as it came to pass)—if not all the time, at least every fifteen minutes.

Turned out, Russell was a more eager spy than Esther. He spent hours (when he wasn't traveling) watching Penny play with the au pair, time he might have spent playing with Penny himself. Attention he might have paid to his lonely, much younger wife.

Keith said, "You look pale again. Did your headache come back? Perhaps you should lie down. Let me help you to your bedroom."

"I'd just assume keep you out of my bedroom," she muttered.

He raised his eyebrows. "Why is that?"

"Esther! Darling! Over here!" a flighty voice rang out, skipping across the great lawn. Esther and Keith turned toward the source, the luscious figure of her neighbor, Ashley Longmead, slinky in a chocolate silk blouse, a creamy pencil skirt, her auburn helmet hair (think Ann-Margret) big and stiff. Ashley waved, diamonds on her wrists catching the sunlight.

Esther waved back, relieved to see her friend. She'd known Ashley since her first day in Short Hares, when Russell brought

her here after their two-week fiery romance and spontaneous wedding. Ashley greeted her that day—twenty-five years
ago—with kisses on both cheeks and a blinding white smile.
Esther received the same greeting now, European buss, tight
hug. Ashley's face hadn't changed much since then, thanks
to her dearly departed husband, a plastic surgeon. Lawrence
was eighty when he died last year. Ashley's age was anyone's
guess. Esther put her somewhere in her early fifties.

In one arm, Ashley carried a bouquet of roses. In the other,
a small shopping bag with the Short Hares Gourmet Bakery
logo on it.

Flowers and food. Exactly what Esther didn't need.

"Sweetie!" said Ashley. "I'm so sorry about yesterday! I
searched madly for you at the hotel to see how I could help,
but no one knew where you'd gone! I'm sure it'll be a comfort
to know that everyone in Short Hares feels absolutely horrible
for you. Really. It's all anyone can talk about."

Esther said, "How kind of you to say."

Ashley held out her manicured hand to Keith and introduced
herself. "The father of the groom?" she asked. "I recognize you
from yesterday."

Keith bowed slightly. "I noticed you, too. That was a stun-
ning dress you were wearing."

Esther hadn't seen it, but she could imagine. Ashley had the
figure of a thirty-year-old, and she loved to show it off—usually
in sweet shades (caramel, toffee, chocolate, etc.). Although sex
was the one topic the two neighbors never discussed (Ashley
was WASPy in her reticence, and Esther had nothing to report), Esther knew her friend had affairs.

"Shall we put these in water?" asked Ashley.

The three walked back into the house through the kitchen
door. Esther asked Ashley to take Keith into the solarium
while she found a vase.

Rummaging in her cabinets, she located a crystal pitcher (a gift from her own wedding). Esther arranged the roses (the smell of which was starting to make her sick) and then checked the bakery bag. Predictably, Ashley brought the shop's signature palmier cookies. Some called them "elephant ears," the cookies were buttery thin pastry rolled into circles and baked with a dusting of raw white sugar. The pastry was light, crumbly with thin layers of deliciousness. Ashley knew Esther adored palmiers, that she could eat them compulsively. She felt a welling in her heart, touched by the kindness of a friend—possibly the only real friend she'd made in Short Hares.

She plated the palmiers and made a pot of coffee. After putting the cookies, pot, mugs, cream, and sugar on a tray, Esther carried it toward the solarium, her favorite room in the mansion, with its floor-to-ceiling window walls and view of her gardens.

As she approached the room, she heard Keith and Ashley talking.

"It's the gray tiled roof," said Ashley.

"You're right next door," he said.

"Esther and I are so close, in so many ways," she said.

A lump formed in Esther's throat. She was glad her friend came over. She entered the room and put the tray on the glass table.

Ashley said, "Your favorite."

"Thanks," said Esther, her eyes wet.

"Darling, your garden looks nibbled," said Ashley. "Oh, that's why."

As the three of them watched through the glass wall, a family of squirrels tore through the garden beds, digging and gnawing. "Not again," sighed Esther. The squirrel overpopulation in Short Hares was fast becoming a major problem. "The state sanctioned black bear and deer hunting. When will they give the go-ahead about hunting squirrels?" asked Esther.

"Allow me," said Ashley, reaching into her jewel-studded purse and removing her pearl-handed .22 revolver, custom-made, a gift from her husband.

"Not before lunch," said Esther, shooing away Ashley's offer.

If Keith found it odd that a middle-aged lady would carry a gun (although, for Ashley, it was more accessory than a weapon), he didn't comment. Esther assumed that, in the waste management business (or whatever it was he said he did), everyone carried a piece. Keith sat on the chintz couch and helped himself to a palmier. As he bit, Esther watched his expression. She smiled when he closed his eyes, licking the flakes of pastry off his lips, and made a yummy sound.

Ashley made a yummy sound, too, watching him.

Keith said, "That is good."

"But messy," said Ashley, pointing at the pastry flakes on his lap. She sat next to him on the couch and brushed the crumbs on the terra-cotta-tiled floor.

If Keith felt ill at ease to find a strange woman's hands in his lap, he didn't let that show, either.

Esther took a seat opposite the couch in one of the matching armchairs, assessing the situation. Ashley was flirting with Keith in her usual, outré way. And why shouldn't she? Keith was a handsome man. Ashley was single.

"So tell me, Keith," said Ashley. "Are you married?"

"I'm a widower."

"That makes three of us," said Ashley.

"I'm a divorcée," said Esther.

Ashley shook her head. "If you really were a divorcée, you'd have nothing. As a widow, you're a wealthy woman. Embrace who you are, darling."

Esther had heard this logic before from Ashley. It made sense. If Russell hadn't gone to the mall—and died—on the way to his lawyer's office, he would have signed off on the unfair settlement Esther had fought for years but finally been bullied into accepting. She would have forfeited all claims to Russell's property, as well as custody of Penny.

Keith stared at Esther with what had to be curiosity or, on an outside chance, concern.

Ashley said, "My Lawrence was an angel on earth. I miss him very much." And then Ashley wiped under her eyes with a napkin, careful not to ruin her makeup.

Keith said, "It's hard, losing someone you love."

Ashley smiled gratefully at him and moved a bit closer.

Esther watched, awed and disgusted. The disgust was new. She was usually bemused by her friend's seduction style. But it felt different, seeing her go to work on Keith.

He's mine, she thought. And then, *He's the father of the man I have locked in the attic.*

Standing abruptly, Esther said, "I'm suddenly nauseated. Ashley, can you show Keith Shiraz out? But don't rush. You seem so comfortable. I'd hate to disturb you."

Keith stood up. Jumped up. Ashley tumbling off of him. "Penny mentioned our having dinner tonight," he said.

"I'd love to have dinner with you," said Ashley. "Since Esther is too sick to do it."

Ashley winked at Esther. The same wink she'd shot her at charity functions and dinner parties as she slinked off with men to, supposedly, stroll the veranda or talk to the chef or find the bar. Often, the men had shown interest in Esther first, only to be intercepted by Ashley in her sugary dresses. Ashley had helped Esther avoid dozens of uncomfortable situations over the years. And every time she threw herself between Esther and a man, Ashley gave her friend that flirty, conspiratorial little wink.

This time Esther didn't return it. "I'm sure I'll feel better after a nap," she said to Keith. "Dinner at six."

Chapter 15

"Allow me to present the legendary Short Hares Mall, known throughout the tristate area as the Ultimate Shopping Experience," said Penny at the entrance to the glittering starship of commerce. "People from Connecticut, New York, even Delaware come for the privilege of walking these hallowed pavilions, browsing in these shops, dining in the famed gourmet food court. The prices might be inflated, but there's no sales tax on clothes in New Jersey, so it all evens out."

"Stand aside," said Vita impatiently, shoving Penny so she could fling open the mall's hydraulic glass doors.

A chorus of angels belted a divine melody.

"What is that?" asked Vita.

Penny pointed at the speakers on the ceiling. "Movement sensors. Whenever the door opens, cherubs sing."

Three steps into the mall they were besieged by nattily dressed women in yellow skirts and blazers.

"Foie gras?" asked one, offering a silver tray with creamy brown wedges on toast triangles.

"Instant facial?" asked another, silver atomizers at the ready.

"We'll pass," said Penny.

"We will?" asked Vita.

Tugging her along, Penny said, "Free mini-makeovers at the Chanel counter, for Mall Members. And that means us. Mom is a Gold Circle Member. For a onetime donation of $5,000, she—and by extension, *we*—can indulge in mini-makeovers, personal shoppers, lunch samplers, free parking, golf cart transport, for life."

"This isn't a mall," said Vita. "It's a country club."

The mall building was designed like a wheel, with a hub and spokes. Penny led Vita into the atrium, until they were standing at the mall's central point, a fifteen-foot-high glass globe fountain.

"You see the five arches?" asked Penny as they walked around the fountain. "Each is the entrace to a separate pavilion."

Penny summed up the pavilions' shopping scheme. "To the immediate right, the Apparel and Accessories Pavilion," she said. "Designer clothing for men, women, children, and very special pets. Watches, eyewear, jewelry, purses, belts.

"Next, the Entertainment Pavilion. Electronics, books, music, movies, including an IMAX theater," she continued. "To the right of that, the Cosmetics Pavilion. Spas and salons, a gym, cosmetics, a laser treatment center—for eyes, skin and hair removal. Onward to the Home Pavilion. Furniture stores, antiques, Sotheby's auction house. Finally, the Food Pavilion. Cookware, specialty food shops, catering services, two three-star restaurants, the world-famous gourmet food court, and the CooKings school. Sponsored by Kings, the local overpriced supermarket chain. Mom once took a class there on how to prematurely age beef."

Vita asked, "How?"

"Tell the cow her teenage calf is pregnant."

Vita laughed. She would laugh at anything, which Penny had always appreciated about her. Smiling, Penny watched Vita take it all in: the great glass elevators, the shiny chrome escalators and handrails, the white marble, gold tiles, and dramatic arches. The Saturday horde of customers. Middle-aged women head to toe in Moschino, their immaculate children eating enormous cookies, their Caribbean nannys loaded down with boxes and bags from D&G, Betsey Johnson, Godiva, Domain. Ponytailed teenage girls in packs wearing identical jeans (Seven), T-shirts (DKNY), and clogs (Birk). Men on cell phones, families cramming the escalators, long lines outside the theater, the restaurants, the salons.

Vita said, "I'm overwhelmed. And what's with the cars?"

She was referring to the line-up of fantasy cars parked inside velvet ropes around the atrium. "They're for sale, of course," said Penny.

They watched as a man in a gray suit circled a yellow Lamborghini. He walked around the car four times before asking the mall hostess for a brochure from a nearby dealership.

"Check out the fountain," said Penny, showcasing the glass sphere, water bubbling inside and flowing out of the hole on top, down the sides, and into a black-bottomed pool thirty feet in diameter. In the pool, pennies, nickels, and dimes twinkled. Every few seconds a coin plopped into water.

Vita asked, "Pennies from heaven?"

Earthbound Penny pointed up, to show Vita where the coins were falling from. On the second floor balcony, in front of Pottery Barn in the Home Pavilion, stood a crowd of people throwing loose change.

"That's the mall-sanctioned coin toss spot," said Penny. "They're aiming for the hole on top of the fountain, to get a penny inside the sphere."

"Why?" asked Vita.

"Because it's there."

"Seems like a waste of money."

Penny laughed. As far as she was concerned, the entire mall and everything in it was a waste of money.

"Look at that kid leaning over the balcony," said Vita, frowning. "Was that where your father was standing when he . . ."

"Fell to this death?" said Penny. "Exactly there. The very spot. He went over the railing and into the fountain hole, head first."

Vita cringed. "Did he drown?"

"Died on impact. Broken neck. He didn't shatter the fountain. The glass is five inches thick. Apparently, it took three hours before firemen could get him out."

"Did you see it happen?" asked Vita. "You were how old? Twelve?"

Penny shook her head. "I was eight," she said. "I did not see the accident; I did see the picture in the *Star Ledger*, though. The headline was 'Fatal Fall at the Mall.' It was the first newspaper article I ever read."

One of the reasons Penny hardly ever talked about the circumstances of her father's death: It was simply too difficult to explain. She drew a picture for Bram on one of their first dates, but she was a horrible artist, and he wasn't clear on the logistics (despite her stick figures and dotted line of trajectory from the balcony). Bram understood when he finally saw the fountain. They'd come here about six months ago, wedding gown shopping.

A quarter plopped into the hole, followed by a cheer from the coin toss area one flight up. The coin floated down, the water magnifying it. Penny wondered if her father's head appeared larger than it was when lodged inside the fountain.

She said, "I was three when he moved out, and I hardly

saw him after that. He was living in the city with his British girlfriend, Jemima. My former au pair. She was with him on the balcony when he fell. They were going to get married later that same day, after he signed the divorce papers. Jemima has since gone Christian. She still sends me letters. Tries to convert me."

Vita said, "This place is just bursting with happy memories for you."

"You have no idea," said Penny.

"None of the others can possibly top the 'Fatal Fall at the Mall.' "

"How you underestimate me."

Penny took Vita by the hand and crossed into the Apparel and Accessories Pavilion. On the first floor, only a few stores in, she stopped in front of the Laura Ashley Bridal Boutique.

"I knew it!" said Vita. "I didn't dare speak the name, but I suspected all along."

Penny nodded gravely. "Oh, yes. I bought a Laura Ashley wedding gown. Bram and I came to the mall to poke around. I figured we'd just get ideas and I'd have something made. But we walked by this boutique, and he insisted I try on a dress in the window. Laughing, hand in hand—it was all so simple then—we went in. He told the shop girl he wanted me to look like the bride on top of the wedding cake. Traditional, over the top *bridal*. The girl would bring out a gown, and Bram said say, 'More ruffles! More bows!' It was hilarious, I'm telling you."

"I can see the fun of trying on dresses," conceded Vita. "But why did you *buy* one?"

Penny shrugged. "I stood on the fitting platform, in the gown that ended all dignity. Bram stepped up next to me, and we looked at ourselves in the mirrors. He kissed me. The kiss that ended all irony. He said, 'There's my beautiful bride.' In a heartbeat, I slapped down Mom's plastic. And the most pathetic part: I rank that as one of the most romantic moments of my life."

Vita took Penny's hand and gave her a little squeeze. "There'll be more."

Penny welled up a bit, and had to turn around to shake off the weeps. Fortunately, her eyes lit on a distracting display window.

"And the hits keep coming," she said, crossing the floor to Precious, a designer clothing consignment store. "Right there, in front of this store, I was kidnapped."

"What?"

"I was seven. Mom took me in and started talking to the saleswoman. And talking, and talking. I got bored and wandered out of the store. A strange woman took my hand and pulled me away, down this corridor, into the restroom. She put her hooded black jacket over me and then walked me out of the Apparel Pavilion and, almost, out of the mall."

"I can't believe this!"

Penny nodded with conviction. "Ten feet from the exit doors, five mall security guards barreled toward us, guns out, screaming at me to get on the ground. They grabbed the kidnapper and threw her against the wall so hard two of her teeth broke. I was lying on the floor, in shock, terrified. Then Mom was down there with me. She was crying hysterically, clutching at me, howling. Completely out of control. When she realized I'd disappeared, she alerted mall security. The guards were on high alert for a seven-year-old girl with dark brown hair in a green jacket and red cowboy boots. In the long black hoodie, though, my hair and jacket were hidden. A smart guard saw the red boots."

"I'm speechless," said Vita, eyes as big as quarters.

"The almost kidnapping made the papers, too. A year before the Fatal Fall. The *Star Ledger* account praised the quick thinking security guards. Mall traffic doubled overnight. Everyone felt safe here."

"Who was the kidnapper?" asked Vita.

"A housekeeper from the Dominican Republic who worked for a rich family in Short Hares. She barely spoke English. Apparently, she went a little nuts from missing her own daughter in Santo Domingo. Loneliness induced madness. She saw me. I reminded her of her kid, and she made the impromptu grab. I never saw her again. She was deported. She also continues to write to me, but it's all in Spanish, and we never bothered to translate. It's just a lot of Jesús Cristos and Dios mios. She went Christian, too. From the guilt."

"So you and your mother are an international Christian conversion tag team."

"Not bad for a couple of New Jersey Jews," said Penny.

Vita shook her head, astonished by Penny's list of Mauls at the Mall. She said, "The biggest drama of my childhood was getting my head stuck in a fence."

"You're lucky," said Penny, thinking of the hundreds of episodes she hadn't mentioned to Vita. "You were spared drama, and now your job is melodrama."

"Not necessarily for much longer," said Vita. "I've fucked every guy in the cast—in real life *and* on the show. They're running out of things—and people—for Cherry Bomb to do on *House of Blusher*. Except get sick and have a beautiful death—full hair and makeup, of course. Or to start fucking women."

"On the show," said Penny.

"Of course!" said Vita. "What I really need is my own show to develop. Get a signature character that can't be killed off—or fucked off—the show."

"I liked you as the girl detective," said Penny.

"Cherry Bomb, the Private Dick," considered Vita. "I'll think about it. Come along now, Penny. We have an urgent errand."

"The dog stuff?"

"We have to buy you a new pair of red shoes."

Vita dragged her into Well Heeled, a top-shelf footwear store. Penny found herself gravitating toward the ballet slippers, as always. At five-ten, flats were a given. She'd been hyperconscious of her height since fifth grade. She was the tallest kid in class, and lost the top spot until freshman year, but only then because she'd learned to slouch, a habit she broke only for dance classes and performances.

Vita stroked a pair of pomegranate red pumps.

Penny shook her head. "Four-inch heels?"

"So?"

"I'll be six-two!" said Penny. "I can't slouch low enough."

"Just try them on," cajoled Vita. "And stand up. For yourself."

Penny groaned, but she relented. A salesperson found size tens. In them, upright, Penny teetered. "Everything looks smaller from up here," she said.

Vita, meanwhile, had tried on a pair of sandals with faux vines as straps curling around her ankles and halfway up her calves.

"Have you always had such great calves?" asked Penny appraisingly.

"They came with the shoes," said Vita. "Two fifty for the pair. Which is about two twenty more than I've got."

Penny looked (all the way) down at the saleswoman and said, "We'll take them both. And we'll wear them out." She handed over her mom's golden card, signed the receipt, gathered their bags.

"And now, we walk," said Penny. "Or try to."

Unable to slouch, forced to pull her shoulders back or topple, Penny was a head taller than most of the shoppers in the pavilion. She could see bald spots, dandruff, dark roots. The air up there was thin and dizzying.

"Here's The Pampered Pooch," said Vita.

Entering pet paradise, Penny and Vita walked through racks of doggie clothing. Rain slickers, booties, sweaters, jackets, Batman capes. Penny plucked a hanger with a little ballet tutu with (four) toe shoes, priced at $150. She said, "This would be adorable, if it weren't obscene." Vita was equally repelled by *cute*. They tut-tutted over a locked glass display case of collars, bracelets, even clip-on earrings.

"Who would spend $4,000 on a diamond necklace—for a dog?" asked Vita.

"How ignorant you are of the local customs," said Penny.

"Actually, this little item is a bargain," said Vita, sifting through a collection of black spiked leather collars. "You'd spend four times as much at the BDSM shops in the Village."

"Look at this," said Penny at another table. "Makeup for dogs."

The table displayed bottles of paw nail polish, liquid nose blackener, brown eyeliner, gum gloss, dusting powder for fur, glitter shampoo. Vita opened a bottle of black Pooch Polish and started to do her nails. She said, "You are aware of the common thread in the wedding gown and kidnapping stories, right? Your willness to go along. Failure to assert yourself."

Penny toyed with the nose and eye pencils. "That looks good," she said of her friend's blackened nails. Penny did her nails, too. The polish was "insta-dry." Made sense. Most dogs wouldn't sit patiently under the fans.

"You need to access your inner bitch," said Vita.

"This would be the place for it," said Penny. She darkened her eyelids with the black nose fixer, and used the gum sheen on her lips. She tried on a studded collar. "Which brings up an interesting quandary."

Vita put on some dog eyeliner, too. "What?"

"If a female dog is a bitch, why aren't male dogs bastards?"

"They probably are," said Vita. "Most puppies are born out of wedlock."

"Which means bitches are also bastards," said Penny.

"What do you call a dog that wears a diamond necklace?"

"A royal bitch."

"You look good," said Vita. "An Amazonian punk."

"And you," said Penny. "Evil nymph."

Freshly made over, the two goth bitches filled a shopping cart with chew toys, biscuits, a beanbag bed, a leash and collar (same one as Penny wore around her neck), and one red knit sweater, size medium (Natasha had said the stray was average).

With their boxes and bags, new shoes and makeovers, the women walked (Penny teetered) toward the gourmet food court, passing the Porsche Spider and the yellow Lamborghini along the way. Mall people stared at the girls more than the cars.

At the food court, they grabbed seats at the Risotto Hut.

Vita said, "How do you like getting noticed?"

Penny shrugged. "Makes me nervous."

"It's what I live for."

"I had no idea."

"See the guy over there?"

"That one?" asked Penny. She pointed at a solidly built man with a crew cut at the Panini Cart.

"I'm going to use a technique I learned in acting class to make him notice me," said Vita. "It's called mirroring. I mimic him. Do whatever he does. Every twitch, shrug, hand movement. Even from across the room, his subconscious will pick up my signals. He'll think I look familiar, like he might know me, but isn't sure how. What he recognizes is his own body language."

"This is bullshit," scoffed Penny.

"Watch."

Penny observed Vita as she jerked her hands around, turned her head nonsensically, swiveled for no reason. Swung her legs, scratched her neck and (sweet Jesus) her crotch. Incredibly, the man clued in and turned toward them. Oddly enough, Penny thought *he* looked familiar.

"Here he comes," whispered Vita. "Told ya!"

Indeed, crew cut stood up and ambled over toward . . .

"Hold the phone," said Penny. "That's Morris Nova!"

Vita said, "Well, well, and so it is. With a shave and a haircut."

Morris's approach was hesitant and squinty. Then Penny realized: He didn't recognize *them*. All that bitch makeup. The out of contextness of it.

She said, "Hi, Morris."

Penny studied his face as recognition set in. He reeled back, confused. Or was he embarrassed to see her again, after he'd been so forward yesterday? Served him right if he was.

He couldn't not come over now, regardless of his mixed feelings. He said, "Penny. You've changed."

"Still want me to break the window?" she asked.

"About that . . ." he said.

"Forgotten," said Penny. "We'll always be good friends, Morris."

Vita listened, but thankfully said nothing about that exchange. "So, Morris. You've come to the mall for a new 'do?" she asked him.

"I had a few hours to kill before my train," he said, self-consciously running a hand over his shorn head.

Vita said, "Your haircut makes me very thirsty," and smiled winningly at the studly-yet-sincere erstwhile best man.

"I'd better buy you a drink," he said, rightly so.

An hour later, having sampled items from the Risotto Hut

and the Belini Buffet, the three mall rats perched on stools at
the Raw Sky Bar, slurping shots.

"No, no, Morris. That's all wrong," said Penny, who didn't
ordinarily (1) drink, (2) criticize, or (3) eat with her hands.
"Do it like this."

A raw oyster on the half-shell in one hand, Penny drizzled
two drops of Tabasco into a shot glass of vodka. She slid the
oyster into the glass and drank the seafood cocktail in a single,
slippery shiver.

"Natasha taught you?" asked Vita.

"She drank vodka in her baby bottles," slurred Penny. "She
can kill a man with a toothpick and a jar of peanut butter."

"Peanut butter must have been a real luxury in communist
Russia," said Morris.

"Shut up and drink," said Penny, letting the dog collar and
black polish do the talking for her.

"I'm not sure I like you this way," said Morris, artlessly
plopping an oyster into his glass.

"You preferred me slouched and passive?" asked Penny
with vodka volume. "Or was the attraction that I was engaged
to another man?"

"You weren't as loud before," he said.

"So tell me, Morris," said Vita, "what or whom do you do?
And have you done enough?"

Penny giggled.

Morris said, "I'm a freelance playwright."

" 'Freelance playwright'? I didn't know such a thing existed." Vita laughed. "You must get a ton of work."

His ruddy cheeks got even redder. "I get enough. I adver-
tise on Craigslist for anyone who needs help writing a speech
or a monologue. I've written marriage proposals for three
different men. And I've written speeches for people who
want to ask for a raise, or confess an affair to their wives.

I've finished a full-length two-act play that I'm trying to get produced."

Penny said, "I thought you lived off a trust."

"A brain trust," he grumbled.

"What's the play?" asked Vita eagerly, soberly. Penny registered the sudden shift in her friend's interest in Morris. Much as she was a seductress, Vita was an actress first. Men came and went (literally). But a good part could last forever.

"It's called *Edina Spanky: Privates Investigator*."

" 'Privates'?" asked Vita.

"She's a sexual investigator. A libido detective. She figures out what's wrong in her clients' sex lives and helps them correct it. In doing so, she fixes all of their problems. She's a hero, a savior. Naturally, her own sex life is fucked up."

"Those who can't do . . . *don't*," said Vita in a schmaltzy Raymond Chandler patter.

Morris gaped at her. "That's actually a line in my play."

Penny said, "Do you really think everyone's problems can be explained by sexual dysfunction?"

He shrugged. "For the purposes of a play, why not?"

"Edina Spanky gets to the *bottom* of every sex mystery," drawled Vita, inching closer to Morris.

"Can I steal that?" he asked.

Vita smiled sweet-and-deadly like Cherry Bomb. "Maybe I should take a look at your script," she suggested. "I'd be happy to offer my professional opinion."

"It's a play," he said.

"So much the better," said Vita, her eyes glowing.

Morris didn't know what he was getting into here. If *Edina Spanky: Privates Investigator* was appealing to Vita, her friend would be all over it, and him. Penny tasted the sour rise of envy in her throat. Not for Morris, or Vita. But for the script, the raw material, the beginning of something that could grow and change and improve. She listened to them talk, faded out of the conversation, into the background like a good chorus girl—pretty in the periphery. Largely overlooked.

Penny's eyes fell to her red patent leather toes. Perhaps Bram wouldn't have left her had she worn these shoes yesterday. They might have saved her, like her red cowboy boots had sixteen years ago. She and her mother had come to the mall that day on a mission. The dip into Precious was supposed to be brief, a quick stop on the way to their ultimate destination. But their big plans were forgotten when she was abducted. She'd never asked her mom if they could try again. Bringing up the subject to Esther seemed like a cruel reminder.

But Esther wasn't here now.

Penny said, "I have to do something." She pressed her card into the bartender's hand.

Vita and Morris turned toward her. They both were startled by her determined expression. "I think the bathrooms are to the left," said Vita.

"We have to leave," said Penny, signing and standing. "Now!"

The three gathered their bags. Penny hurried down the stairs, out of the Food Pavilion and around the hub into the Accessories Pavilion. Vita was looking at each storefront as they passed, asking repeatedly, "Is that it?" as they blew by store after store.

"I know it's around here . . . ah-ha! This is it!" she said, stopping short in front of Glimmer, the place for all things pink, purple, shiny, sparkly. A bangles and barrettes store galore.

The three looked up at the shimmering signage over the glass doors of Glimmer. "You have an urgent need for a furry notebook?" asked Vita.

"Come on," said Penny, dragging her into the tweenage mecca. Morris reluctantly followed, as if stepping into the den of adolescent femalia would make him sprout pubescent tits.

To Vita, Penny said, "You might have noticed, over the years, that my ears are not pierced."

At the counter in back they found a pimply teenage girl, her diamond-studded nose buried inside an *InStyle* magazine. The name tag on her shirt read DAWN D."

Lazily closing the pages, Dawn asked, "Who's first?" She reached for her piercing gun.

Penny suddenly felt the oyster shots. Backpedaling, she said, "Second thoughts."

"I could get another hole in my ear. Show you how easy it is," said Vita.

"I'll do it," said Morris, stepping forward.

"You will?"

"Guys with earrings are hot," said the teen.

"If it would make you happy," Morris said to Penny. "It's the least I can do for you. After, you know, what happened."

Dawn asked, "What happened?"

Vita said, "She got left at the altar yesterday. At the Plaza across the highway."

"That was you?" asked the puncturer. News of a disaster traveled turbo in New Jersey.

"The *old* me," said Penny.

Dawn readied her alcohol swabs. To Morris, she asked, "One ear or two?"

Morris looked from Vita to Penny. "What do you think?"

In unison, they answered: "Two."

The teen sat Morris down in a high-backed metal chair. She drew dots on his lobes with a fine point Sharpie. "Definitely two. One is queer," she said as she assessed her dot work. "Now hold still. A little antiseptic. A little nanomicrosecond of pinch, punch, and . . . one down."

"Jesus Christ!" cried Morris, reaching to cradle his lobe, a gold ball nestled against it.

"Another convert," said Vita.

Penny laughed. She loved Morris at that second, puncturing himself to lend her moral support. And Vita, holding both of their hands.

"A pinch, a punch . . . you're done," said the girl. "Want your nostril, too?"

"No!" shouted Morris and Vita.

He turned toward Vita, curious about her vehemence.

She said, "I don't date men with metal on their faces."

"You'd date me?" he asked, his thoughts of Penny's closed window disappearing in Vita's green eyes.

Vita kissed each of his lobes in response. Morris got out of the chair, stumbling charmingly. Penny took his place. She drew back her hair and let the teen swab her with alcohol and make dots on her ears with the Magic Marker.

"Hokay," said Dawn, loading the piercing gun with silver ball earrings. "Here we go."

At the first sharp prick, Penny felt herself swoon. She breathed deep, deciding to let herself feel it, not fear it. How many times had she prevented herself from feeling because she was scared of what would happen if she did? She flashed to that day at the mall. Men with guns, stomping toward her. Esther hysterical. Penny herself a mute limp doll in her mother's arms.

"Hold still now," said the teen. "Hey, she looks kind of weird."

"Get on with it," said Vita, locking eyes with Penny.

"A pinch, a punch . . ."

Penny screamed. Not a dainty yelp, either. A window-rattling, air-compressing, eardrum-popping explosion that flowed out of her mouth like a sonic river. People in the parking lot looked up. Birds flew off trees. Wineglasses shattered half a mile away. She screamed for the pinch. The punch. Her father's magnified head in the fountain. The ten minutes of terror when she was taken by a stranger.

Customers gathered outside the store to see who was being tortured.

"Do the other one!" Vita yelled at the girl. "Hurry up!"

Five seconds later it was over. Dawn leaned back and said, "And we're out."

Penny closed her mouth and the silence became a vacuum, sucking up all the mall sounds. The angel choir, the pings and dings of the elevator, shuffling feet, crinkling shopping bags, tinkling change in a fountain.

Penny grinned, touched her earlobes. The teen held up a mirror, and she saw the evidence. Her tasteful studs were perfectly symmetrical.

"You do good work," said Penny, going into her wallet and giving the teen a hundred dollar bill.

"It's ten bucks a pierce."

"Keep the change."

"You, too," said Dawn, a braver and wiser girl than Penny had thought. "Twist the posts and clean with witch hazel three times a day for a month."

"You hear that Morris?" asked Penny.

"I can't hear a thing," he said. "You've got some lungs, Penny."

The three walked out of the store. Penny had never felt taller, or lighter. She floated through the pavilion. "I couldn't have done that without you two," she said to her friends. They were heading toward the atrium, passing the yellow Lamborghini. "What a rush!" she added.

"It was a rush for me, too," said Vita. "Seems a shame to waste it. Tell me, Morris. What would Edina Spanky think of a woman who likes to fuck in cars?"

His chin crunched in thought, he said, "I guess Edina would . . . *what are you doing*?"

Vita had him by the belt and was yanking Morris toward

the Lamborghini, which was, as luck would have it, presently unguarded. She opened the car door and pushed Morris down in the passenger seat. Vita sat on his lap and closed the door.

The blackout windows ensured privacy. Penny stood guard. When the car started shaking, a mall hostess in trademark yellow (matched the car), rushed over and wanted to know, "What the hell is going on here?"

Penny folded her arms over her chest, stood at her formidable height, and said, "When the Lamborghini is a-rocking, don't come a-knocking."

"We'll see about that," said the hostess, taking out her walkie-talkie. "Security!"

The passenger side door opened. Vita spilled out first, then Morris.

Penny said, "That was fast."

Vita said, "Lamborghini." She straightened her skirt. "Although, to be honest, I'm not sure if I just gave a hand job to the stick shift or the guy."

"The stick shift," said Morris. "But it really liked it."

And they ran (giggling, serpentine) out the mall's exit. Penny's feet felt puffy as eggplants. The handles of her bags cut into her fingers. The dog makeup was making her eyes itch. Her ear holes were throbbing ever so rhythmically. She hadn't been as exhilarated in months.

When they reached the safety of the parking lot, she asked, "You know what's supposed to come first?"

"The woman?" asked Vita.

"*Safety*," said Penny. "Safety is supposed to come first. But when it does, it's also last and everything in between."

"So you're in a dangerous mood," said Vita.

"I could kill something!" Penny proudly proclaimed.

"How about a fifth of scotch?" asked Morris. "We could

drive into the city, hang at my apartment. Just don't judge me for the filth. I wasn't expecting guests."

"As appealing as that sounds," said Vita, "why don't we go to my hotel room? I haven't checked out yet."

"Actually, would you take me home?" asked Penny. She wanted to show her mom the earrings.

Chapter 16

"*What have you done?*" asked Esther, her finger shaking with disbelief at the bundle in Natasha's arms. The two women were in the mansion kitchen on Overlook Lane.

"He is Moscovian miniature terrier," said Natasha. "Also called Russian toy terrier. One-year-old male. Only at Short Hares animal shelter you find rare purebred dog."

"Take it back!" shrieked Esther, who was not fond of dogs, even a pocket-sized, spindle-legged, Martian-eared mutant like this squirming canine thing.

Natasha stroked the pup in one hand and pressed his miniature snout into her cheek. "We had dog like this in Moscow. Nikita. He had favorite spot, on big armchair by furnace in living room that was also bedroom for my five brothers. We lived nineteen people in one house."

"Where as, in Short Hares, middle-aged women live alone in mansions," said Esther. "Correction: Make that two middle-aged women."

"Thirty-six is not middle age," said Natasha, making a correction of her own. "So Uncle Vanya—he lost one leg in second war, with bad heart and psoriasis. He would peel skin and throw pieces at furnace. So one day he sat in armchair without looking and crushed Nikita to death. We kept chair. Threw away dog."

Esther said, "I don't care if your uncle lost both legs. And an arm. You cannot keep this dog."

"He did lose arm!" said Natasha. "He was hit by bus in Red Square in winter. He waited five hours for ambulance to come, and his arm went frostbite."

"I so love your colorful stories of the motherland," said Esther.

"I want this dog," Natasha declared. "So does Penny."

"Why would she want a dog she's never known?"

"This is nature of wanting! Everyone wants things they've never known," said Natasha. "Hold him. Look at little face!"

The Russian shoved the petite pup at Esther, but the stench made her stumble backward. "He smells like rot."

"I wash him," said the Russian, stealing up to her room to lavish soap and love on the dog.

"We're not naming him Nikita," Esther called after her. "For one thing, he's no La Femme. Which reminds me: Is he neutered?"

Natasha, voice trailing as she got farther away, said, "If he's not, I'll do it myself."

Vita's green bug appeared outside the kitchen window. Esther instinctively ducked under the counter. She hated that Vita, and had since Penny brought her home from NYU. She was a negative influence on Penny, with her man-chasing and that idiotic soap opera. Some performing arts majors were destined for Broadway, thought Esther. And some would have to settle for basic cable. Besides, how dare Vita accuse her of bad driving? Even if it were true?

A shadow fell over the kitchen door. Someone walked into

the kitchen. From her crouch, Esther could see only a pair of bright red pumps clicking across the terra cotta tile. And then the woman came fully into view. Esther observed her from the bottom up. Slutty heels, tattered jeans, shopping bags hooked under each black-nail-polished hand, too-tight T-shirt, dog collar as a necklace, black lipstick, black eyeliner, mussed hair.

She did a double take. Egads, it was her own daughter.

"Hi, Mom," said Penny. "Lose something?"

"Getting there," she said, standing up.

"I got my ears pierced. Do we have witch hazel? Vita had sex with a car. I used your golden card. Freely."

"The girl at the Chanel counter did this?" she asked, refering to Penny's bitchin' makeup.

"I did it myself," said her daughter with pride.

"You look awful," said Esther. "Go upstairs and wash your face."

"How could you let a seven-year-old wander off at the Short Hares Mall? Why weren't you keeping a closer eye on me?" asked her daughter.

When Esther didn't respond (she was having trouble breathing from the mere mention of that hideous day), Penny said, "We've never spoken about it. You like to pretend it didn't happen, or that I don't remember. But I do. Clearly. You were haggling over a price at Precious. I got bored and walked out of the store. And then she grabbed my arm and pulled me into the bathroom."

If physiologically feasible, Esther's jaw would have dropped off its hinge and rolled ten feet across the floor. She was shocked and cut by Penny's accusation. By guilt, too. Finally finding her breath, she managed to say, "I wasn't haggling."

"Then what were you doing?"

"I was trying to sell a Valentino suit," said Esther. "The

saleswoman offered me a quarter of what it was worth, and I wasn't in the position to take less than half."

"Selling your clothes? Why would you do that?" Penny asked, incredulous. As far as her daughter knew, Esther only accumulated. She held on to everything. A habit she'd picked up when her divorce settlement fight began.

Russell had cut Esther off as soon as he left the mansion, taking the au pair Jemima with him. He closed joint accounts, cancelled her cards. He consented to pay the mortgage and the bills from Kings, the supermarket. But otherwise Esther was completely on her own with a three-year-old. Penny wasn't in preschool, and Esther couldn't afford babysitting, so she couldn't get a job.

His strategy had been to make her crack so she'd agree quickly to his terms. But Esther held on, selling jewelry to buy clothes and books for Penny, to pay the phone bill. After four years Russell got tired of waiting for Esther to crumble. He announced (via his lawyer) that he would no longer pay her Kings bills. Russell intended to starve Esther (as well as his own daughter) into a settlement. She got that news with one foot out the door, on the way to the mall so Penny could get her ears pierced. With no more jewelry to sell, Esther went up to her room and grabbed some couture suits.

"I needed the money," she said.

"You were so focused on bickering over a few hundred dollars that you let me slip away," said Penny.

Esther had come to this junction before. Should she tell Penny about her father's cruelty, or let her go on believing that Russell was a flawed but decent man? She itched to tell Penny every way he'd twisted the knife. But she also wanted to shield her daughter from the truth about the murky water in her gene pool. Much as she wanted to forget that time in her life, she had kept the memories fresh, waiting with both terror and anticipation for the day she'd have to share them with Penny.

Has the moment finally arrived? she wondered. Her ribs felt tight, crushed, like her secrets were being squeezed out of her.

"I don't know why all this is coming up now," said Esther explosively. "It's Bram's fault somehow. The tension between us started the day you met him. And it keeps on coming even now that he's . . ."

"He's what?" asked Penny.

"Gone," said Esther. "Bram is gone, gone, gone. And good riddance. He's the one you should be angry at. I never did anything to hurt you. I've protected you from a thousand hurts. And that afternoon, by the way, broke me. Broke me in half. I woke up a different person the next day. I was fighting for our lives, Penny. You have no fucking idea what you're talking about."

Penny gaped at Esther, her pretty mouth a perfect circle. The overhead kitchen light glinted off her new earrings. Even in the full flower of her anger at her ungrateful daughter, Esther hoped that the piercing hadn't hurt too much.

"I was thinking of selling my ring, actually," said Penny, twisting the bauble on her finger. "Or sending it back to Bram."

"Oh," said Esther.

"I can't. Not yet anyway. The ring makes me feel close to him. Being in this house makes me feel close to him. Can't explain that, since we hardly spent any time here."

Their talk was interrupted by the pitter of hairy wet feet, followed by the clomp of Candies. Penny said, "You found him!" Her face lit up and she clicked out of the kitchen toward the commotion.

Esther pinched herself to settle down. Then she followed

her daughter into the foyer in time to see the dog scramble across the floor, slide on his slick wet paws and crash into the wall of gift boxes, knocking one off with a crash.

"Ceramic platter," guessed Esther.

Natasha picked up the box and shook. "Ten bucks says crystal candlesticks."

"You're on," said Esther.

"Ha!" snorted Natasha when the candlesticks were revealed.

"You wouldn't've paid me if I'd won anyway," said Esther.

"Hello, little guy," said Penny, catching the shivering, suds-covered dog. "Soaking wet, he's four pounds."

"I catch him in trap outside," lied Natasha.

"A mouse trap?" groused Esther.

"You said 'average size,' " said Penny, letting the animal lick her face (which, Esther was thankful to see, cleaned away some of her ghoulish makeup).

"Small, medium, no difference," answered Natasha.

"This dog ate three roast chickens?" asked Penny. "He's hardly bigger than a drumstick."

"He poops bigger," said Natasha, holding up a plastic Baggie, as if confirmation was needed or appreciated.

Esther groaned. "Do you intend to bronze it?"

"For vet," said Natasha. "To check for worms."

Closing her eyes tight (but seeing ringworms under her lids anyway), Esther said, "I hate this dog."

"I love him," said Penny, holding him in the air and spinning around and around. "I want to be with him forever and ever. He's everything I've ever wished for, and wanted, and waited . . . oh, God. I need to sit."

Natasha sniffed. "You are drunk," she said to Penny. "You had vodka and oysters." Her nose twitched again. "Seven."

Esther wondered if she was hard of smelling; she hadn't

detected an atom of alcohol in the air. Drunkenness would explain Penny's bold outburst in the kitchen, the tottering, the maudlin sobbing as she clutched the fragile terrier.

They'd have to keep him now. "What should we name him?" she asked

"Nikita." This from Natasha.

"No way."

"How about Snuggles?" asked Natasha snidely.

"Bram!" shouted Penny.

"Where?" said Esther, spinning around to look up the stairs.

Penny said, "I meant we should name the dog Bram."

Esther touched her rampant heart, which was straining against her blouse. She wasn't sure she could stand any more of this. "How about Boris?" she suggested.

Natasha said, "I like Boris."

"Hello, Boris!" said Penny, her nose to his snout.

Chapter 17

"How much shrimp can one man *eat*?"

The overflowing tray sagged under the weight of fifty shrimp, a vat of cocktail sauce, forty halved red potatoes, an entire sockeye salmon, a liter of San Pellegrino, and the top tier of the wedding cake.

Bram frowned when he noticed the white plastic fork, knife, and spoon. He'd been hoping for a replacement set of steel utensils. The knife and fork he'd been working with were bent and mangled. He'd made good use of them, though, dismantling the bookshelves. He'd had to work in the dark, in a fury, afraid that he'd be caught. But then, as the hours went by this morning without a visitor, he slowed and concentrated, making every minute count.

The bookshelves were propped back in place now, had been for at least an hour. He must have dozed on the couch, and woke up to find the food by the door.

"Anyone there?" he asked, assuming someone was on the other side of the mirror.

No response. Mrs. Bracket and her Slavic henchwoman

hadn't bothered to talk to him all day. Solitary confinement was taking its toll. He'd gone two days without seeing another human being. Bram was lonely.

"Be careful what you wish for," he said to himself, although he was hoping for some response.

Nothing came back but silence.

Bram slid the tray onto the table. He pulled up the tiny chair, arranged his knees alongside the table's corners, and dug in. The food tasted marvelous, and he scooped bigger and bigger bites. He could choke on a shrimp, and no one would rush in to Heimlich him. He could have a heart attack. He could suffer a stroke. Who knew what kind of blood clot was forming under the goose egg on his head? He might be hemorrhaging.

He stuffed a wedge of salmon in his mouth. People overeat because they're bored. They overeat because they're lonely. Because they have no one who loved them to tell them to stop. People in love have someone watching their back. And their backside.

Penny had long, strong thighs she'd wrap around his ribs and squeeze. She had a high, round ass so tight you could bounce a quarter off it. He thought of her reclining on his bed on Sullivan Street, her legs parted slightly, just a shadow visible between them.

Bram put down his fork. He surveyed the tray and saw that he'd all but polished off the shrimp, salmon, and potatoes. He'd consumed three days' worth of calories in fifteen minutes.

He dropped the tray back by the door and lay down on the couch, his legs hanging off the side. He unbuttoned his pants, put his forearm over his eyes and realized with surprise that he was about to cry.

Bolting upright, he said, "This is fucking crazy! Let me *out of here!*"

Prowling as best he could with a grossly extended belly, Bram returned to the bookshelves, and searched them again for some toy or tool he could use to pick the lock, not that he knew how to do that. He caught a glimpse of himself in the two-way mirror. He patted his stomach. Already, he'd gained weight. He'd roll out of this room, if he could fit through the door.

He badly needed a distraction. Scanning the video selection, he found only classic little girl romantic fantasy. *Sleeping Beauty. Cinderella. Snow White.* Stories of princesses held captive, set free by hard-won love. The stuff Penny grew up on. The fairy tales had been absorbed by her formative brainpan. He was not her prince, that was for fucking sure. He wondered if anyone could satisfy her or know what it would take to make her happy.

Bram closed his eyes and pinched the bridge of his nose. He had to stop returning to these depressing thoughts. He grabbed the *Cinderella* video, put it in the VCR. He retrieved the cake plate and settled down on the couch for dessert and a flick.

Somehow, he'd managed to exist on Earth for twenty-five years without having seen this movie. Ten minutes into it, Bram was impressed by the pitiful orphaned girl. "Cinderella had pluck," he said to himself.

"Glad to see you've made yourself comfortable," said a voice over the PA system.

It took him by such surprise, he dropped the cake on his lap.

"Go to hell," he said, wiping at his jeans.

"Okay," she said, switching off the PA.

"Wait," he said, hungry for conversation.

Nothing.

"You have to tell me if Penny's okay," he demanded.

"She's fine," said the voice. "She's happy. Relieved. You did her a favor by leaving, and she's starting a new life without you."

"What does that mean?" he asked. Was Penny already seeing another man? He felt sick, the shrimp and salmon wrestling each other in his stomach. Morris Nova's face flashed across his mind. He'd always had a crush on Penny. Had he acted on it? Had Penny been receptive?

"It means she's moving on," said the voice. "Listen carefully. I'm going out to dinner. While I'm gone, I expect you to finish the return mailing labels."

"I have to know about Penny," he said, standing, cake crumbs tumbling on the floor. "Where is she? Is someone taking care of her?" *Someone other than you, soulless maniac,* he thought, but didn't say.

"She went back to New York," said the voice. "And I can assure you, she's getting all the TLC she needs."

Bram felt a surge in his throat. He started hacking, coughing, doubled over. Violent spasms rocked his chest. "Help!" he wheezed. "Help me! I'm sick! I need a doctor." Chock, sputter, writhe. "You can't let me die in here!" One hand clutching his chest, the other extended, fingers rigid, desperate.

Esther laughed, a wicked cackle. "Nice try," she said. "And clean that tray. You've still got another hundred and fifty servings to get through."

Bram sighed. He sat back down on the couch, temporarily defeated.

Esther said, "Are you ready to admit you beat up my daughter?"

"That is *not* what happened," he insisted.

"So what did?"

He bit his lip.

"I'm leaving," she said. "If you notice a green toxic gas oozing through the vents, just ignore it."

"One more thing," he said.

"Hurry up," she said.

"If I could do it over, I would marry her."

"Big of you," she said. "Shithead."

She switched off the PA system, killing the hum.

He was alone again. Esther said she was going out. Penny was back in the city. The Russian was probably locked in her room, swilling vodka. He would attempt to escape tonight, but then again, it might be an unnecessary risk. Sunday morning would come soon enough.

Bram imagined what his rescue would look like. A battering ram at the front doors. A SWAT team bursting into the house.

Soon enough, he thought. He'd have to be patient, bide his time. He turned his attention back to Cinderella. At present, her stepsisters were in a mad, lusty frenzy, tearing off Cinderella's party dress.

"In another context, this scene could be hot," Bram said to himself, licking the frosting off the plate.

Chapter 18

At six in the evening Penny eavesdropped on her mother and Keith from the second-floor landing.

"I hope you don't mind if we go out for dinner," said Esther, holding the front door open for him. "I wasn't in the mood for anything on the wedding menu."

"Are you feeling better?" asked Keith, natty in a suit. "Did the nap help?"

"Very much, thank you."

"Where's Penny?" he asked. "She's not coming?"

"She's . . . tired and emotional."

Keith laughed and said, "That's how the English describe someone who's had too much to drink."

"Penny doesn't drink," replied Esther crisply. "She's tired and emotional because of everything that's happened."

Penny frowned. But she *was* drunk. Had been, anyway, before the hangover set in. Her mom was always such a hothead. Why couldn't she relax? Penny had spent half of her childhood trying to calm her mother down when she flew into a rage about the slightest thing, a missed appointment, a teacher's note, a leaky faucet.

Keith smiled into Esther's face of fury, not indulging it. He said, "Perhaps you're also tired and emotional?"

Esther said, "I certainly am!"

"Then I've got some catching up to do," said Keith, taking Esther's elbow—which was, perhaps, the first time, in recent or distant memory, she'd seen a man touch her mom—and pulled her out the door.

Finally, she and Boris, her new love, were alone.

"It's me and you tonight, Boris," Penny whispered into his mud flap ear.

Penny held him like a babe in her arms. "From what I understand of dogs, if I feed you, you'll be devoted to me forever and stare at me with worshipful, moist loving eyes."

Men were so often compared to dogs. Penny had seen a handful of self-help books with titles like *Men: A Training Manual* and *How to Make Your Man Sit Up and Beg*. Last year she read a novel with the opening line: "Peg Silver could make a man come, but she couldn't make him stay."

Penny tickled Boris under his triangle chin and decided the comparison between men and dogs wasn't apt.

"It's an insult to dogs," she said to Boris, who seemed to smile.

She took him into her private lair. Her entire apartment in New York could fit inside her bedroom in New Jersey. When she was a kid, she'd called it "the ballroom" because the vaulted ceilings and elongated, rectangular layout reminded her of ballroom scenes from princess movies. By the time Penny was fifteen, she realized calling her bedroom a "ballroom" might give people the wrong idea. As a point of fact, she'd never balled anyone in here—or in this house. Her high school assignations were always outside, in the pool cabana or on a blanket in the woods. She and Bram never spent the night here. He refused to. Said he'd be afraid Esther would try to kill him in his sleep.

The no-balling policy applied not only to her own bedroom. The whole house was a sexless manse, a palace of abstinence.

"And yet, I want to move back in," she said.

Penny decided to shed her goth makeup and jeans, and she changed into soft cotton lounge pants and a tank top. Possibly nap. She lay down on her bed, king-sized with a cushioned headboard for, as her dad once said (a distant or imagined memory?), "his little princess." Boris scampered on the quilt. He sniffed and pranced in circles. She hoped he'd settle down. As it just so happened, she *was* tired and emotional. Mainly tired.

But Penny couldn't sleep a wink. Not with Boris hurdling back and forth across her body. He chewed on her hair, her shirt. He licked her face, panted in her ear.

"You're a hyper puppy. Maybe you have doggie ADHD," she said. He fixed on her with these big wet eyes, wagging his tail, waiting and watching, demanding strokes and coos. It was enervating, to be stared at like that. And how much cuddling did one creature need?

"Maybe you have to go out?" asked Penny. Boris immediately bounded off the bed and scratched at the door. Groaning, Penny hoisted herself out of bed, into slippers. She opened the door—he'd been hurling himself against it—and trudged down the hallway as he ran ahead. Instead of going downstairs, though, the dog made an abrupt left turn and raced up to the third floor.

"No, Boris. Come. Come!" said Penny.

A memory flash: she and Bram in his bed, him on top of her, screwing her slowly, whispering "Come, come," in her ear.

Penny swallowed hard and shook the image out of her

mind. She would not think about Bram. And definitely not about sex.

She called up the stairs again. "Get your dog ass down here!" Boris barked back. And then kept barking, with impressive volume, given his size.

He smelled something. Probably squirrels or a raccoon in the attic.

Looking upward, into the darkness of the third floor, Penny couldn't believe this was her life. She was supposed to be on her honeymoon, not chasing after a frantic, emotionally greedy pet.

Perhaps Boris would eat the squirrels. Or they'd eat him. A fat Short Hares squirrel might outweigh the dog. Penny took a step upward, then another. Boris was going berserk, high-pitched yelps alternating with low growls.

There really was something up there. Maybe bigger than a raccoon. She felt cold suddenly, a shiver of nerves, her back muscles rippling. Penny paused. If a woodchuck or a raccoon was up there, she should be in jeans, boots, and a long-sleeved jacket. That would be prudent. The animal could be rabid. She should be safe.

Natasha will know what to do, she thought.

Penny turned back around, skipping down a flight of stairs.

But halted, mid-step. "Fuck safety," she said. "The woman is supposed to come first."

Penny marched all the way up to the third floor. She'd deal with the creature by herself. However big and rabid it might be.

Chapter 19

"Where are we going?" asked Esther from the passenger seat of Keith's Town Car.

They'd been driving south on the Garden State Parkway for nearly an hour already. Keith had been taciturn. He didn't fill the dead space with chatter, which Esther appreciated. Chatty men reminded her of Russell (aka Liar). He could talk for twenty minutes about any subject, since he knew everything about everything. When they'd first met—Esther was twenty years old at the time and easily impressed—she thought Russell was the smartest man she'd ever met. She once loved to listen to him expound. Russell wasn't so chatty anymore.

Keith said, "We're going to see the ocean."

Full moon. The boardwalk would be breezy in June. The lapping of the waves on the empty beach at night. Shoes in their hands, they could walk barefoot on the sand. So this was to be a romantic adventure. Esther hadn't been on one of those since she was in her early twenties.

She said, "Were you planning this?"

"Snap decision," he said, eyes off the highway briefly to smile at her. "When I found out Penny wasn't coming."

Esther looked out her window, away from the handsome widower next to her. The lights of oncoming cars blipped by. She was hypnotized by them. Every mile away from Short Hares made her feel freer, lighter. Younger.

"I thought it'd be nice to take a drive," he said.

"Very New Jersey of you," she said. "We're a car-loving people. You know the opening credits of *The Sopranos*—Tony in his Range Rover? Says it all."

He nodded. "So the beach is okay with you?" he asked.

"Sure," she said. "I'm always up for a clam roll." The last time she'd been down the shore (in NJ, one never said "to the beach") was on her impromptu honeymoon in Atlantic City. She and Russell stayed in the Maharaja Suite at Trump's Taj Mahal Casino, where and when she lost her virginity. She added, "I haven't been down the shore in quite a while." (As it were.)

"Good to know," he said, sounding pleased.

"You like clam rolls?"

"I like spontaneity," he said. "Same as you. I knew you'd like getting in the car and driving."

He thought she was spontaneous? Esther didn't bother correcting him. Let him think what he wanted. It was his car.

Keith said, "This is the first time I've had breakfast and dinner on the same day with the same woman since my wife died."

"The real milestone would be having dinner and then breakfast," said Esther. "Which isn't going to happen."

He nodded. "I said you were spontaneous, not easy."

"I'm definitely not easy," she agreed.

Keith laughed. *He's the easy one*, thought Esther. "My wife Alice wasn't impulsive *or* easy. She needed advanced warning about everything. She'd study menus before making reservations, read ten reviews before going to a movie, laid out her clothes before going to bed. She researched for a year before making travel plans. I loved her meticulousness when we first met. I was a little too spontaneous myself at that age, if you know what I mean."

"I haven't the slightest," she said, deadpan.

He smiled, eyes on the road. "I trusted her judgment. If she were on the case, the restaurant would be clean and good. The movie would be smart and funny. The resort comfortable and convenient. Alice took care of everything outside of work, let me build the business. She was a loving, warm woman, but compulsive about planning in advance. Shames me to say, when the oncologist said her cancer was 'advanced,' I almost laughed."

"I thought she had a heart attack," said Esther.

"She did," he said. "Her heart was weakened by months of chemotherapy. She was in treatment when she died. Classic case of, 'If the disease doesn't kill you, the cure will.' "

"Funny how what attracts you to someone at first is usually what you grow to hate about him—her—in the end," said Esther.

They stared straight ahead out the windshield. The black highway curved.

Keith said, "I never said I hated anything about Alice. I loved my wife until her last breath."

She'd said the wrong thing. Esther groaned inwardly. Her inexperience with men was only glaringly obvious. What did it matter, anyway? Her goal should be to repel this man. Keith Shiraz was not just some guy with a broad chest and powerful pheromones. He was father of her enemy. Therefore, he was her enemy as well, no matter how much his physical presence made her light-headed.

Suddenly claustrophobic in the Town Car, Esther said, "Take this exit. Right here. Take it!"

She tugged the wheel to the right. Keith swerved across two lanes to get off the highway. They screeched around the ramp and came to a jerky stop at the red light at the bottom.

"Pull over," said Esther, pointing at a boxy clapboard building, a six-foot metal lobster on the roof. The neon sign in the window buzzed ABRUZZI'S.

Keith parked the Town Car. Esther pushed her door open and flung herself out. The briny sea air helped. She greedily inhaled the salt and sand, the gritty essence, she thought, of New Jersey. Appropriately enough, they'd landed in the shore town of Sea Grit.

"What's the matter with you?" asked Keith, slamming his car door behind him, stomping toward her, red in the face.

"I wanted a drink," she said, and walked into the restaurant.

The place was dark and dank; the only light came from the seven or eight neon signs for Budweiser, Miller, Pabst, Heineken. Esther took a seat at the splintered bar and waved at the bartender. In his early twenties, he wore skintight acid-washed jeans, rips in the knees, a white T-shirt with the Rolling Stone lips logo. The left sleeve was cut off, and the right rolled up around a pack of Marlboros. His hair was brown, long and puffy in back, short and puffy on top. In the back pocket of his jeans he'd stuffed a wallet on a chain. In the other pocket, a metal hair pick.

"A glass of water, please," said Esther.

"Just wawtah?" asked the bartender.

"Yes. Wah-ter. Thank you."

"Bottle or tap?"

"Actually," she mused, "make it a double gin martini with two olives." Keith sat down next to her. She said to him, "Alcohol should kill the germs in the glass."

To the bartender, Keith said, "The same."

He fixed and brought their drinks. She took a sip. "This is the worst martini I've ever tasted."

Keith tried his. "Disgusting," he agreed.

The bartender said, "Ten bucks apiece. Cash only."

They drank. Esther said, "I'm sorry about your wife. I didn't mean to imply anything about your marriage."

"I got defensive," he said. "Besides, I'm pretty sure you were referring to your own marriage."

She nodded. "It was short and long ago," she said dismissively, trying to change the subject.

"I don't know how you avoided remarrying. I bet you were swarmed by men when you were newly single at—how old?—in your late twenties?"

"I was twenty-five when he . . . when we separated. I was thirty when he died. And there wasn't much of a swarm." A lot of potential suitors stayed away because of the lingering suspicion—perpetuated by gossip—that she had some hand in Russell's deadly plunge. He died an hour before signing papers, after all, conveniently making her a very wealthy woman. Esther didn't like being thought of as a murderess, but she was grateful to be left alone. She couldn't have trusted anyone after what she'd been through, especially considering her new status as an obscenely wealthy widow. She was a target for any fortune hunter. Any man—fortune hunter or otherwise—who'd shown interest over the years was diverted by Ashley Longmead.

"I didn't—don't—want to remarry," she said. "I have a child to protect."

"You've done a great job with her," he said. "Penny is a wonderful woman." He'd emphasized the word "woman," implying Penny was too old to be mothered.

"She's as naive as I was at her age," snapped Esther. "And I made some pretty big mistakes."

He asked, "Where were the people who should have helped you? Your family?"

"My parents live in Columbus," she said. "When I married Russell—spontaneously, a week after meeting him—they cut me off."

"Because it was so rushed?"

They hated him on sight. He was twenty years old than Esther. And slick as an otter. But the real reason they objected: "He was Jewish," she said.

Instead of taking offense (Keith was also Jewish), he laughed. Then he shook his head in disbelief. "So you're not a member of the tribe after all," he said. "I wasn't sure. Esther is a classic Jewish name."

"Tell that to my Catholic parents," she said. "Russell was adamant about raising Penny Jewish, and I didn't really care one way or the other. I never told Penny I'm not Jewish. I didn't want to confuse her when she was young. And now, I don't see why it would matter anyway. I'd appreciate it if you didn't tell her."

Keith seemed surprised to hear it. He looked at Esther strangely, sadly, like he wanted to ask what else Penny didn't know about her mother, her identity, her childhood. Or what else he didn't know and couldn't possibly imagine about Esther.

Uncomfortable about the unspoken questions, Esther drained her glass. She hadn't talked to anyone—except Natasha—about Russell or what she'd kept from Penny. Ashley was her friend, but not entirely trustworthy.

He said, "I've got to excuse myself." To the bartender, he said, "Men's?"

Esther peeked at his rear view when he walked toward the restroom. Like all of Keith, his ass was solid, masculine. Esther had large hands, for a woman, and she pictured them fanning wide across his cheeks.

Abruzzi's door swung open, the gust of salt air sweeping away her randy thoughts. A couple of men came in. They could be the bartender's brothers. Same shore style, the frizzy mullet, too-tight T-shirt and jeans, big basketball sneakers. They bellied up to the bar, high-fived the young man behind it and ordered a round of Budweisers. Instead of showing the common courtesy of giving Esther a one-stool-over cushion of privacy, the taller acid-washed idiot sat immediately to her right. Where Keith had been seated.

She smiled condescendingly at him (couldn't help it) and said, "That seat's taken."

"Whoa!" he said, recoiling. "From the back, I thought you were a lot younger. Shit, you could be my mother."

Esther didn't dare imagine what this kid's mother looked like, but she was certain, given his extreme buckteeth and scar-ravaged skin, that his comment was not a compliment. She said, "If you don't mind moving."

"I do mind," he said. "This is my stool. I sit here every night. And if you've got a problem with that, you can kiss my bony white ass." Which more or less spoiled Esther's thoughts about Keith's derriere.

Having learned as a Lady of Short Hares that the best way to handle unpleasantness was to ignore it, Esther turned away from the lout and fixated on her empty glass.

He said, "Well, you're not leaving. So that means you like me. I usually don't go for anyone over twenty-five, but there's not another woman in here. And you're a decent looking old lady."

The cretin dared to put his hand on her knee, which, as they say in NJ, skeeved her out.

She threw Keith's martini in his face. The kid pawed at his eyes and screamed, "It burns!"

She said, "Keep your unmanicured hands to yourself, or I'll

hit you on the head with a bottle and dump you in the Pine Barrens!"

"You bitch," he snarled, coming at her with a hair pick.

He didn't lurch an inch. Keith Shiraz, back from the john, had the ruffian by the neck of his T-shirt. The kid struggled, but Keith had fifty pounds and thirty years of experience in his favor. Once the kid stopped jerking, Keith whispered in his ear.

The kid's face drained of color, youth, cock, bull.

Keith let him go. The kid fell on the floor and race-crawled out of the bar, his friend and the bartender snorting at his expense as the door hit his bony white ass on the way out.

"What did you say to him?" asked the bartender.

Keith shrugged. "I told him he'd left his headlights on."

The shore guys laughed heartily (they were also easy).

Esther asked, "What did you really say?"

Keith shook his head.

"Come on," she pleaded.

"Piss me off and you'll find out."

A thrilling and frightening suggestion. Esther was not immune to flattery. Being avenged by Keith was a huge turn on. Even more, being at his mercy.

She asked, "Can we go?"

Keith took out his wallet and left two twenties on the bar. He didn't ask her why she wanted to leave or where she wanted to go. He probably assumed she was having a fit of her alleged spontaneity. But Esther was not an impulsive person. With two major exceptions (the little Bram-bashing moment; marrying Russell), she had lived a rigid if cushy life. Either Keith had a limbering influence on her. Or, perhaps hitting Bram over the head had knocked something loose in her own mind.

They went outside. The block was quiet. Keith unlocked the Town Car doors. Instead of getting in the passenger seat, Esther opened the rear door and slid into the back seat.

He said, "I'm your chauffeur now?"

"Sit next to me," she said, patting the spot.

He slid in and closed the door behind him. Then locked it with his fob.

Keith said, "I never know what you're going to do next."

Esther said, "Bullshit."

They went at each other, mouths first, hands a fast second. Esther hoisted herself onto his lap. He was so large, thuggish, he made her feel small. A hand on the back of her neck, Keith lowered her onto the seat. He bent over her, mauling her lips, bruising her tits.

Pulling back, he said, "Does this mean we *are* going to have breakfast together?"

"How can you be thinking about food?" she asked.

Chapter 20

"For fock's sake, shut up!" Penny yelled at Boris, still frantically barking and hopping up and down in front of the door to her old playroom.

Pressing her ear against it, Penny thought she heard faint voices. Barely audible. But they seemed to be high-pitched, squeaky, singing.

She turned the knob. Locked. Penny tried to look under the crack, but the doorjamb was sealed with a foam-rubber strip.

"Raccoons get in, but they don't get out," she mused. "There must be a key somewhere."

Groping along the door molding, she searched for the key. Finding none, she tried the knob again, rattling it, attempting to force it open. She leaned against the door and pushed with all her weight, slamming against it twice to test the lock's strength.

Boris watched her approvingly. He cocked his head and yelped whenever she grunted with exertion, cheering her on. One final smack failed. "Ouch," she said, rubbing her bicep.

Hands on hips, Penny looked up and down the third floor

landing. Furniture was piled along the walls, stacks of chairs, nesting tables. She noticed something on one of the tables. It looked like a wedge of cheese. She went over to inspect the object.

"Not a wedge," she said, "a wedg*ie*." Penny tightly gripped the right shoe, remembering exactly when she'd seen the left.

Her eyes lit on the door opposite the nesting tables, or more particularly, the smudge above its knob. Bending closer, she saw that the smudge was white, frosty. She sniffed.

"Not frosty," she said. "Frost*ing*."

From her wedding cake.

The knob on this door turned. She opened it, slapped on the wall light switch, and surveyed the space she'd never seen before, didn't, in fact, know existed.

A console with a microphone and a dozen buttons and switches. A big window, but not to the outside, to the neighboring room. Two chairs. A suitcase on the floor. A framed photo on the console. She picked it up to see what it was.

Her own face smiled back at her.

She looked up, through the window. Even in the dim light she immediately recognized her old playroom. The tiny table, the bookshelves, the glowing TV, the pink couch.

And then something unexpected. A dark shadow, against the wall by the door. The shape of a man. His arm was raised over his head, something in his hand. A plastic doll?

The shadow moved. Just slightly, a shuffle of feet an inch to the right. He was real. Alive. It took a moment for Penny to process the information. Strange man in room. Poised to bring down the wrath of Barbie on whoever walked through that door.

Penny screamed. Her skin went cold, her blood ice. She instinctively backed away and bounced against the opposite wall, falling on top of the suitcase on the floor. Boris barking in her ear, jumping on her stomach. Scrambling, she tried to get up, her feet without purchase, her hands flailing. She rolled off the suitcase, clutching it, holding it like a shield against her chest. Except it wasn't latched and fell open, the contents—cotton clothing, mostly—spilling onto the floor at her slippered feet.

The smell of Bram was everywhere in the small room now, overwhelming her nostrils.

Penny threw the clothes off of her and stood up. She glanced again at the man shadow, leaned over the console for a closer look, and inadvertently toggled a switch.

Suddenly, an electronic hum filled the room. Over the hum, she heard breathing. Shallow, rapid—and *familiar*. She recognized its depth and rhythm, the slight catch at the end of an inhale. That same sound had filled her ears as she lay in bed, writhing beneath the man she loved.

"Bram?" she asked. He looked toward the window, startling her. But he didn't seem to see her. "I don't understand. What are you doing here?"

He lowered his arm and said, "I was doing . . . some stretching exercises."

"You were going to cudgel me with a Barbie!"

He approached the window, stood close to it, talked at it, but four feet to the left from where she was. She could see him, but he couldn't see her.

"I didn't expect you back so soon," he said.

"Back from where?" she asked, mystified.

"Wherever you went," he said impatiently. "You told me you were going out."

She'd told him nothing! She hadn't exchanged a syllable with him since the rehearsal dinner. "You're deluded," she said.

"An hour ago, you told me you were going out to dinner. You wanted me to write the return address labels. And I'm going to start on those just as soon as Cinderella gets her foot massage from the Grand Duke."

And then it hit her. *He thinks I'm Mom.* Ergo, her mom knew Bram was here, in her old playroom. Hiding out? No, he was locked in. Imprisoned. Against his will.

"Holy shit!"

The same words Penny had just been thinking came from the open door. Natasha stood in the threshold. Throwing her weight into the room, she toggled a switch and the room fell suddenly, vacuously, quiet, the hum silenced.

The two women stared at each other for ten seconds before both started yelling at once.

"You're in on it!"

"It's not what you think!"

"This belongs to you!" Penny shook the wedgie at Natasha.

"Your mother is going to have a basket case."

"You don't have a basket case," said Penny. "You *are* a basket case. And you are!"

"You should see yourself," tsked Natasha.

Penny caught her reflection in the window, the crazed expression, her hair a hive, the saggy tank. She immediately ducked, afraid Bram could see her at her worst.

Natasha said, "He can't see you. Or hear you, unless you push button."

"This one?" she asked, her index finger hovering over a red switch. Natasha nodded. Pushing it, Bram's voice flooded into the little room. ". . . you there? It's inhumane to leave me alone like this, completely cut off from the rest of the world. At least give me a radio. Or a TV antenna. Or a telephone."

"A telephone?" chortled Natasha, switching the microphone off. "He can dream on."

"How did this happen?" asked Penny.

"I know nothing."

"Tell me!"

Natasha shrugged. "Your mother was angry after he dumped you. So she hit him on head and brought him here."

Penny said, "Oh, well, that makes sense."

"It does?"

"In the Twilight Zone."

Penny stared at Bram, astonished by his proximity. He was only inches away. He looked kind of puffy. She toggled the switch. "You look bloated," she said.

"What do you expect?" he asked. "I'm eating twenty meals a day!"

Penny whispered to Natasha, "Those trays were for him. There was no stray! *Bram* is the dog—which is an insult to dogs, I realize." She paused, letting it all sink in. "So where did Boris come from?"

"Short Hares Animal Shelter."

"You adopted a dog to cover up a kidnapping conspiracy?"

"When you put like that, it sounds wrong," said Natasha, cradling Boris in her arms. "You begged for dog, Penny. He needed a home."

"He is a pookie," said Penny, massaging his little noggin.

Bram, meanwhile, said, "You think it's funny that I'm getting fat? It makes you laugh to see me stuff my face with wedding cake? This should amuse you. Go ahead. Bust a gut. Chuckle up a lung."

He picked up a plate on the floor by the couch and crammed the creamy confection into his mouth, not pausing to catch his breath or chew. Penny watched with horror, half disgusted, half fascinated. He'd cracked in isolation. And so quickly! She started laughing at the absurdity of it, his manic cake-covered face, his imprisonment, that her mother was a criminal, Natasha her conspirator. Penny's laughter excited Boris, who leapt out of Natasha's arms and ran in excited circles at their feet.

"That's right," said Bram, white cream all over his face. "Laugh, cow. Laugh, bitch."

And then Bram dropped the plate, cake chunks rolling on the carpet, leaving white trails. He grabbed his throat and doubled over. His eyes bulged dramatically as he attempted to hack up what was, apparently, clogging his throat.

"He's choking!" cried Penny.

"He's faking," said Natasha.

"We have to help him! He's turning red!"

His face was a tomato, fast becoming a beet. Bram fell to his knees, his hands in a ball, thrusting upward under his rib cage.

"He's trying to Heimlich himself," said Penny. She pushed passed Natasha to get to the playroom door. Then she remembered she didn't have a key, couldn't get in there to help him. "Unlock the door!"

"He's faking. I know what choking looks like."

"He's turning purple!" shrieked Penny. And then, "You've seen someone choke to death?"

"Many, many times," said Natasha, with second-world weariness. "They don't go red. They go blue."

Penny spoke into the microphone. "You're faking."

Bram stopped twisting and contorting. He lay on the floor, cake smeared on his cheek, motionless.

"Now he's playing dead?" Penny whispered to Natasha.

"Badly," whispered the Muscovite. "Soon, he will roll over."

After a knuckle-biting thirty seconds, Bram flipped over.

"Now, he will sit."

Bram leaned upright.

"Now stay."

He stood and flopped on the couch, the TV glow flickering on his resigned face.

Penny studied his dejection, the pathetic globs of frosting on his face and jeans, the slumped posture. She felt sorry for him.

Natasha toggled the switch to off and said, "When your mother comes home, we will talk about what to do next. I like sleeping pill, blindfold, dump in Pine Barrens."

"I've never seen him like this. Vulnerable, desperate, at the mercy of others. He looks so sad," said Penny.

"He made you sad," said Natasha.

"What, this is an eye for an eye?"

"In Moscow, it is leg for eye," said Natasha. "Bram got very good deal."

Penny nodded, toggled, and had to ask, "Bram, why did you do it?"

He sighed, heavily, frostily (or was it frost*ing*ly?). "Do what?"

"Bail out on the wedding."

He looked away from the TV, at the glass, right where she stood, as if he could see her. Penny gulped.

"Don't act like you care, Esther," he said. "You're glad the wedding didn't happen. Not only because you hate me. You'd love it if Penny never got married. If you had your way, you'd lock *her* in this room."

He might be on to something there, she thought. "The question on the table is why did you leave Penny at the altar?" asked Penny, pretending to be her mom.

"I've already told you, it's none of your business. And frankly, I don't understand why you want to know. Penny is all yours again. That's what you care about. More than you care about Penny herself. If I ever get the chance, I'll explain myself to Penny directly."

"Tell him it's you," whispered Natasha.

She could do that. She could demand Natasha give her the keys to set him free. She could then confront him face-to-face, no glass wall between them, get her answers and boot him out of her house, her life, her future.

But he'd insulted Esther. He'd impugned their mother-daughter relationship. Granted, in this case, it might *seem* a bit tense, but their bond was sacred nonetheless, and above criticism from anyone on the outside. He had no right to speak to (whom he thought was) Esther that way.

Penny picked up the microphone and said, "You're not going anywhere, you selfish, heartless, chickenshit bastard. You don't understand the first thing about my relationship with Penny, what we've meant to each other over the years. I've done everything I could to make her happy, which is a lot more than I can say for you. Ass. Hole."

Bram's frosted jaw dropped.

Penny switched off the mike.

Natasha's pencil-thin eyebrows rose nearly to the hairline. "You are angry," she said. "About time."

Penny grabbed Boris, held him tight, and stomped into the hallway. She gave the playroom door a swift kick on the way downstairs.

Chapter 21

Keith detached his lips from Esther's and said, "Making out in the backseat makes most of me feel like I'm seventeen again. Except my back. It still feels fifty."

Esther's spine had turned to Jell-O, so she couldn't complain.

He said, "Let's go back to my hotel. We can order room service. And champagne. I can open that bottle you gave to Bram and Penny. I've still got it."

At the mention of Bram's name—and her weapon of opportunity—Esther stiffened.

"You don't like champagne?" he asked.

"I love champagne," she said. "The hotel sounds great."

They got into the front seats and Keith sped back toward the highway. The movement gave Esther a chance to mentally clean house, putting Bram, Penny, and the wedding mess into a box, and slipping that on a high cranial shelf. She would not think of anything but Keith, this night, her own long-ignored sexuality. Tomorrow she'd face the reality she'd created, try to sort it out.

"It's a long drive back," he said. "I might have to pull over and attack you."

Esther said, "Hands on wheel; eyes on the road," and then she proceeded to give him an over-the-pants hand job for the entire drive back to Short Hares. He was splendidly erect, silent and focused on driving (as focused as possible).

They made excellent time. Esther hadn't realized how fast Keith had been driving.

Keith zipped into the Plaza driveway. They kissed passionately until the valet knocked on the passenger side window and the two broke apart, guilty smiles, blushing cheeks.

Keith said, "Don't move."

He stepped out of the Town Car and walked around to Esther's side. He opened her door and offered his hand. She took it, and he gallantly lifted her out of the car. Keeping a tight grip on her arm, Keith escorted her up the steps and through the hotel's front doors as if she were as fragile as blown glass.

The full treatment. How long had it been? Women of her era had been trained to react negatively to chivalrous behavior. Esther remembered her earnest insistences to Russell that she could open her own doors and pull out her own chair. It seemed ridiculous now, to take a political stand over a show of courtesy.

Negligence had helped her see the light. She'd take any courtesy, any chivalry Keith had to offer, and she'd bask in the courtly attention.

"Now it's your turn," he said once they'd entered the lobby.

"My turn?" To show him chivalry? Had he been reading her mind?

He smiled mischievously and placed his hand against her dress in a strategic spot.

"Hey!" she cried, drawing glances from the concierge and a bellboy.

"In here," he said, tugging her toward the Plaza Bar.

"Let's go upstairs," she said.

"I want to play with you under the table first," he said.

He's a perv, she thought. Although, the idea of him fiddling with her in partial view of other people made her genitals twitch.

I'm a perv, she thought. All those years of abstinence, only to learn she was kinky. Or maybe Keith brought out the kink in her, not that she had any clue it existed to be coaxed.

The Plaza Bar was perfect for the task. The room had old-world style—polished, staid, super preppy. Saxon-patterned carpeting, oak wainscoting, hunter green wallpaper, paintings depicting a fox hunt on the lush green nineteenth-century English country-side. The room was crammed with strategically organized navy velvet couches and low mahogany tables. This bartender, an im-maculate middle-aged mustachioed man in a black vest, trou-sers, and white shirt, wiped the bar with a clean white rag.

He said, "Good evening, sir. Ma'am." A dozen people, all expensively dressed for evening, sipped brandy or iced cock-tails in highball glasses from atop stools.

Keith whispered to her, "From Abruzzi's to this orgy of preppiness. It's a different planet."

"Takes all kinds in New Jersey," said Esther as they settled into a love seat in a dark corner. This bar, to its credit, smelled like wood oil and peppermint, and not like cooking grease and mung beer.

Keith said, "We need a tablecloth."

"Should I ask the bartender?" said Esther, surprising herself with her brass.

"Put my jacket on your lap," he said, helping her arrange it. "That's good."

Esther was glad she hadn't worn hose. In June, it would have been gratuitous chastity.

Keith arranged himself at her side, his right hand finding its way underneath his jacket and up her thigh.

He said, "Hands on the table; eyes on . . . me."

She sighed when his fingers found their mark. She may have moaned lightly, her eyes exactly where Keith wanted them. She stared at his mouth. He was speaking softly to her, nonsense, nothing, might have been a nursery rhyme, just to make it appear like they were having a real conversation.

"You are sopping wet," he said, and she felt a flutter in her groin, a twang of sensation, the beginning of something big.

"Oh my God," she moaned.

"Oh my *God*!" someone else shrieked.

Esther and Keith both looked up.

"Hello there, you two. I can't believe it. What a coincidence, finding you here!"

"Ashley?" gasped Esther at the sight of her friend.

Keith withdrew his hand, and Esther actually whimpered a little. He said, "Good evening, Ashley."

"I thought I might find you here, Keith. But I didn't expect to see you both. And you look so chummy. Just sitting here talking. You don't even have drinks yet."

Instinctively, Esther scooted a few inches away from Keith. She said, "Would you like to—"

"I'd love to," said Ashley, and lowered her heart-shaped rear into the love seat, a tight squeeze now for three, Keith in the middle.

Ashley leaned across his lap to kiss Esther on the cheek. When she pulled away, Ashley gave Esther a conspiratorial wink. Esther shook her head. *No,* she mouthed. But Ashley had already turned the wattage of her attention to the man on the couch. There had been a couple of times, years ago, when Ashley staged a similar "rescue" for Esther when she hadn't necessarily wanted saving. But she'd never figured out a polite way to tell Ashley to back off. But she hadn't much cared then anyway.

With Keith, however, Esther cared.

"I'm still floored that I actually found you!" Ashley sang.

"Is it really so surprising to find Keith at his hotel?" asked Esther rudely.

Ashley gave her friend a quizzical glance. "Am I interrupting something? Were you two having a heart-to-heart about your children? The wedding? The misery of it all?"

Yes, the heartbreak, thought Esther. The headache, too. And just like that her mental housekeeping was ransacked. Bram, Penny, the wedding, thoughts in boxes flying off their shelves, right onto Esther's lap, now cold and impenetrable.

"Okay, I confess. I came looking for you. I hope you're not angry. I was sitting in my big house, bored out of my mind." To Keith, Ashley continued, "I get lonely at night, since my husband died."

"I know how you feel," said Keith.

So did Esther. Not about missing the dead spouse. She'd danced a jig when she got that phone call. But of the nightly sting of alone, she could relate. That was Ashley's seduction specialty: empathy. She had the uncanny ability to sense whatever her target was feeling, and reflect the feeling back at him. Instant rapport. Except Keith wasn't a dupe. He wouldn't be sucked into Ashley's seductive vortex.

Or so she thought. She turned toward Keith, expecting him to be watching her. But he was stealing a gawk down the gaping front of Ashley's toffee silk shirt.

"That's a lovely top," said Esther to her friend, jealousy flaring.

On cue, Ashley plumped up her breast implants, pushing them against her blouse. "This old thing?"

They laughed together, like the dear old friends they were.

"Aren't we all cozy?" asked Ashley, slapping her hand on Keith's knee.

"And to think, when I first met Esther, she hated my guts," he said.

"You did?" asked Ashley.

Esther was not in a mood to walk down memory lane. Even the short walk.

Keith said, "I tried to make a good impression on her by telling a little joke. And I bombed completely."

"Was it funny?" asked Ashley.

He said, "I gave her the 'What exit?' line."

"Oh, poor, poor Esther," sympathized Ashley.

"I knew I'd bombed in a heartbeat. If looks could kill," he said, laughing. "So I decided then and there that I'd use whatever means necessary to change her mind about me."

"You like a challenge?" asked Ashley.

"You like to talk about someone as if she's not sitting next to you?" asked Esther.

"I wanted to make you happy," he said, looking into Esther's eyes, "because it seemed like you couldn't manage it on your own."

"I've always needed a man to make me happy," said Ashley. "All women do. Except the lesbians. But that's not our Esther."

Esther wasn't sure how to take this. Keith had decided to come to her emotional rescue? Who said she needed saving? Esther hated the idea that she was a woman like Ashley. She rejected the notion that a woman couldn't be happy without a man. Often, the opposite was true.

Ashley collected men. Esther turned her gathering instincts elsewhere, to rugs, chairs, sewing machines, violins, chess sets. But, contrary to conventional wisdom, some of the items in her collections (the antique quilts, for example) could keep her warm on cold winter nights. What did Ashley have to show for her man collecting? Unlike Esther's chairs, a man wouldn't necessarily stay put. For all her man chasing, Ashley was left with an empty bed. At least she had gotten accustomed to hers, Esther thought.

"She's right," said Esther. "I'm not a lesbian. But I am very tired." She stood up. Sleeping with Keith had been a lovely fantasy. Seeing Ashley, though, had been like the Fates firing a warning shot. If she were to go through with it, like a hit of crack, would sex make her an addict? Would a night with Keith turn her into Ashley Longmead? The prospect made her shudder.

"Where the hell do you think you're going?" asked Keith sharply, standing, too.

"Home," she said. "And you're leaving town tomorrow, so I won't be seeing you again. Take care now!"

"We had other plans for tonight," he said.

"Which have since changed," said Esther. "But I see no reason you can't make the better of it." Her gaze flickered over Ashley.

"No change in plans," he said. "I'll have to insist." He squared off with Esther. She wasn't sure if he wanted to slug her or kiss her.

Ashley said, "Now, now, friends. Let's not argue, especially not with dry throats. Joffrey!" she said. "A bottle of champagne. And charge it to Mr. Shiraz's room. You two, please sit down."

From the bar, the tender said, "Yes, Mrs. Longmead."

Esther and Keith remained standing. Their chests only inches apart, Keith's eyes roiling and intense. Her crotch (she couldn't deny) was throbbing. Esther said, "Joffrey. Cancel the champagne."

"Yes, Ms. Bracket."

Keith said, "Joffrey."

"Yes, Mr. Shiraz."

"Send the champagne to my room."

"Yes, sir."

Ashley stood, clapped her bejeweled hands like an excited five-year-old and said, "Excellent idea! I'd love to see your suite. Esther, do you really have to go home? Ah, well, if you must, you must."

Keith put his hand on Ashley's creamy breastbone and pushed her back down on the couch. She bounced on the cushion. He said, "It's been nice seeing you again, Ashley. Good night." Then he grabbed Esther's shoulders, spun her around, and pushed her out of the bar and toward the elevator bank.

He jabbed the Up button. Then, under the gold and crystal chandelier, Keith encircled Esther's waist and pulled her against him for the meatiest kiss of her life. The porterhouse of smooch, it was bloody, chewy, heavy, and fortifying. A meal. A kiss that could sustain her for days, or for the rest of her life, should that be necessary.

The couple, pressed together, not a sliver of space between them, barely noticed the elevator doors opening with *ping*, a handful of people exiting around them.

"Well, well. Will you look at this, Morris. I'd tell them to get a room, but I guess they already did."

Esther opened one eye and saw her daughter's degenerate friend Vita standing behind Keith. The girl's spindly arms were folded across her chest. Next to her: Bram's best man, the Neanderthal who'd delivered the letter bomb to Penny the day of the wedding. Esther and Keith parted and faced their children's friends.

"Vita," snarled Esther.

"Mrs. Bracket," she replied.

"Hello, Mr. Shiraz," said the young man.

"Hello, Morris," said Keith, shifting behind Esther to hide his trouser tent.

The foursome smiled awkwardly at each other. Seeing Penny's friends—who'd obviously just made use of a hotel room themselves—dampened her lust completely.

"Have you heard from Bram?" Keith asked Morris.

"Nope," said the young man.

"Sounds like you weren't expecting to," said Keith.

"No, I mean, I figured he was . . . busy, whatever."

"Busy? You said he was probably on a beach something." That was Vita.

"What beach?" asked Keith. To Esther, he whispered, "Not Sea Grit."

To Morris, Vita said, "What did you think Edina Spanky would make of this scene? The mother of the bride with the father of the groom? Curious. And demented, considering the circumstances. It's like Juliet's mother balling Romeo's father."

Morris said, "Edina would be intrigued by the sexual motivation."

Vita nodded. "Opportunism? Lust borne of stress and anxiety? Sex as a distraction from problems too big to deal with?"

Esther noted, during Vita's speech, that the girl's mouth was pink, compact, adorable, and her green eyes sparkled like the Irish Sea. She really was a lovely little thing, petite and sugary. A cupcake.

"You presumptuous self-righteous wretch," said Esther, who loathed cupcakes.

"Just exploring a role," said Vita. "Don't take it personally. By the way, does Penny know about this? She might have some issues."

"There is no 'this,' " said Esther.

Keith said, "There isn't?"

"It's my obligation as her best friend to tell Penny what I've seen. In fact, I'm heading there now. Penny just called. She wanted me to come over."

Esther checked her watch. Ten o'clock. Was Penny okay? Calling for an emotional boost (however lightweight) at this hour? Why not just talk on the phone with Vita? What reason could Penny possibly have to demand Vita's physical presence at the house? Did she have something to show her?

Esther's stomach plunged to her knees. *Penny's found him*, she thought.

"I'm coming with you," said Esther to Vita.

"You are not," said Keith, more exasperated than forceful.

"Penny clearly needs support," said Esther. "I'm her mother. I need to be there for her."

"I can handle it," said Vita.

Esther snorted.

Morris said, "Vita, if Mrs. Bracket wants to go, you can stay."

The girl smiled and said, "I promise I'll be back soon. If not later tonight, early in the morning. Oh, here, before I forget," said Vita, handing the young man her hotel room card.

"I have to be in the city by ten," said Morris. "I've got a, er, business appointment."

"On a Sunday?"

"It's . . . yes," he said abruptly, looking at his sneakers.

"You got a real job?" asked Keith.

"Still freelance playwriting," said Morris.

"And you have a business meeting," said Keith. "On a Sunday."

"It's a new client," said Morris vaguely. "He wants a speech."

"About what?" asked Keith, his eyes intense and demanding.

Esther imagined those eyes staring down at her as Keith pinioned her to the bed.

"Mrs. Bracket," said Vita, "you're breathing in my ear."

Morris said, "The speech is, er, about a work thing."

"Tell me more," said Keith.

Vita said, "I'm leaving."

"Me, too." That was Esther.

Keith kissed each woman on the cheek. He said to Esther, "We'll have breakfast another time."

Vita smirked, mentally recording the scene for Penny's benefit. Esther followed her through the lobby.

"I hate to cut your evening short." The girl walked quickly.

"I was just leaving anyway," said Esther, scrambling to keep up.

"Seems a shame to rush you."

"Not at all."

"The hotel can call you a cab later if you'd rather stay."

"The house is two miles from here, for God's sake, Vita," said Esther. "Surely you can stand to be alone with me for three minutes."

"*I* can stand it," said Vita, hand to chest. "I was concerned about your comfort. Given your age, I don't want to put undo stress on your heart."

Esther cast a glance over her shoulder at Keith. He had his bear hand on Morris's shoulder, holding him to the spot. Morris seemed nervous. Keith was asking him something. Morris's eyes darted left and right, as if looking for an escape.

Vita and Esther walked through the revolving doors. The valet drove up in the green bug just as they descended the hotel steps.

Chapter 22

Penny cradled her aching foot. Natasha cuddled Boris, smoothing down his floppy ears.

"Next time, wear boots," said the Russian, who had, allegedly, some experience kicking in doors.

Bong.

"Who's this now?" Penny asked as she hobbled down the steps. After finding Bram in the attic, she was prepared for anything. "Perhaps it's my dead father, come to take me away from it all."

"Maybe it's my dead husband," said Natasha as she swung the door open.

"Good evening," she said to the woman on the other side.

"Hello, Ms. Molotov. And nice to see you, Penny," said Ashley Longmead.

Ashley kissed Penny on the cheek. "You look . . . like you're holding up well," said the chemically preserved woman in toffee-colored silk. "You just need a spa day, Penny. Make that a spa *weekend*. I'll call Reynaldo at Short Hares Wellness. I'm sure he'll squeeze you in."

To the left, the kitchen door swung closed. Natasha had made herself scarce. Boris also reacted badly to the tawny-haired neighbor, yapping at her with adorable hostility. Penny scooped him up and (gently, lovingly) pinched his little trap shut.

"Mom's not home," said Penny.

"I thought she was having dinner with that wonderful Keith Shiraz." Ashley peered over Penny's shoulder, scanning for signs of a man.

"They went out."

"You don't happen to know where they might have gone, do you?"

Penny shrugged.

"Is Keith still staying at the Plaza?" asked Ashley.

"I guess."

"Thanks ever so, Penny. And don't forget. Reynaldo is a genius. And he'll do anything for me. I just have to say 'boo!' "

"Don't you mean 'boob'?" said Penny.

Ashley paused and then smiled. "You've always been a strange child, Penny. Good luck with being alone. I hope you have an easier time of it than your mother."

Penny kicked the door shut.

And immediately flung it open. "Sorry about that," she blurted.

But Ashley was already in the front seat of her Porsche. She waved a sparkling hand, tooted her horn, and was gone.

The guilt set in immediately. She'd slammed the door on Ashley's nose job. As satisfying as that had been, Penny knew she'd live to regret it. Esther would be furious when she found out.

Penny went into the kitchen. Natasha was nowhere in sight. She picked up the wall phone and called Vita's cell.

She got her in one ring. "Come over," she said.

"I'm with Morris," said Vita. "We're reading through the script. I mean, the *play*. It's not bad, Pen. This might be the part I've been looking for."

Should she tell Vita about Bram in the attic? *God*, she wanted to. It was juicy news, after all. And the delicious irony of it all! Bram had sought freedom. And look at him now. She opened her mouth to speak such thoughts, but something made her hesitate.

"Are you okay?" asked Vita into the phone.

"I'm fine," said Penny. "Good."

"Something's wrong."

"Forget it." Penny thought better of confiding in Vita. The actress tended to overreact; she and Esther didn't get along. If she were to find out about Bram, Vita might do something insane, like call the police.

"You sound bad," said Vita. "I'm coming over. Give me twenty." And then she hung up.

Penny tried to call back, but Vita had turned off her phone. Too restless to wait in the kitchen, Penny walked through the kitchen and headed down the narrow short hallway, making a sharp left to take the seldom-used back stairwell. It deposited her on the second floor, just outside Natasha's bedroom.

Boris under one arm, Penny knocked.

"Is she gone?" asked Natasha, opening her door.

"With the wind," said Penny.

"That woman"—Natasha spit on the floor—"she treats me like a maid."

"What, exactly, is your job description?" asked Penny.

"I am house manager," sniffed Natasha.

"And co-kidnapper," said Penny. "Co-criminal. Co-tormenter."

"Yes, but I'm not a maid!"

Penny stepped into the dramatically decorated room, admiring as always the apple-red oriental rug, a plump strawberry-colored bedspread, and glossy cherry walls. Her dresser was an antique Asian armoire, lacquered as dark and shiny as a pomegranate.

Natasha liked red. And fruit.

And Penny loved this room. When she was younger, she begged Esther to let her paint her then (and now) purple room red, too, but her mom refused, saying, "Red is for hookers and communists, and not little girls."

Penny would say, "So why does Natasha get to have red?"

Which would make Natasha and Esther share a belly laugh, and thusly ended the conversation.

Natasha was still ranting about the neighbor. "Ashley Longmead is never so happy when your mother is miserable."

"She does seem to show up whenever things go wrong," said Penny, reclining on the strawberry bed. Ashley was over in a flash the day Russell moved out, as if she'd been waiting at the bottom of the driveway for the van to hit the road. She arrived on cue again the day Russell died. It felt only natural she'd make her presence known in the wake of the botched wedding.

"And Esther thinks Ashley is her friend," scoffed Natasha. "Maybe you understand your mother better now."

"Yes, I realize that she was a powder keg just waiting to blow," said Penny. "A criminal late bloomer."

Natasha said, "Your mother is alone in the world, except for you. And me."

Sympathy plucked Penny's heartstrings, but not loudly enough to hear over the roar. "I stand corrected," said Penny. "Mom is a *sad and lonely* criminal."

"In Russia, mobs would have set Bram on fire and fed his smoking corpse to the rats for what he did."

Penny knew Natasha was capable of ruthlessness and dastardly deeds. The Russian made an excellent accomplice. But

Penny never would have thought her Mom could hit a person over the head and kidnap him. Then again, people had whispered for years that Esther was somehow involved in Russell's deadly dive.

Penny hugged a red pillow, remembered how Esther tried to talk her out of the engagement. The more Esther discouraged her, the tighter she had held on to Bram. She'd had enough therapy to realize that, someday, something would have to come between her mother and herself. Bram had been her love—and her wedge. But what, Penny wished she knew, was she to him?

"If I pretend to be Mom when I talk to Bram," said Penny, "I can say whatever I want without any consequences."

"You won't get chance," said Natasha. "Esther will let him go when she comes back."

"No!" said Penny.

Natasha said, "If there are arrests, you can't be involved. Now you know, so it's over. But fun while it lasted!"

"We won't tell her," said Penny.

The Russian could be as unyielding as an iron curtain. "He has to go," she insisted.

Penny said, "Tell me about the playroom. The two-way mirror? The PA system? Mom used to spy on me?"

"Not your mother," said Natasha. "Your father. And not to spy on you. To spy on *her*."

Her, Penny instantly understood, was Jemima, her English nanny. The woman he'd left Esther for. The one he was with when he died.

Natasha added, "He was very sick fuck."

Her mom had a screw loose, and her dad was a voyeur. The news was both upsetting and reassuring. Penny had been itching to go back upstairs and spy on Bram since she left the control room not twenty minutes ago. She enjoyed watching him. She always had. This way, she could gaze all she liked without the pressure and anxiety of him looking back.

"Maybe I'm a sick fuck, too," said Penny.

"Maybe you are," said Natasha. "You have his genes. You could go evil. It could happen—to anyone, at anytime, if pushed. Look at Esther and what she did to Bram. One day, my brother Misha make nest out of newspapers he find in gutter, and started to sleep in it. He said he was pigeon. He jumped off roof to fly."

"Was he hurt?" asked Penny.

Natasha shook her head. "Our broken-down hovel was one story high. Me and my brothers jumped off roof for fun all the time. There were no playgrounds or parks in Moscow. We had to stay close to home anyway or else be captured by police and sent to Siberian juvenile work camp."

"Just once I wish you'd tell me the truth about your life before New Jersey," said Penny.

"Every word is true!" insisted Natasha.

"You were *not* a mail-order bride."

"I was! I was cover of very first catalogue. My brother Sergei took naked pictures of me and my cousin. This was 1991, the day after wall in Berlin came down. Two months later, I get letter from American man. He sends money, papers, plane tickets. I fly to Chicago and we get married."

"And he died?"

"He is very dead," said Natasha. "Stupid man. Electrocuted in bathtub by plug-in razor. I find body. I cry for long time."

"You? *Cry?* Now I know you're lying," said Penny, shaking her head and grinning.

"Okay, that part is lie." Even Natasha couldn't keep a straight face.

"You won't tell Mom I found Bram, will you?"

They heard a door slam.

"Someone here," said Natasha.

"I called Vita before," said Penny.

"You can't tell her!" said Natasha.

"I won't!"

"I get rid of her."

Penny didn't like the sound of that. She said, "I'll ask her to leave."

The two women jostled each other through the doorway, fighting and racing down the hallway toward the main staircase.

"Stop pushing," said Natasha.

"Back off," said Penny.

These sentiments were matched by two *other* women, jockeying and jostling each other to get *up* the steps.

"You can't stop me," said Vita, surging forward.

"This is my house," replied Esther.

The four of them converged on the second-floor landing.

"Your mother and Keith Shiraz were making out in the lobby of the Plaza Hotel!" said Vita to Penny.

"We were not making out," said Esther. "We kissed each other good night."

"He had a huge hard-on!" declared Vita.

"You shouldn't stare at men's groins," said Esther.

"I couldn't help it. We're talking flagpole. The mighty oak. He could have poked my eyes out with that thing."

"Like father like son," said Penny.

Esther blushed and said, "This entire exchange is grossly inappropriate and I won't listen to another word. Natasha, care to join me in the kitchen? I'm starving."

"I thought you went out to dinner," said Penny. "Hours ago."

"What are you implying?" demanded Esther.

"Forget I asked!" Penny said.

Her mom opened her mouth, but she couldn't think of what to say, or was too hungry, embarrassed, or confused to defend herself. Esther seemed sad, emotionally spent.

Penny's heart constricted. With a start, she thought, *Mom looks old*.

Chapter 23

Midnight. *Only twelve more hours*, thought Bram in the shower, shampooing with Barbie Bubble Gum scented liquid. He could last another twelve days—twelve weeks!—if he had to. But if everything played out as he expected, he'd be free in half a day.

Bram inhaled the scent of the lather, letting it take him back to baseball cards, two-wheelers, skateboards. The long ago days when he didn't care about girls—or have to deal with their pathological, soon-to-be-locked-up mothers.

His first act as a free man? Bram fantasized about hiring a team of lawyers. And a few expert witnesses, psychiatrists who were ready, licensed, and able to declare Esther Bracket demented but accountable for her actions. He chuckled to himself, imagining the soon-to-be-arriving SWAT team cornering Esther Bracket as she sipped tea in her solarium.

He laughed and lathered. Cleansing suds slid down his muscular back, glided along his legs. For the first time since his capture two days ago, he felt good, clean, *cleansed*.

But when he heard a creak and shuffle in the playroom,

the magical spell in the shower broke. "Shit!" he yelled, and banged out of the shower, out of the bathroom, into the playroom, where he flung himself at the door as it closed. He collided with it as it locked, nearly kicking over the new tray. The food was piled in a proteinous mountain upon it, a single potato balanced precariously on top.

Bram leaned against the locked door, giving it one last slam with his hand. He did his modest best to cover himself with his hands (which, though large, weren't adequate for the job) on his long walk back to the privacy of the bathroom. "I'll catch you next time," he promised.

Getting no response, he returned to the shower to rinse.

And heard another creak and shuffle from the playroom.

"Fuck!" he yelled. Shampoo dripping in his eye, he hurtled back into the larger room, his penis slapping against his thighs, arm outstretched. He grasped for the knob, trying to get a grip. But his fingers were slippery. The door shut again. The locking sound was a taunt.

"I hope you're enjoying yourself!" he yelled, trying to hide his parts with his mitts again.

"Check the bag," said a voice.

"What bag?" he asked.

"Next to the tray," she said. Her voice was scratchy and distorted as usual, but lighter tonight. Friendlier.

Bram looked at the floor and saw a shopping bag from a place called The Pampered Pup. He peered inside. Right on top he saw a fresh, white bath towel, which he wrapped around his hips. Underneath that: a razor and shaving cream, a hairbrush, a toothbrush, clean jeans, a T-shirt, a pair of boxers. Each item, except for the towel, had been in his suitcase.

"Thank you," he said, smiling at the mirror.

Nothing. He walked up to the glass and tried for the millionth time to make out what was behind it. But he could only see his own (visibly thicker) reflection. He gathered the razor and shaving cream and took them into the bathroom.

"You're welcome," she said softly, a tender afterthought.

Taken by surprise, Bram spun around too quickly. The towel loosened and fell to his ankles.

"You're in a revealing mood," she said, laughing at his fumbling to recover the wrap. "Let's talk."

"About my release?"

"We'll get to that."

"I've made a fascinating discovery," said Bram, sitting on a chair.

"Go on," she said.

"No-more-tears technology works. Barbie shampoo *is* as gentle on the eyes as pure water."

She laughed. The sound warmed and soothed him like the hot shower he'd just stepped out of. A strange response, given that Esther Bracket was his sworn enemy. Penny's laugh used to heat him from the inside. Only logical that a mother and daughter had similar tones.

"I've never heard you laugh before," he said. "You should do it more often."

She ignored his comment. "Did you talk to anyone about your decision to leave Penny?" she asked. "A friend, a shrink. Your dad?"

Bram crossed his legs, pulling the towel discreetly over his knee. "I didn't talk to anyone."

"Why?" she asked softly. "Pretty major decision to make on your own."

"I didn't think anyone would understand."

"Why didn't you talk to Penny?"

He shook his head. "Talking about my problem with her would only make it worse."

"You'll have to explain."

"I can't," he said, standing up, the conversation getting uncomfortably intimate. "I'm going to shave and get dressed."

"Okay," she said.

The static stopped. "Wait," he said, suddenly gripped by the prospect of more alone time (how had he ever thought he'd want so much of it?).

The PA hummed back on, and she said, "Yes?"

"I would explain."

"But?"

"It's personal."

"I should think so!" she said patiently.

"You hate me," he added.

"All hatred comes from misunderstanding."

Bram craved understanding, as much as he'd ached for a confidant. He'd thought about finding a shrink in the months leading up to the wedding. But he knew a therapist would urge him to confront Penny with the problem. Night after night he'd sit across the table from her, eating the dinner she lovingly prepared, feeling her eyes on him as he took each bite, worried if he was enjoying the meal and why he was so quiet. He was paralyzed in her presence.

"If you confide in me," said the voice of Esther Bracket, "I'll let you go."

"When?"

"In the morning," she baited.

She was lying. It didn't matter. He was getting out—one way or another—in the next twelve hours. She had no idea the hell that was about to fall on her, and much as Bram would have liked to free his thoughts as well, he couldn't do it.

"I'm too tired now," he said. "But why don't we meet here for lunch tomorrow. I'll explain everything. Including Penny's injuries."

"It's a date."

"And now I'll be able to dress for it," he said, pointing at the just-delivered jeans and shorts. "I thought you weren't going to allow me a single shred of dignity—or clean clothing."

"Change of plans," she said. "I've decided to be nicer."

"What have I done to deserve—"

"Good night," she said, switching off the PA system.

Bram waited a minute, but he sensed she was gone. She seemed borderline human tonight. The fresh clothes and warm tones softened his antipathy.

She knocked me cold and locked me up, he reminded himself. *You're Stockholm syndroming.*

After shaving, Bram unfolded the jeans to put them on. Something heavy was tucked inside them. A silver picture frame.

He stared at the photo of Penny in her urban hiking clothes, taken the day they got engaged. He rubbed his thumb along the frame, across Penny's smile. She was beautiful, especially on that afternoon when she was as cool as the autumn air. He propped the picture up on the table, finished dressing and then hauled the tray over. As he ate his late third dinner, Penny's picture smiled at him across the table.

Penny in the picture didn't worry or stare. She existed, which was all he'd ever wanted or needed. For Penny to simply be near him, to share his space, their lives. Double the joy, half the pain. She didn't have to cook his dinner, suck his dick, or wash his socks. He could have been perfectly content, a goblet overflowing with bliss, if Penny could just be with him. If the limber dancer who could bend into amazing shapes were capable of simply unwinding.

Bram ate his broccoli florets in congealed Hollandaise, sopping up the excess sauce with the increasingly stale rolls. He smiled at Penny's picture, relishing her in two dimensions, regretting with every chew that, somehow, they'd lost that great day along the way.

Chapter 24

"Sorry to call so early," said Keith to Esther, who'd stayed up late talking with Natasha last night.

She checked the night table clock. Nearly nine.

"No problem," she said, still groggy.

"I know where Bram is," Keith gleefully announced.

Which woke up Esther like an air raid. "I'm stunned," she said.

"It is a shocker," he agreed.

"I don't know what to say," she stammered.

"Get dressed," he said. "I'm coming over."

Flop sweat made the phone slip from her fingers. Time to pay the piper. She hoped the fee wouldn't be steep. Perhaps she could bash Keith as well, put them both in the attic . . .

"I'll be ready," said Esther.

"See you in ten," he said, and hung up.

Nine minutes later Esther was dressed in a pretty white sundress and ballet flats, a wrought-iron candlestick in her fist.

Keith pulled up in his Town Car and honked the horn.

Natasha looked though the front window. "He's waving you out."

"Should I hit him?" asked Esther.

"See what he says first," said Natasha. "Keep candlestick behind your back."

Esther nodded, and opened the front door. Keith waved from the driver's seat. "Hurry up, Esther. We've got to go."

Natasha whispered, "Ask him where you are going."

"Where to?" shouted Esther.

"Just come on," he said.

"I'll be one minute." Esther closed the door and conferred with Natasha.

"Can we assume he thinks Bram is somewhere other than here?" asked Esther. "Or perhaps he's taking me to a dark alley to make me an offer I can't refuse."

"Put candlestick in purse," said Natasha.

"Good idea," said Esther. "If I'm not back in a few hours, make the prisoner a 'special' drink."

Natasha nodded gravely. "Cyanide or strychnine?"

"Whichever tastes worse," said Esther.

She wrapped a silk scarf around her hair, stuffed the candlestick in her tote, took a deep breath, and joined Keith in his car. This morning adventure would test her mettle. She wasn't sure she had the strength (the candlestick was heavy).

Keith beamed when she got in the car, and immediately pulled her in for a hot smooch. Esther crumbled against him like a paper lantern.

A squawk erupted from the Town Car radio. "Charlie here, sir."

Keith picked up the mouthpiece. "Charlie. Go."

The radio—a CB, she surmised—said, "Checked on the radar. Best route to Manhattan: Route 24 to 1–9, over Pulaski Skyway to Holland Tunnel. No delay at the tunnel."

"Got it."

"Out," said this Charlie.

"So we're going into the city," said Esther, buckling up.

Keith eased the Town Car into Drive and rolled down the driveway. "If you want to amuse yourself, you can always give me another hand job."

Esther said, "Not before noon."

He smiled. "Then I've got something to look forward to on the drive back."

The trip to Manhattan took about forty minutes. Esther used the time to extract the story of how Keith "located" Bram.

"I could tell Morris was holding out," said Keith. "After you and Penny's friend left the hotel last night, I urged him to join me for a drink."

"Did you whisper in his ear?"

"Only a little," he said. "It took half a gin and tonic. Then Morris spilled his guts. He can't resist me. I've known him since he was three. I'm like a second father to him." Keith was practically squirming with pleasure at his own detective work and the upcoming excitement of seeing his son (which, as Esther knew, wasn't going to happen).

"So what'd Morris say?" Esther asked, relief growing as the story unfolded.

He must have sensed her mood, dropping a palm on her thigh and giving her a squeeze. "Why don't you relax, Esther? Lean against the headrest," he said. "I can look at your beautiful neck that way."

She let her skull fall against the cushion, exposing her throat for his viewing pleasure.

He said, "I took him into the bar—your friend Ashley was still there, by the way, and I had to be rude to her again to get her to leave me and Morris alone."

She shook her head. "What did Morris tell you?"

"Seems Bram and Morris had a plan," said Keith, getting more into his story. "To rendezvous in the city on Sunday morning—today—at Bram's apartment. Morris had keys. Between Friday night and this morning, Bram wasn't to be contacted. Morris was supposed to stick around Short Hares, keep an eye on everyone. Essentially, see if the coast was clear for Bram to come out of hiding."

"No offense, Keith, but your son is a weasel."

"Which the two of us can explain to him together. We're going to keep Morris's appointment with Bram. Me and you. We'll get the explanation we both deserve, and then we'll take him to Penny to apologize to her. I want to clean up this mess," he said. "For our sake."

They were an "our"? Esther gulped hard. "He's been hiding out in his own apartment," she said, achieving *fancy that*. "All this time, he's been in the most obvious place!" His big plan had been to go home? Proof Bram was an unworthy ninny, she thought.

"Morris promised not to warn Bram about the switcheroo," said Keith triumphantly. "He won't see us coming!"

"How right you are," said Esther over the sound of motors echoing inside the Holland Tunnel.

Keith put his fingers on his lips in the international "shush" position. He put his key into the lock of Bram's SoHo studio, twisted, and then pushed the door wide open.

He sprang into the room, and yelled, "Busted!"

Deep silence.

"Maybe he went out for breakfast," suggested Esther.

Keith checked his watch. "We are a bit early. He and Morris were meeting at ten."

"We can wait, or come back later."

"If we wait, we lose the element of surprise," said Keith,

who'd clearly been looking forward to springing himself on his son.

"So we go."

"No," he said. "He might see us leaving the building on his way in. We should wait. Have a seat. I'll make coffee."

Esther arranged herself at Bram's fifties-style dinette table and chair set, cerulean blue with silver sparkles. The set was genuine, not a cheap reproduction, and Esther was impressed. Her eyes drifted around the airy, bright space. The astro-star wall clock, retro white fridge and stovetop. His loft bed, expertly constructed with only one supporting beam. Esther assumed Bram custom built it for himself. He had a Noguchi amoeba-shaped couch (lime green) with a matching frosted glass table (Esther believed they were also originals) on a white shag rug. Built-in shelves (also custom made) on one wall were filled with books, objects, CDs, and DVDs. Loaded, but not cluttered. No messy laundry piles or dirty dishes in the sink. The apartment was clean and orderly, impeccably decorated. One might think the resident was a tasteful, conscientious, stylish, and talented man. One might think.

Keith handed her a diner-style mug and poured her a cup of steaming coffee from a Robert Graves pot. He sat down at the dinette table with his matching mug and scooped sugar from a kitschy blue and white checked bowl.

"I wish he were here," he said mournfully.

Esther felt for the guy. Keith missed his son. An empathetic yearning for Penny tightened Esther's chest. She wished she'd woken up her daughter before she left the house this morning.

"He'll surface," she said.

"When?" asked Keith.

Esther swallowed hard. "Any minute."

She would have to let Bram go. Today. This had gone on

long enough. She'd made her point (if she ever had one). Bram got what he deserved, and so would she, eventually. The truth would come out. Keith would hate her, that was guaranteed. Their "our" status would soon expire.

She said, "I really like you, Keith."

"I like you, too, Esther," he said. "I wish we could have started without all this bullshit."

If only he knew how big a pile it was.

They held hands, sipped coffee.

"It's after ten," he said, standing and pacing the studio.

"Let's give it a few more minutes," she suggested.

"I'm taking a leak," he said.

Esther blushed. He was uncouth. At least, since they were on the verge of breaking up, she would be spared the daily chronicle of his leaks and dumps.

"Esther, you've got to see this," he called from the bathroom.

"I'd rather not."

"Bram left a note!"

Another note. Bram was a veritable postmaster general. Esther got up and found Keith in front of a sparkling white (with gold flecks) vanity. He pointed at an envelope propped behind the sink faucet.

The envelope had writing on it: *In Case I'm Not Here.*

Curious, thought Esther. When could he have left this? Before he came to Short Hares on Thursday.

"He's not here," Keith said. "I'm opening it." He reached for the letter.

Esther said, "It's obviously meant for Morris. We should give it to him."

He said, "It doesn't say Morris's name on it."

He tore the envelope open and removed two pieces of white paper with black ink script.

"Definitely Bram's handwriting," said Keith.

Esther watched his face in the mirror as he read the letter. His eyes narrowed to slits, brow crinkling with concentration. He exhaled steam from his mighty nostrils, fogging the mirror.

"What's it say?" she asked tentatively.

He looked at her. His eyes were not kind.

"Read it yourself," he said, handing her the letter.

To Whom It May Concern:

As of this writing—it's Thursday morning, and I'm going to New Jersey for the rehearsal dinner in a few hours—I still haven't decided what I'm going to do. If I wind up calling off the wedding, I'll be able to retrieve and destroy this letter tomorrow. If I do marry Penny, I'll destroy it after the honeymoon. If this letter is found and read by someone else, however, it can mean only one thing. I have not been able to return to my apartment. Something bad has happened.

I may put my personal safety at risk if I leave Penny. There are people in her family who would do me harm. Esther Bracket, for one, hates me and wishes me dead. I believe she could do it. She has killed before. I've researched the circumstances of her husband's death. I've read the police reports and all the newspaper stories. The death was ruled an accident, but only due to lack of evidence. Although the police believed Esther Bracket had motive to kill her husband, she wasn't a suspect because she had an alibi. Penny, only eight years old at the time, would have been a dubious witness at best.

I also fear the revenge of Natasha Molotov, a woman I've also researched. I believe she is a killer, too. Her huband, Stanley Gorp of Evanston, Illinois, was electrocuted in his bath. The police suspected Molotov, but they couldn't prove her guilt. She stayed in Illinois only long enough to collect the life insurance money, and then she moved to New Jersey to reunite with her cousin, Alexia Flushenko, also a Russian mail-order bride. The insurance money didn't last long. She took a job with Esther Bracket, and found a kindred spirit in her new boss.

Penny doesn't know I've investigated her mother and house-keeper. I pray to God this is all wild speculation on my part. I'm sure no one will ever read this letter. When I come home, I'll re-read it and laugh myself sick at my own paranoia. But on the off chance I'm not paranoid, I just had to write down my theory.

If I do call off the wedding, and should I go missing afterward, look for my remains in Esther Bracket's mansion on Overlook Lane, Short Hares, New Jersey.

Belatedly,
Bram Shiraz

Esther lifted her eyes to meet Keith's. She giggled nervously. "Well, this letter speaks for itself," she said.

"What is it saying?" asked Keith, his lips clenched.

"Bram is delusional and paranoid," she declared. "He's not well. We have to find him and get him the professional help he clearly needs."

If Esther had any guilt about what she'd done to Bram, it was gone. *The little shit*, she thought. Assault and kidnapping were one thing (two, whatever). Murder was way off the charts. Oh, what she would give to clobber him again. She'd hit much harder.

"He sounds sane to me," said Keith.

"He accused me of murder!"

"Yes, I can read," said Keith, snatching the letter back.

"My husband fell over that balcony. There were dozens of witnesses."

Keith wouldn't look at her. "We'll give him ten more minutes. If he doesn't walk through that door, we're driving to your house and I'm searching every room."

"I can't believe this!" said Esther. "Do you really think I'm capable of murder?"

"Given the right motivation, anyone is capable of anything."

Even though he was absolutely right, Esther was insulted to hear it. "Go ahead," she said. "Search my house. Tear up my garden, drag my pool. I just need to make a phone call, if you'll excuse me."

She stomped out of the bathroom (as much as she could in her flats), plopped down at the dinette table and searched her tote for her phone. Finding it, she tried to dial home.

Keith followed and said, "No phone calls." He snatched the cell from her hand. "What about this Natasha Molotov?"

"She's the only person who's never betrayed me," said Esther, who could barely speak. Rage sizzled all the way down through her fingers and toes. Was Bram psychic or brilliant? Either way, she hated him even more. He'd somehow predicted his own capture before it was a naughty glint in her eye. How dare he anticipate her actions before she did them! It was an invasion of privacy.

"It's 10:45," Keith said tersely. "We're leaving."

As Esther stood, the swing of her purse (lighter in her rage) knocked her coffee mug off the table. She watched with pleasure as it shattered on the floor, fingers of brown liquid stretching to the shag carpet.

Chapter 25

As soon as she was up, showered, and dressed, Penny hurried to the kitchen to make a tray for Bram. Natasha beat her to it, filling a gravy boat of sauce au jus as Penny burst through the door.

"How do you know when to put the tray in the playroom?" asked Penny.

"I watch and wait for him to go into the bathroom," said Natasha as they ascended to the attic, Boris trotting behind. "Since Bram eats so much, he goes in a lot. And he always closes the bathroom door."

Penny knew that already. He was particular about his bathroom privacy. She'd always believed it was just one more way he held out on her, denying her the stripped-to-the-bone intimacy she wanted from him.

Parking themselves in the control room, Penny and Natasha watched Bram with the sound off for about ten minutes before he went to the can. Penny held onto Boris while Natasha, sly as a fox, opened the playroom door and slid the tray inside.

He must have heard the door open. Bram slammed out of

the bathroom, his pants around his knees, and hurled himself at the door to catch it before it closed. He stumbled on his pants and crashed at least four feet from the door. He slammed his fists on the carpet and screamed, *"FUCK!"* (Penny didn't need to have the sound on to get that.) Then he gathered up his pants, went back into the bathroom, and slammed that door behind him.

Natasha returned to the control room. "He does that every time," she said, snickering. "He will never learn."

"Dense," agreed Penny.

"I have things to do, people to see," said the Russian. "I take Boris with me."

"Good," said Penny. "He's adorable, but so demanding."

"You are staying here?"

"For a few minutes."

"You will talk to him?"

Penny shrugged. "Just watch. He's my own private surreality show."

Natasha pinched Penny's cheek in a loving, if painful, way. Penny listened to the Candies' clomps fade. She waited for Bram to come out of the bathroom. Then she turned on the mike and addressed him.

"Luncheon is served," she said liltingly into the microphone, hoping to set a pleasant tone.

"What time is it?" he asked snippily, not even looking at the mirror, ignoring his food.

"Noonish."

He scowled.

"We had a lunch date, remember?" she said. "Or perhaps you made other plans."

He paced, raked his hair.

She reminded him, "You promised to tell me why you left Penny. And then I'll let you go."

Bram said, "Yeah, right."

"What have you got to lose?" Penny asked.

"Why don't you let me go first," he said finally, "and then I'll talk."

"You can understand my reluctance."

"And you can understand mine."

"We seem to be at an impasse."

"We sure do," he agreed.

"Come on, Bram. Just admit that you left Penny because you're scared of commitment."

"That's bullshit."

"You left her because you hate her mother—*me!* You hate *me*, and you wouldn't marry into our family."

"I do hate you," he said. "But I figured, if you didn't kill me, you'd only make me stronger."

"Then you're just an egomaniacal bastard. You think you can do better than Penny. You don't think she's good enough for you. She knew it all along. You never really loved her."

"Shut up!" he boomed, making the PA system buzz. "She didn't love *me!*"

Penny probed her ear with her index finger. She must have misheard him. "She did love you. She was madly in love with you."

"She wasn't. Isn't. She can lie to herself, but I know how she really feels."

"You arrogant shit. What makes you think you know Penny better than she knows herself?"

"She's a fake!" he said, standing, pacing, clearly pushed to the brink. "A phony. She lied to me when the truth matters most."

"When she said 'I love you,' it was the God's honest—"

"Penny. Faked. Orgasms," he said deliberately. "Not once or twice when she was tired or drunk. She did it night after night for as long as we were together."

The blood drained from Penny's face. From her whole head. She was dizzy and disoriented and feared she'd faint or die from embarrassment.

Bram mercilessly continued. "She thrashed all over the bed, moaning and groaning. She put on hundreds of Academy Award-winning performances. And afterward, Penny kept on lying, saying how the earth moved, or how she saw colors and stars. She always said she loved me then, too."

Penny froze at the console, unable to speak, move, breathe.

Bram said, "Hello? You still there."

She forced out a grunt. "Uhh."

"The truth sucks, doesn't it?" he said. "I felt like a failure, again and again. It ate at me. The longer the faking went on, the harder it was to confront the problem. I tried to rationalize it. What difference did it make if I loved her and she was available for sex whenever I wanted? If she was okay with the situation, then I could live with it, too. But when the wedding date got closer, I realized I couldn't pretend as well as she could. It's not enough for me to love her and want her if she didn't love me—want me—just as much. I started to have doubts about her integrity. How could she stand to fake like that? Why would she marry a man who didn't excite her?"

"How could you tell?" she asked, her voice thin, fragile, a robin's egg about to crack. "About the faking."

Bram sighed. "Do I really need to spell it out, Esther? You're a woman. There are physiological signs."

"Such as?"

"Vaginal contractions, facial flush, nipple erection—what I'd noticed in other women I'd been with. I asked my friend Morris and he said all women were different. So I did some research, called a few gynecologists. They said 'no contractions, no orgasm.' Orgasm is defined by contractions set off by stimulation of the clitoris, which is a lot longer than most people think. It's not just the little nub you see on the outside. It's forked, with two prongs that—"

"You talked to Morris about this?" she asked. "But you never said a word to m—to Penny. You should have called her on it."

"How exactly? 'Penny, love of my life, you know the hundreds of times you moaned and thrashed and scratched at me like a tiger in heat? Were you full of shit?' "

This was almost too mortifying for Penny to bear. She felt dipped in filth, coated in the gunk of shame. Defensive, too, since she had no other option. "So what if she faked?" she said. "Penny was willing to do whatever you wanted in bed. And out of bed. You didn't seem to object to her marathon blowjobs. And all those positions, the ceiling swing."

"Penny told you about that?" he asked, his skin graying. "I think I'm going to be sick."

"Mothers and daughters tell each other everything," she lied. Again.

"I thought it was *private*," he mocked. "If Penny told you about our sex life, I can't see why you'd be offended that I told Morris. Besides which, since we're getting into the nitty gritty, I tried all those crazy positions *for her*. To see if anything would make her happy. And the blowjobs. I am human! I'm not going to turn her down. Besides, she'd act insulted if I did. She liked giving them! For Penny, our sex life was about my pleasure."

"That must have been awful for you," Penny said sarcastically.

"Look, Esther, I don't know what kind of men you've been with. Maybe it's a generational thing. But what excites *me* is pleasing the woman I'm with. Penny and I were together for two years. I asked her a million times, in a million ways, what I could do for her. But she'd always turn the attention back to me. And if you asked me—to save my fucking life—what turns her on, I couldn't tell you. I'd die."

At this point in the conversation, Penny thought she might die, keel over, her last breath a ragged draw of shame. Bram looked equally depleted, but relieved. He'd unloaded his burden. That must have felt fantastic.

He called gynecologists, she marveled. He did the research. She already knew he investigated new sexual techniques—oral, manual, coital—since he tried them on her unrelentingly. If only she'd done her homework, she wouldn't be here right now on the verge of death by humiliation. She'd be in the bridal suite at the Short Hares Plaza, making love with Bram, faking it more convincingly.

"Are you going to let me out, or what?" asked Bram.

In the hallway, Penny heard garbled voices. They seemed to be getting louder. She switched off the PA system and put her ear to the control room door. She heard Esther and a man. Keith? They were on the second floor, arguing.

Bram was still talking, his mouth moving. He stood at the mirror, trying to see through, rapping the glass, demanding a response.

The voices got louder. Penny peaked out of the control room and saw Keith Shiraz marching up the stairs to the third floor. Mom was a few steps behind him. She looked frantic and furious with an undercurrent of panic. Esther reached into her purse and pulled out a big black candlestick.

A visceral kick propelled Penny out of the control room, down the corridor to the top step and into a surprised Keith Shiraz's arms.

Chapter 26

When her daughter flung herself into Keith Shiraz's arms, Esther Bracket was convinced she was hallucinating. For one thing, Penny had bolted from the control room, where she would have undoubtedly seen Bram locked up next door. And yet, Penny wasn't demanding an explanation from her. She was hugging Keith, purring like a well-fed kitten. Gesturing over his shoulder for Esther to put the candlestick *down*.

"Keith!" said Penny. "Just the man I wanted to see! I've been thinking about what a wonderful person you are, how Bram is lucky to have you for a father. And when he shows his face—and he will—he'll need your love and support more than ever."

Esther realized she must have looked stricken, because Penny mouthed, *It's okay,* to her. She pointed again at the candlestick, which Esther continued to hold aloft. Penny nodded as Esther lowered her (shaking with fatigue) arm, and quietly put the candlestick on the nesting tables in the hall.

Penny said, "If you can be half the parent to Bram that my

mommy has been to me, then Bram is the luckiest guy in the world."

To Esther's continuing admiration, Penny loosened her grip on Keith and was now slowly guiding him down the hallway, toward the stairs and, most importantly, away from the playroom door.

The girl continued to ramble excitedly. "I'm just so grateful that the two of you have been spending time together. My mommy has had a lot of tough times, Keith. Did you know that? No matter what, she's always loved and protected me. Isn't it just fantastic that Bram's little stunt brought the two of you together?" Penny's bright eyes shone with (real?) tears of joy.

Keith said, "You're a sweet girl, Penny. Bram is an idiot."

A little louder, thought Esther, glancing at the playroom door.

Keith let himself be led toward the stairs, but he did look back a couple of times—at Esther. He said, "I'm an idiot, too."

Penny asked, "What's wrong?"

Esther said, "Nothing."

Keith shook his head violently, stepped toward Esther and clasped her hands. "Everything is wrong. I made a terrible mistake. I'm ashamed I doubted you for a second."

Esther said, "What's done is done," and started down the stairs.

Keith said, "Wait!" And, "What's this?" He picked up the candlestick. "This wasn't here a minute ago."

Penny said, "I put it there."

"You did?" he asked.

"Don't talk to him, Penny," said Esther. "He thinks I'm capable of violence. That I'd intentionally harm Bram."

"What?" screeched Penny, with Vitaesque drama. "Mom is the kindest, most gentle . . . she's nonconfrontational. She

wouldn't hurt a bug. I've seen her catch mosquitoes and set them free." With extra indignation, her daughter added, "How *dare* you accuse my mother of such lies!"

"I'm sorry!" pleaded Keith. "I wasn't thinking rationally. A woman who is so beloved by her daughter couldn't hurt anyone."

"You got that right," said Penny. "Hold on, now. What exactly were you doing, storming up to the third floor? Were you about to search the attic for . . . for a body? Bram's *corpse*?"

Keith covered his face with his hands and said, "I can't begin to apologize. It sounds insane now."

Esther and Penny locked eyes. The women each took one of Keith's elbows and practically dragged him down the stairs and up to the mansion's front door. He babbled the whole way. "I'm ashamed of what I thought," he said. "I'm begging forgiveness, Esther. Put yourself in my shoes! How rational would you be if Penny were out of touch?"

By now they'd gotten him outside and to the driver's side of his car. Esther said, "I accept your apology, but I don't think we should see each other again."

"Esther, please," he said.

"Goodbye," she said.

"Reconsider! I'll wait at the hotel for you," he said. "Come for dinner. Promise me you'll think about it."

"I'll think about it," she said before taking Penny's hand, backtracking into the mansion, closing the door behind them and locking it three ways.

Then Esther sank to the floor. Penny sat next to her. "I don't know if I should thank you or commit you," she said. "I kidnapped your fiancé, and still you protect me?"

"I should—I am—*thanking* you," said Penny. "Whatever you've done, however illegal and/or emotionally unbalanced, was out of love for me."

Sunlight came in through the front windows. Esther's eyes clouded with mist. She smiled at her little girl. "Not so little anymore," she said to herself.

Penny rested her head on her mom's shoulder. "I need to tell you something about me and Bram."

"You never really loved him?" tried Esther.

"The time I dislocated my jaw," said Penny. "It happened when I was blowing him. I was trying to break my own record of forty-five minutes. And Bram is a big guy. I mean *wide*. Around. I was doing it for about twenty minutes, and my jaw spasmed and then I heard this pop sound inside my head. Bram rushed me to the hospital. We had to tell them something, so I said I fell and hit my chin on the counter."

Esther was flabbergasted. "He made you do it!"

Penny shook her head. "I made *him* do it. And I suggested the tantric position that caused my slipped disc. And I insisted on giving him the hand job at a weird angle that sprained my wrist. Bram never hit me. Wouldn't, couldn't. He'd sooner chop off his own fist than use it on me."

"So you didn't fall downstairs either," said Esther.

"They were all sex injuries, Mom," said Penny. "Maybe you can understand now why I didn't tell you the truth."

"You let me think the worst of him."

"I'm sorry," said Penny.

Regardless of the deception, Esther was deeply relieved. It'd been nearly impossible to resist stealing Penny in the night, despite her daughter's insistence that Bram was blameless. As grateful as she was for the truth, the idea of Penny performing certain acts made her queasy. Was sex an extreme sport to everyone in her daugher's generation? Or did Penny have particular tastes?

Esther said, "I'm sorry, too. About kidnapping your fiancé."

"If you hadn't, I wouldn't know why he left me."

"He told you?"

"He told *you*," said Penny. "Mistaken identity. I doubt he'd've told me. Ever."

"And what did he say?" asked Esther.

Penny shook her head. "Only one true confession per hour."

"If you're satisfied, we'll set the bastard free."

"We can't," said her daughter.

"You saw how close Keith Shiraz came to finding him," said Esther.

"If we let him go, what will happen?" asked Penny. "To you?"

Esther sighed. Regardless of when or how Bram was sprung, she'd pay for this crime, most likely with her freedom, reputation, property. "Doesn't matter," she said.

"How hard did you hit him?" asked Penny.

"I don't think I did any permanent damage."

"Maybe if we hit him again, he'll get amnesia, and won't remember where he's been."

Esther laughed. "That occurred to me, too. But where to strike?"

"I'll google 'amnesia,'" said Penny. "You go to the Plaza. Hook up with Keith."

"What's the point?" asked Esther. "He's going to find out about Bram eventually."

"So what? You don't have to marry a guy to fuck him," said Penny.

"This is not an appropriate conversation," said Esther sternly. "And, for your information, Penny, I grew up in the seventies. Love was freer then than it is now."

"We were talking about love?" asked Penny.

Esther raised her eyebrows. "Cynical already? Love ruined for you at twenty-three?" It'd been destroyed for Esther around the same age.

"If I ever have another relationship—and I'm sure I will—I'm going to focus on my own happiness," said Penny. "I'm going to take."

"I'm going to take, too," said Esther. "Take a bath. A hot one. Have you seen Natasha, by the way?"

"She had errands."

Curious, thought Esther. Natasha often disappeared on mysterious errands. Probably spending her salary on pedicures.

Esther stood up and climbed the stairs to her bedroom. After cranking the tub faucets all the way on, she slipped out of her dress, took the pins out of her blond hair, and sank down in the water until she was in over her head.

Chapter 27

Aman couldn't know what he was capable of until he found himself in the given situation. And now Bram knew: After confessing his private heartbreak to the woman he hated most in the world, he was capable of tremendous wallowing, greater than any wallowing he'd ever experienced before. He sank into it, as if his misery were a deep, bubbling bath, and he went in over his head.

In his pathetic state, he watched a double feature. *Snow White* and (hello, old friend) *Cinderella*. "Birds in hats," he grumbled to himself, sprawled on the couch. "Mice in vests." When Cinderella was locked in the attic, a bunch of birds and mice scurried to her rescue. When Snow White was in danger, a swarm of bunnies and fawns flocked to save her.

Bram flashed to the day he and Penny got engaged. The day of the photograph, when they'd been chased by tough-ass city squirrels.

He laughed at the absurdity. Talking rodents. Evil mother figures, locked up innocents in towers. He wished that, just once, he'd had the courage to confront Penny. If he ever got the chance, he would initiate the talk. And if the truth was what he suspected—that Penny just wasn't attracted to him—he'd bow out the graceful way. Try to fix the damage of his inelegant previous exit, if possible.

He checked his watch for the hundredth time. Where the fuck was Morris? He must have read the letter about Esther Bracket and Natasha Molotov by now. It was late afternoon already. The sun would go down in a couple of hours. If Morris didn't ride in with the cavalry by then, he'd set his escape plan into motion.

Bram waited until he felt certain no one was watching him on the other side of the glass. Esther hadn't come to talk to him since lunchtime. She was probably busy contemplating the means of his death. Esther's deal—information for freedom—was bogus. He'd suspected as much all along. But she'd pushed and needled and gotten him to the point where, if he didn't get the truth out, it would explode inside and damage organs. His organs were safe from the inside. But Esther had to be feeling her own internal pressure. He was a growing (especially around the waist) problem.

He turned the lights off. He'd work in the dark. Using his makeshift screwdriver (the bent fork), Bram removed the bookshelves from the wall. He arranged them in the center of the room in the shape of an H. Using Dr. Seuss books, he wedged the shelves together, creating a firm base upon which he stacked the little white table and the two kiddie chairs on top. The chairs were back to back, touching, so he could climb on top of them, one foot on each seat. The shelves, table, and chairs, by his estimation, would get him eight feet off the ground.

Although the bookshelf base wasn't as sturdy as he'd hoped, Bram successfully climbed to the standing position on the table. Now to get on the chairs. One foot up. And then . . .

"Argh!" he screamed when he slipped and nearly toppled the entire structure.

"Steady," Bram calmed himself. He put one bare foot (for traction) on the first chair. Balancing, he lifted himself up and placed his other foot squarely in the center of the second chair. He straightened himself and stood at his full height of six feet, the chairs rickety beneath him. The top of his head was now fourteen feet off the floor.

He didn't dare look down.

With arms stretched over his head, he was still a couple of feet short of the ceiling. Bram removed the coil of jump ropes from his shoulder and unwound it. He tied a lasso on one end. Taking a deep breath, squaring off, he flung the noose at the latch of the skylight above.

Missed. The swing motion nearly sent him toppling off his platform.

Second attempt: smoking, but no cigar.

Before his third attempt, Bram closed his eyes and channeled the force. He flung the rope.

The lasso caught the latch and he pulled hard to close it tightly around the window hardware. Flop sweat and relief spilled out of his pores. He yanked the jump rope to see if it would hold. It was firm, but his hands were too slippery to climb.

He dried them on his jeans. Gripping the rope tightly, he pulled himself up. Thanks to pounding nails and hauling lumber, Bram had impressive upper body strength. With quick hand over hand motion, he scaled the short distance of rope in seconds. He clamped his fingertips securely inside the skylight window frame and kicked his legs up to get purchase with his toes.

It took all of Bram's courage to let go with one hand to unlatch the skylight and push it open.

But the glass was stuck. He nearly cried. He was shaking with effort, hanging like a cat on the ceiling, using all his leg and hand muscles to hold onto the window frame. If he let go, he'd fall and break his back.

With a blast of adrenaline, he slammed the stuck window with his forearm, springing it open. The lasso slipped off the latch and fell eighteen feet to the ground. His right foot also gave way. His body weight pulled him down, and he started to fall, hands grasping, legs cycling in the air.

One finger caught the edge of the open window. He hung by that finger until he could inch up with his hand. Then he got his other hand in the edge, kicked his feet through the hole and his legs out onto the roof of the house.

In this position, he easily hoisted his upper body through the hole. Then he collapsed on the roof, exhausted. The exertion made him breathe rapidly, his pulse jackhammering in his ears. He rolled onto his side, and looked down through the open skylight. He frowned at the jump ropes he'd tied together, now on the floor of the playroom. He'd planned on using them to scale down from the roof.

He shifted onto his back. The stars were not yet visible in the early hour of night. But the view was beautiful from the top of the mansion on a hill. He could see the town of Short Hares laid out like a movie set, the wooded areas like patches of trees, the streetlights in a glittery grid. The houses in curved rows, the glowing blue swimming pools.

Swimming pools.

Without a rope, it was the only way. Bram crawled like a crab along the slanted roof to its edge. Lying flat by the gutter, looking over the side, he saw the Brackets' swimming pool. It appeared to be a straight drop down. A three-story drop.

Bram once dove off the high board in college. That had been thirty feet. This jump would be over fifty.

"No problem," he said to himself. "Kids on PCP do it all the time."

Out of the corner of his eye he noticed a squirrel on the roof. It was nosing around the open skylight.

"Better you than me," he said, watching it climb down into the hole.

He stood up, toes off the edge of the roof. He eyed the smooth surface of the pool. Underwater lights made it glow radioactively.

Bram cupped his balls and jumped.

Chapter 28

Night was falling. Penny wandered into her mom's suite. She'd spend the last few hours in her room replaying a few of her finest Academy Award–worthy orgasm performances. The irony: She thought she'd been good. Wildly convincing. Once or twice, while in the throes of faux climax, it occurred to her that she should forget dancing and try her hand at acting since her talent was going to waste.

Of course, Bram's confession had cast her acting chops into doubt. She hadn't fooled her audience of one. Vita's "fake it to make it" advice had never made sense to her anyway, but she was willing to keep trying until it worked. She'd had orgasms, of course, jerking off, or positioning herself under the bathtub faucet (naturally, she knew about vaginal contractions; she just hadn't realized Bram knew). But in the presence of a man, she couldn't manage to get off. Not only Bram. But every guy she'd been with. Since her first several lovers didn't seem to care whether she came or not, she hadn't bothered to pretend. But Bram cared. Man, did he care. He was relentless about it. He was on a fucking mission, literally. The pressure made it impossible for her to relax. He'd fuck and fuck, flip her around, dive between her legs. She didn't want to tell him to stop since he might take it the wrong way. Faking seemed like the best option.

And thus the cycle of deception began. Penny figured she'd have orgasms with Bram eventually. She was wildly attracted to him, couldn't keep her hands off him. Her skin flushed under his touch and she loved his release, the feeling of him coming inside her. She firmly believed, God's honest, that after they got married, she'd be secure enough to make suggestions, or show him what she liked. Or go vibrator shopping together. They could have lunch. Make a day of it. If she'd had any clue he was in on her act, she'd have stopped, of course. There'd have been a long talk. As horrified as she felt now, Penny was also glad. She'd never fake again, that was for damn sure. So the truth might set her free. *What about Bram?* she wondered. He should be free, too. But it wasn't her decision to make.

"Mom?" she called softly.

"In here," replied Esther from inside the master suite.

Penny poked her nose inside the giant bathroom. "Have you been in the bath since Keith left? Jesus, Mom, it's been hours."

Esther was sprawled in the tub, bubbles glistening and popping on the water surface. "I am a bit pruney. Hand me that towel."

Penny gave her mom the terry bath sheet and faced the wall. She listened to the splashing and ruffling sounds of her mom exiting the tub, and turned back around. Esther was wrapped in fluffy white plushness, the towel secured under the arms. Her damp shoulders were broad but bony. Her neck was long, but not gnarly like a lot of older women. Penny smiled at her mom's rosy cheeks and the dew on her forehead. She looked beautiful like this, she thought. Younger without the makeup, done hair, tailored outfits.

"Any sign of Natasha?" asked Esther.

"No." She had been gone for a while. "I wonder what she's doing. With Boris."

Her mom shrugged. "Does it matter?"

"Are you going to the Plaza to be with Keith?"

"Yes," said Esther.

"Good."

"I haven't been with a man in a long, long time."

"You're gorgeous, Mom!" said Penny. "If I look half as good as you do when I'm your age, I'll be milking it."

"I'm not worried about how I look," said Esther, a bit impatiently.

"It's like riding a bike, Mom."

"Although sex is a dim memory," said Esther as she sat down at her vanity and started drying her hair, "I don't remember it having anything to do with riding a bike."

Penny laughed. She wished she had the guts to ask if her mom had ever faked, but she didn't dare. It was just too embarrassing.

Esther stopped toweling and turned abruptly to Penny. "You will visit me in prison?"

"Every day," she said.

"This night is my last hurrah."

"You picked a good man for the job," said Penny.

"I'll live off the memory in the big house."

"Please, Mom. You're not going to jail," said Penny. "Rich white people don't get convicted. You'll hire the best lawyers. You'll claim temporary insanity. Whatever works."

"Or we could just kill him," said Esther. "Dump the body in the Meadowlands marsh."

"Bram and Jimmy Hoffa," said Penny, laughing. "You're a regular comedienne, Mom."

Esther smirked. "Yeah, me and Sarah Silverman."

"I'm stunned," said Penny.

"By my macabre sense of humor?"

"That you know who Sarah Silverman is."

Esther frowned and said, "There's a lot you don't know about me. And when you come to visit me in prison, I'll correct that. We'll talk about things I should have told you years ago. If it has to be with a pane of glass between us, so be it."

Penny felt antsy. Whatever her mom was alluding to, whatever secrets Esther kept, she didn't want to know (although the details of Russell's fatal fall came immediately to mind). Penny had only just concluded another uncomfortable conversation through a pane of glass, concerning matters that should have come out years ago. She wasn't sure if she could handle another.

"I'm going to take a swim," she said, changing the subject.

"I gathered," said Esther. "The bikini was a giveaway."

"See you in the morning," said Penny. "And good luck."

Penny padded outside, around the stone path, along the gardens, and up to the edge of the kidney-shaped pool. The water was heated to a warm 76 degrees, and cleaned weekly by the best pool guys in Short Hares. Esther hardly ever went swimming anymore, but she kept the pool well-maintained from June to September just in case Penny dropped by to use it. How many times had she gone swimming in the five years since she left home? A dozen?

Penny dipped a toe in the water, testing it. If the temperature had dropped when she'd dumped the ice sculpture into the pool, it'd returned to normal. She scanned the pool bottom for any icy remnants. Seeing nothing but water, she tossed her towel on the lounge chair behind her.

She stretched her back and neck muscles and prepared to

jump in. Half a second before she took the plunge, a giant bird or animal or *something* dive-bombed into the water at screaming speed, creating a fountain of back-slash that slammed against her, knocking her off her feet.

Sputtering, partially in shock, she crawled to the edge of the pool. A dark and motionless figure floated on the surface. Facedown.

Chapter 29

"I knew you'd come," said Keith Shiraz when he opened the door of his hotel suite at the Plaza.

"You're sure of yourself," said Esther. She loathed conceit, almost as much as she despised the idea that he'd been lying around, buffing his nails, or whatever it was men did to demonstrate the passage of time with the smug certainty that she would soon appear.

"Please," he said, inviting her in, grinning widely at her red cocktail dress and matching silk pumps.

Esther stepped into the immaculate room, bed clothes tight as a rubber band, a table set with china and crystal, a champagne bottle chilled in a silver bucket next to a bud vase with a single red rose.

"I was sure, not of myself. I was sure about *us*. I knew this was going to happen—eventually. All afternoon I found myself relishing the memory before it's even happened."

"I pictured it, too," Esther admitted. Their (one and only) night of lust seemed destined. They'd been pushed together like chess pieces by fate. It was only logical that they'd collide.

Keith smiled. "Shall we eat?" he asked. "Or would you rather get in bed?"

Esther blushed (she hoped charmingly). "Can't we do both?" she asked, trying to match him easy for breezy.

He answered by grabbing her with his bear (and bare) hands around the waist, squeezing her ribs, lifting her off her pumps, and pressing his lips against hers.

Esther's breath stolen, she held on to his neck, letting him take control. This hotel suite would be his control room—and their playroom. Keith was larger than her, and she was a tall woman. She felt small and delicate in his arms, soft and cute and squeezable—a dramatic shift from her usual stately solidity. She liked this feeling better, being a warm and cuddly pet Keith was so eager to play with.

When he broke their kiss to take in air, she asked, "Hate to bring this up, but what about birth control?"

"Are you still . . . I mean, how old are you, anyway?"

"I'm forty-five," she said. "Pregnancy is unlikely—absurd, certainly—but a physiological possibility."

He smiled devilishly at her. "I'm fixed," he said, and snipped the air with his fingers. He held her by the hips and rubbed himself against her.

"Fine middle-aged couple we are," she observed. "I'm still ovulating, and you're hard as a rock."

He laughed. "I can't believe Bram described you as a humorless shrew."

"He was right," she said. "I was for a long time. But I'm making a comeback."

"Should I ask what turned you around?"

You, she thought. Kidnapping Bram, a new trust with Penny. A break from years of routine.

"Definitely not," she said, and pulled his face down to her lips. He cupped her ass with his hands and lifted her high enough to wrap her legs around his hips. Taking a step backward, he sat down on the bed, Esther straddling his lap.

"Hold on," he said, and flipped her over. She was suddenly flat on her back, Keith Shiraz and his muscular bulk pinning her to the bed.

Esther smiled. She wanted him to flip her around, throw her this way and that, to be his rag doll. She pecked at his neck and chin. He was smooth. She could smell the minty residue of shaving cream.

He propped himself up on his elbows. "I have to ask about something," he said. "Russell Bracket."

"What about him?"

"We have to talk about how he died," he said. "You can't expect me to just pretend that letter from Bram doesn't exist. He made spurious accusations, but they were based on something. I need to hear what happened. From you."

She sighed and pushed him off. She sat upright. "A bit of a mood killer."

"I'm sorry," he said. "Has to be done."

"I didn't kill him," she said. "I wished him dead. I prayed he'd be hit by a truck. I fantasized about him having a massive heart attack while fucking his girlfriend. I didn't want him dead—abstractly—out of revenge alone. Had he lived, he'd have taken full custody of Penny."

"The mothers usually get custody," said Keith.

"That's true," she agreed. "But during the settlement battle, there was an incident. At the mall. I looked away for a second, and someone snatched Penny. She was rescued in time, but it was a close call. Russell found out about what happened—it was in all the papers, how could he not?—and he used it against me. He called me an unfit mother, he accused me of alcoholism, drug abuse, neglect. He'd previously stopped paying for our food, and then he accused me of starving Penny to spite him."

"Jesus," said Keith. "Sounds like he deserved to die."

Esther nodded. "He ground away at my strength. After almost losing Penny, whatever fortitude I had was gone. I agreed to his terms. No money, no custody. I'd already traded my family and ambitions for Russell. He was bent on destroying me. By then, I thought I deserved it. The day he died, I was packing to vacate the mansion. I was supposed to take Penny to Russell's lawyer's office, sign the papers and hand over my daughter. And then the phone call came. Russell fell off the balcony at the mall."

Esther paused, afraid to look at Keith's face. She continued, "I laughed and laughed. I laughed so hard, I pulled a muscle in my stomach. When I calmed down and realized that Penny would be safe with me, and that everything was now mine—the house, the money—I cried. With joy, but Penny thought I was sad for Russell. She believed—still does—that her father was a good man and not the scum-sucking pig who got what he had coming."

Keith seemed momentarily taken aback by her tone. She said, "I'm still working through some of the anger."

"You're better now," he said. "Since you met me."

She smiled weakly. "You're right."

"Natasha Molotov," prompted Keith gently.

Esther said, "Russell cut me off during the settlement fight, and I didn't have money to pay a housekeeper or babysitter. As soon as he died and I had access to the funds, I called an agency and they sent over Natasha. The Soviet Union had only just fallen, and there was an influx of Russians into New Jersey. Penny loved Natasha immediately, was fascinated by the accent. She moved in after a month or two. It's been fifteen years. She's the only person I've trusted completely since Russell betrayed me. Frankly, if Natasha did have something to do with her husband's death, I don't care. Whatever she has or hasn't done, I would protect and help her with everything I've got."

"I'd best not cross swords with the Russian."

"If you value your life," agreed Esther.

"I admire your friendship with Natasha," he admitted.

"It's more than a friendship," said Esther. "We saved each other. And she's like another mother to Penny."

"I was looking forward to being Penny's father-in-law. Maybe I'll get to become something else to her."

A stepfather? Esther didn't dare ask. A ludicrous notion. Once Keith found out what she'd done to his son, he'd never forgive her. She had tonight with him. And then it would end.

"I think we've done enough talking," she said.

"I agree. Let's have a quick drink." He bounced off the bed and opened the champagne. He handed her a flute.

She sipped. A fine vintage. Keith, a man she'd met only a few days ago, reached under her dress and stroked her thighs.

She said, "Fair warning: I may look my age naked."

"Me, too," he said.

"I do exercise," she said. "Every day."

"I've heard that exercise lengthens your life, but only by the amount of time you spend exercising," he said.

"Does sex count as cardio training?"

"Not for me," he said. "I like to go slow."

Chapter 30

"Breathe," screamed Penny as she labored over Bram's prone body. She'd hauled him out of the pool and was performing CPR. His lips were warm, soft. Lifeless.

He lay beneath her. She leaned away from the body to see if his chest rose and fell. She put her hands over his lungs, tried to detect movement. She put her ear to his mouth and listened for breathing. She searched for a pulse on his neck. Flailing, unsure what she was doing, blanking on the hours of CPR training she'd logged at sleepaway camp, Penny felt helpless. And she was royally pissed off that he'd stupidly jumped.

In a panic, she stood up to go call 911, then plopped back down at his side, not wanting to leave him. She stared at the face she'd fallen in love with. "Wake up!" she demanded, and slapped him, hard.

Bram yelled, "Hey!" and cupped his cheek.

His sudden movement made her reel, and she fell backward into the pool. Surfacing, she sputtered, "You bastard! I thought you were dead!"

Bram, now seated cross-legged on the pool's lip, said, "You deserved that."

"You deserved what you got!" she said, hoisting herself out of the water to sit next to him.

He pushed her into the pool again.

"Mother fucker!" she hollered at him.

He was laughing now. He said, "Ahem, your bikini."

Penny looked down to see that her right tit had popped out of her top. Bram was staring at it, transfixed as he always was by her breasts. She took her top off and threw it at him, hitting him on the forehead.

Bram held the skimpy gingham in his hands and said, "I always loved this bikini."

"It's yours to keep," she said. "My parting gift."

He frowned. "Don't say that. I'm sorry about what happened."

"Sorry you called off the wedding?" she asked. "Or sorry you got kidnapped?"

"Both," he said, watching her tread water. "I've had a couple days by myself to think—as you are, apparently, aware. I fucked up ten different ways, and I regret all of it. We should have talked."

"About what?" she asked innocently.

Bram pursed his lips. "Come out of the pool." He held her towel open for her.

"No."

"I won't push you in."

"For the record, I had nothing to do with the kidnapping. I only found out about it an hour ago."

"But that was you on the intercom at lunchtime today," he said. "I didn't realize at the time, but I kind of figured it out."

"It wasn't me!" Penny said. And then she stopped. Why lie *more* at this point? "It was me. I've known about your, shall we say, 'confinement' since last night. I gave you the bag of clothes."

He smiled at her. "I wondered about that. I thought it might be you, but then I rejected the idea. And then, at lunch, it was easier to pretend I was talking to Esther. But, subconsciously, I knew it was you just the same."

"I understand," she said.

"We've got to work at having direct conversations."

"Why bother?" Penny asked, climbing up the pool steps, letting Bram drape the towel across her shoulders. "We're done, Bram. You left me to go up on the altar and tell the wedding guests what you did. I was naked up there!"

"I'm sure you felt terribly exposed," he said.

"No, I was literally naked. My gown fell off."

He said, "I'd have liked to see that."

She smiled. "If I were in the audience, I would have laughed." Then, bitterly, she added, "But I wasn't."

"Why did you fake?" he asked softly, lowering his eyes.

"It seemed easier than admitting defeat."

"Were you ever attracted to me?" His voice hitched.

She gathered the towel under her chin. "No, you disgust me," she said. His face caved in. "Of course I'm attracted to you! What woman isn't?"

"Then what was wrong?" he asked.

"I don't *know*," she said. "I just couldn't flick the switch. The harder I tried, the more impossible it became. Don't you think I wanted to come? Believe me, I did. More than you wanted me to." Penny's eyes filled, completely against her will.

Bram pulled her into his arms. She let him comfort her. It felt good to be hugged and touched—always had with him. Bram was an affectionate person. Perhaps one of the big reasons she'd wanted to marry him. She'd had an affection-deprived childhood. Esther didn't kiss her good-night or snuggle while watching TV. Penny mourned the lost opportunities to be close with her mom. She wondered what kind of mother Esther might have been had circumstances been different for them both. A child measured love in hugs. She had always wondered about Esther's.

"The truth is," said Penny against Bram's wet T-shirt, "I wasn't convinced you really loved me. I was afraid you'd leave me, and then you did. In the worst way."

At that, she shoved Bram into the pool. He had quick hands, though, and pulled her in with him.

"I'm sorry!" he said when their heads were above water. "But you're going to have to forgive me." She tried to swim away, but he held onto her wrist.

"I won't," she said, struggling and splashing.

He said, "Stop fighting and I'll let you go."

She complied. He dropped her arm. And she went for his eyes. In a mad tussle, Bram snagged both of her wrists and lifted them over her head. They were in the shallow end, the water at waist level. She was topless, breathing hard.

Bram tried to keep his eyes up but he couldn't help himself. He said, "Tell me exactly what you want me to do."

"It's hard to use words," she said.

"You could draw pictures," he suggested. "Or blink twice if you like it, once if you don't."

Bram lowered her arms. She put them around his neck and pulled him close. Couldn't help herself. As they kissed, Penny felt him get hard through his soaked jeans.

"It's going to be a struggle," she said, gripping his waistband. "Getting these off."

He said, "We're not alone."

She followed his eyes and saw the pair of squirrels by the edge of the pool, their hands folded over their stomachs, noses twitching in the air.

Bram splashed some water at them. They moved away, but came right back.

"We're a live sex show for rodents," he said.

"Maybe they want to help us," she said. "Like Cinderella's mice."

"No, these rodents are from New Jersey. They're degenerates. Peeping squirrels."

Penny laughed and they resumed making out. She kept one eye on the critters, who kept their beady eyes trained on the couple in the pool.

"Five of them," she said.

"Come on," he said, then led her up the steps of the pool and into the all-weather cabana. Before he closed the door, Bram said, "Listen up, squirrels. Don't let anyone in here. If Esther Bracket shows up, go for the jugular."

Penny stretched out on the cabana's queen-size lounge chair. Bram stared at her body as he pulled off his wet shirt and yanked out of the jeans. His boxers were plastered against his erection. He peeled those off, too, and lay down next to Penny on the lounge.

"I'm at your service," he said. "Tell me what you want."

Penny opened her mouth but simply couldn't speak. Then, an idea. "Have you ever heard of 'mirroring'?" she said.

"Is it fucking in front of a mirror?" he asked. "Which might be exciting down the road. Frankly, I've had enough of mirrors—one- or two-way—for a while."

She shook her head. "It's an acting technique. Vita showed me. She imitates people's movements—mirroring them. It might be useful for us."

"You want me to do what you do," he said.

"Precisely," she said, and kissed Bram on the lips, lightly.

Bram matched her, kissing her slowly and thoughtfully, their heads close, noses rubbing.

She kissed him along his neck, sucking on his ear, licking down to his shoulder, always feather light. Bram let himself accept her attention. Usually, whenever she tried to slow down, to enjoy the taste and smell of him, he'd get too excited, flip her over and maul her (which had its merits, too).

Penny moved to his nipples. She took one in her mouth, and the other she rolled between her fingers. She circled his nipple with her tongue, exactly the way she wanted him to do to hers. The idea alone—that he would soon be imitating her every stroke and suck—flooded her already wet bikini bottom. She found herself getting into it, feeling power as well as building excitement.

She knew Bram was having a hard time being passive. But he'd get his turn. Meanwhile, what she did to him, anticipating his reciprocation, inflamed her, inspired her. As she teased and taunted, worshipping his gorgeous body inch by inch, she found herself becoming dizzy with desire and anticipation.

Penny swallowed him whole. Bram cried out and started to throb inside her mouth. To stop him from coming, she encircled the base of his penis with her fingers and squeezed. He seemed to calm down. Then she tickled him softly with her tongue.

Bram said, "I can't take much more of this."

Penny released him and lay back on the lounge, ready (and eager) for her turn.

A good student, Bram returned her kisses with the same gentle, slow, lingering pace and pressure. He was holding himself back. She knew he liked to ravage, not savor. His restraint excited her, too, knowing he'd been paying attention. When he put his lips on her nipples, brushing his tongue against them, sucking shallowly, she gasped. Pleasure streamed across her skin, sinking into her body, humming along her spine until it melted.

As he licked along her belly, he would speed up, catch himself and slow down. The arrhythmic pace was tantalizing, and when he finally reached the hot spot, she nearly burst from the slightest contact, just as he had. While he swirled with his tongue and brushed his fingertips on her bottom, Penny thought she could come at any second, as easily as Bram, as any man. She pictured herself gasping, her hips buckling, muscles spooling in the tension of the years.

Bram slid a finger inside.

Penny screamed and released, twitching and rocking on the lounge, filling the small cabana with the sounds and smells and happiness.

It was her first genuine orgasm with Bram. And even though he'd made it happen, she knew she'd done it, too.

He crawled over her and lowered himself on top. He kissed her cheeks and chin, smoothing the wet hair from her forehead. In the dim light, his eyes shimmered. Bram looked misty, unglued.

She said, "Much better than faking."

"I can't believe how beautiful you are," he said. "It's not human. It's alien beauty. I've never seen you like this before."

"It is pretty dark in here," she said.

He laughed. She spread her legs and he let himself in, staying up on his elbows so they could watch each other. No glass wall between them now, Penny kept her eyes and emotions open to Bram, letting him all the way in.

Bram seemed to understand that she was present, in the moment with him, not mentally hovering over their entwined bodies, watching herself struggle to relax. This time they were connected mentally and physically. She felt every inch of him. Every thrust had a beginning, middle, and end. Each sigh told a story.

When he quickened and came, she held him tightly, and registered his gratitude in her core. An unexpected coiling between her legs sprang open into another explosion. She gasped and spammed, couldn't believe what was happening. As soon as she stopped trying, she came thoughtlessly, effortlessly.

Bram said, "Did you come again?"

She nodded, as dumbfounded as he was. Dumbfounded, and exhilarated. This wasn't a breakup, she realized, holding him close. It was a breakthrough. She'd finally figured out how to turn off her mind, silence the mental chatter, and let her body take over.

She'd wasted years.

Bram's head was resting on her shoulder, his eyes closed. He was almost asleep. Penny, however, was wide-awake. Awakened, one could say.

He'd been right to end it, she knew now. Perhaps Bram hadn't done it the right way. But now she understood all he'd wanted for them. A marriage of any less wasn't enough.

Understanding led to forgiveness. She might be able to forgive him. But Penny wasn't so sure she could forgive herself for her deception. Bram would be a daily reminder of all the faking she'd done.

Half sleep, he muttered, "I like your earrings. I wish I'd been there when you got them." And then he fell asleep.

Penny slid his head off her shoulder. She got off the lounge and went to the cabana closet to fetch a dozen beach towels. Before draping them over Bram's sleeping body, she took in the sight of him. Tried to memorize it, paint a mental picture and frame it.

It would be the last time she saw him naked.

She covered him with the towels, and hung his wet clothing on hooks. She wrapped herself in a dry towel and went into the house. Penny walked up to the playroom and saw how he'd escaped. He'd gone through the roof. Up and out. He'd earned his freedom, and she would let him go, in every way.

She gathered Bram's possessions, his toiletries, his sneakers, the dirty clothes. The photo of her. She packed them all in his suitcase, along with the video of *Cinderella*. She stopped in her room to write a note. She sealed it in an envelope. She carried it and the suitcase back out to the cabana.

Bram hadn't moved an inch. She kissed his nose, left the suitcase by the lounge, and taped the envelope where she knew he'd find it.

Chapter 31

Dear Bram:

Last night was incredible. We finally got to say what needed to be said, and to be together one last time. I don't regret a second of it.

I saw what you did to escape. You could have killed yourself. Says a lot, how far you were willing to go to get away from me.

Too much has happened between us. I'm not ready yet to forgive you for leaving me—or myself for lying to you. You had the right idea, ending it. This way, we can both start over fresh.

Fondly,
Penny

P.S. If you press charges against my mother, I'll kill you.

Bram found the note taped to his chest hair. He ripped a few of the hairs out to read it. Inside the envelope, along with this bitch of a note, was Penny's diamond engagement ring.

Bram put the ring on his pinkie. It stopped between the first and second knuckle. He flopped back down on the lounge, exasperated.

The note hit him like an anvil. Hadn't—couldn't—have seen this coming. As far as he was concerned, last night had been their triumphant reunion. Penny, apparently, regarded it as a "fond" farewell. She had two very real orgasms, and still she didn't want him. Penny was as batty as her mother. To think, as he'd drifted off, he'd felt grateful. If Esther hadn't kidnapped him, he and Penny wouldn't have had their moment(s) in the cabana.

In the cold light of morning, Bram's gratitude toward Esther was gone. He could see how Penny was still angry about the wedding. She should be. And he deserved some suffering for what he did, but he'd paid that price in full already, by his reckoning. He'd been knocked unconscious, locked up like a dog, stuffed with overheated leftovers. Worst of all, he'd been forced to examine his psyche, to count his mistakes, to see how he'd created the horrible situation with Penny, where he remained still. He'd isolated himself by not confronting her. His escape plans (from the wedding and his imprisonment) only landed him more stuck than he'd been before.

"So what am I supposed to do now?" he asked himself.

No one answered. Not even the degenerate peeping squirrels.

Bram found the suitcase on the floor by the lounge when he tripped over it. He put on the clothes Penny hung up for him. They were dry and smelled of chlorine. Once dressed, he picked up the suitcase and strode toward the house.

He wanted to talk to Penny. If Esther or the murderous Russian opened the door, he had a few words (slurs, snarls) for them, too. He tried the kitchen door first. Locked. He banged on it. No response. He stormed around to the front entrance.

Rang the bell, pounded on the door until the meaty part of his hand was red and numb.

He felt the rising tide of anger, the flash of rage that gripped him in traffic and whenever he witnessed public abuse of animals and children. Bram closed his eyes and forced himself to count to ten.

Two hundred and forty-three counts later he was calm. He was serene. And determined. Penny might lock herself in her castle, but he'd find a way in.

So now he was plotting and scheming for a way into the mansion, he thought ruefully.

He was seriously considering knocking Penny on the head with a bottle and kidnapping her.

Deciding to regroup, Bram pointed his sneakered feet down the driveway. He'd go back to the Plaza. Find his dad, or Morris, or just get a room to figure out his next step. Then he'd come back for Penny and wouldn't leave without her.

As he hoofed down Overlook Lane, he relived his time in the cabana with Penny, warm and soft in his arms, grabbing and clutching him from the inside when she came, squeezing the last drops out of him. He'd waited two years for those few seconds. And, if he had to, he'd wait ten years to feel that again.

She said she'd kill him if he had her mother arrested. What *should* he do about Esther Bracket? Sane, rational people did not smash skulls with bottles. Maybe Esther should be institutionalized, for the public safety. Esther was a negative influence on her daughter as well. If Penny hadn't been under her roof and influence, wouldn't she have let him go as soon as she found him?

He trudged, moving fast and furious. Bram reasoned that he could somehow broker a deal. In exchange for his pardon, Esther would have to agree to sever her relationship with Penny. That seemed fair. Or not. He wasn't sure. Maybe threatening him was Penny's way of testing him. If he let her mother off, would Penny give him another chance?

He reached the Plaza before long. He walked up to the concierge desk.

He smiled at the young woman behind it. She smiled at him. He'd expected her to recoil. He knew he looked tired and rumpled.

"Good morning, sir. How can I help you?"

"Is Keith Shiraz still here? Or Morris Nova?"

She checked her computer screen. "Mr. Shiraz is registered. And I believe Mr. Nova is taking calls in the room of a friend. I'm sorry, I can't give you their room numbers. I can call them for you."

Bram grinned with relief. Dearly beloved were near. "Not necessary," he said. "Thanks."

He pretended to head toward Coq et Boule, the restaurant. When he was certain the concierge wasn't watching, he snuck over to the elevator bank.

Unless Keith had changed rooms, Bram knew where to find him. He'd rather go straight up than deal with Keith's reaction over the phone.

Bram rode the elevator to the twelfth floor. Walking down the hallway toward his dad's room, Bram got weak, woozy. The events of the last three days were finally taking their toll. As he neared his father's protective orbit, he felt deflated, weak. He allowed himself to fully grasp the danger he'd been in. The fact of the matter: Esther Bracket was a pathological, murderous woman. She'd been living like a shrew since she offed her husband, the violent urges had been building and growing. Had he not risked his own life to escape, Esther would have killed him.

With a shudder, Bram stepped up to Room 1214. He knocked gently on the door. It was early morning, eight o'clock. Keith seldom slept this late. Bram wondered why his father was still in Short Hares. Perhaps his use of brown crayon on yellow paper had tipped off his Dad to the foul play after all. Bram knocked again, louder.

A voice from inside the room: "Come in, it's unlocked."

Keith. The sound of his voice made Bram well up. Wiping his eyes, he flung the door open and nearly fell into the room with relief.

From the bed, from under the covers, his father said, "Just put the tray on the table. Give yourself a big tip."

A woman giggled. Lumps under the sheets wriggled.

Bram dropped his suitcase where he stood. "Dad?" he said.

The bodies in the bed froze. Keith flung the covers away and stared at his son. "Bram!" he shouted. He was naked, apparently, because he started to leap out of the bed and then thought the better of it.

Next to his dad on the bed lay Esther Bracket, his tormentor, the sheets pulled up under her chin.

Bram spun backward at the hideous sight, knocking a lamp off a table.

"Bram, what's the matter?" cried Keith, suddenly at his side. Thankfully, he'd found a robe.

"What the fuck are you doing with *her*?" demanded Bram.

Keith said, "Son, I know what you think of Esther. But you're wrong. She's a loving, kind, generous woman. I'm falling in love with her."

That news made Bram gag. He would have vomited, but he was too flummoxed, too stunned.

Keith clasped his son by the shoulders. "Bram! You look green! Are you sick? What's wrong?"

"*What's wrong?*" Bram spit. "That woman *thing*, that human *pustule*"—he pointed the finger at Esther—"that *creature* you think you're falling in love with, *tried to kill me*!"

"That's ridiculous," dismissed Keith.

"Ask her!" demanded Bram.

"You need to calm down," warned his dad.

"You goddamned *witch*!" bellowed Bram. "What have you done to my father?" To Keith, he added, "She's crazy. She's got no conscience, completely sadistic, bent on my destruction. Ask her, Dad. *Ask her.*"

Keith sighed heavily and turned to face Esther. With an apologetic expression, he said, "I'm asking. Esther, did you try to kill my son?"

Chapter 32

Esther could see Keith was torn. He thought she was a spontaneous, whimsical, red-hot lover. But, in reality, she was dangerous, plotting and way out of practice.

Keith thought he was falling in love? That was news to her.

"Lemme at 'er!" grunted Bram, in a shoving match with his dad.

Esther, from the bed, said, "I didn't try to kill him."

"Liar!" screamed Bram.

"Bram, please. Settle down."

"You believe *her*? That vile, loathsome snake? Fuck her and fuck you, too," railed Bram, who then hurtled himself out of the room, banging the door so hard the walls shook.

Keith stared at Esther in shock and dismay. She'd unwittingly pitted a parent and child against each other. Collateral consequences?

"I didn't try to kill him," she repeated. "I did, however, brain him with a champagne bottle. Then I kidnapped him, and held him prisoner. But only for a few days. And I was very nice to him. I never tormented him—I categorically deny that. Well, maybe a little psychological torment. But nothing he couldn't handle."

"*What?*" roared Keith.

Esther could tell by his volume that Keith needed to cool off a bit before they could have a productive conversation. She swung her legs over the side of the bed and collected her strewn clothes. She dressed quickly. Esther figured she had approximately thirty seconds to get out of there before Keith's top blew off.

"You've known where Bram was," he stated. "All this time."

"At my house. On the third floor, in a sealed room," she said, zipping her dress.

"I was there yesterday," he said.

"A close call."

"The time you spent with me, the assurances and attention. It was to keep me from searching for Bram. To distract me. That note he wrote, with crayons."

"I made him write it," she said, slipping on her pumps. "So you'd stop being suspicious about the missing bedspread and the champagne bottle on the floor of the bridal suite."

Keith said, "Penny was involved, too?"

"She had nothing to do with it," Esther said sharply. "It was all me. You have to understand, I snapped. I did a bad thing. But he's free now. Seems intact. No harm done."

"How could you do this?" he said.

She sighed. "I admit that there might be something wrong with me. I might be ethically challenged. But I'll go to the grave—or prison, whichever comes first—believing Bram deserved what he got. I acted as a mother seeking justice for her daughter."

"You've been lying to me for days."

"I was practicing self-preservation," she defended. "It's a basic, animal instinct."

"How could you kiss me, make love to me, knowing you had my son locked up in your attic?"

Good question. "I put Bram in one mental box, and you in another," she explained. "It was as if his kidnapping and our relationship had nothing to do with each other. That was the lie I told myself."

Esther, dressed, lifted her purse by the handle and took a few baby steps toward Keith. Anything could happen. He could punch her. Or restrain her and call hotel security. He could spit on her. Kiss her. Whisper in her ear (and not the nice way). He might give her a big hug, which would be lovely since she was feeling extremely vulnerable right now.

When she got within arm's reach, much to her surprise, Keith put his hand on her waist. He reached down and put his other hand behind her knees. He lifted her off her feet and smiled, their faces only inches apart.

Esther flung her arms around his neck and dropped her head on his shoulder, closing her eyes with gratitude and relief. He forgave her! He understood that she'd been temporarily insane. She wouldn't be someone's bitch in prison.

She heard a creak, and opened her eyes.

Keith had opened the hotel room door. And then he threw her out of it. She landed hard on her ass in the carpeted hallway.

She stood up, dusted herself off, smoothed down her hair. Keith seemed bemused by her pantomime. "You're not going to call the police, are you?" she asked.

He showed her his teeth. "In my business, we like to handle . . . things . . . internally," he said.

"Internally, as in internal injuries?" she asked.

"You'll find out soon enough," he said, and slammed the door shut.

Chapter 33

Penny woke up in her own cozy bed to the bong of the mansion bell and Bram's repeated pounding. Pulling her comforter up high, she ignored him. It was surprisingly easy to do. She fell back asleep for a few minutes, and woke up again to banging.

But this time it came from inside the house. She padded in her pajamas toward the noise in Natasha's room.

"Good morning," said her live-in whatever of fifteen years. The bed was covered with half-packed duffels. On the floor, half-filled boxes of books and tchotchkes. Some of them, Penny noted, were Esther's.

"Hello, Alexia," said Penny to Natasha's cousin, who was helping Natasha pack. Alexia was shorter than Natasha, and scrawny, not curvy. Both women had matching pert noses, sandy stringy hair, overplucked eyebrows, and Candies. Alexia nodded at Penny, but didn't speak a word of English.

"Going somewhere?" asked Penny.

Natasha said, "I always said I would return to Moscow one day. One day is today."

Boris bounced around on the bed, trying to nuzzle into bags as Natasha stuffed clothing into them. The Russian knew how to pack in a hurry. Penny leaned on the door frame and watched, transfixed by the whirling, bustling women as they emptied drawers and closets.

"You have fifteen pairs of Candies," observed Penny. "What is it about Russian women and toe cleavage?"

"I give you red pair," said Natasha, "to remember me."

Penny slipped on the sandals and instantly felt like a cheap slut. "I love them. Thank you," she said.

Alexia said, "Sputnic gravlax borscht." That was what it sounded like to Penny anyway.

Natasha responded in Russian, and then turned to Penny. "I show you something." She handed Penny a slip of paper.

A fax, from Moscow. Penny didn't recognize a single letter in the Cyrillic alphabet. She blinked helplessly at Natasha and said, "I can't read it."

"I translate. 'Dear Natasha, I am dying with brain cancer. Doctors say six months. Your brothers are useless. I need you. Signed, Mama.' "

"I'm so sorry!" said Penny, then slowly, "Is this for real?"

"I would not make up dying mother," said Natasha.

"Didn't you tell me that your mother already died? She was attacked by nuclear mutants from Chernobyl?"

"That was *other* mother," said Natasha. "My stepmother from my dead father's second marriage."

"Oh," said Penny. "Your leaving doesn't have anything to do with Bram's escape. And the imminent arrival of the Short Hares police department."

"How could you think this of me?" asked Natasha.

"You did notice he escaped, though."

"Last night. I come home to empty house. Take food to empty room."

"You have enough money for plane tickets and shipping to Moscow?" asked Penny, starting to feel sad. Whatever was making Natasha run didn't matter. She was leaving.

"Lucky coincidence," said Natasha. "Alexia's American husband died this week. Fell asleep with car running in garage. Tragic. So she has money to buy tickets. Timing is very good shit."

"My condolences," said Penny to Alexia.

The two cousins exchanged a few lightning quick words in Russian. To Penny, Natasha said, "She thanks you for your sympathy. We also thank you, if police from Lodi come for Alexia, to say you never heard of her."

"Alexia who?" said Penny.

"Good. I take Boris with me," said Natasha. "I told you my family had dog just like him. We loved him until he got sucked into a sewer drain and drown in river of shit."

"You said your dog was crushed by a one-legged uncle," said Penny.

"That was *other* dog."

Penny started to protest and insist that Boris stay. But then again, she and Boris hadn't exactly bonded, despite her life-long dream of having a pet. What she thought she'd always wanted turned out to be a giant pain in the ass. Yet another case of expectation exceeding reality. Just once it'd be nice if it were the other way around, she thought. She flashed back to last night in the cabana, on the lounge, Bram's head between her legs, her jolting orgasm, unexpected and sublime.

"Boris'll be happier with you," said Penny. "Just keep him away from uncles and sewers. I'll go find his stuff. The Mr. Woofers Grooming Brush, the Pampered Pup Nap Pad, and his Dharma Doggie shampoo."

"I packed them already." Natasha looked around her room. It was bare, except for the red on the walls. She'd stripped and packed the bedclothes, even though Penny was sure Esther bought them.

The three women piled the boxes and bags on a hand truck, maneuvered the load down the back stairs and into the kitchen. From there it was a short haul to a van parked by the kitchen door. They loaded up the van.

Alexia got in the driver's seat. Natasha pulled Penny into a tight embrace.

Penny said, "You can't leave without saying goodbye to Mom."

"She's not here," said Natasha, "and I can't wait for her. I have much to do."

"She'll be heartbroken."

"Esther will understand," said Natasha. "My only regret about leaving today is that I have nothing to show for my years in America except many pairs of shoes."

Penny knew her mom paid Natasha a hefty salary, and covered her living expenses as well. "You blew it all?" asked Penny, shaking her head.

"When you grow up with nothing—no privacy, no possessions, no dignity, no hope of doing anything with your life—and then you have money, you spend it. All of it. As soon as you get it. I know that sounds flat to you."

"Flat?" asked Penny. "You mean superficial."

"Superficial." Natasha nodded. "Restaurant dinners not so superficial when you grow up eating dirt and drinking water from dirty rain puddles. My mother will never get the chance to live like an American. I wish I could show her some of the beautiful things I've seen here. Before she dies. Of cancer. In the brain."

Penny took hold of Natasha's wrist and tugged her through the kitchen and into the foyer.

"I want you to take this," said the young American, sweeping her arms like a game-show hostess at the wall of gift-wrapped boxes.

"You are sure?" asked Natasha.

"Now I won't have to send them back," said Penny.

"Thank you!" said Natasha, embracing her weepily, gratefully.

The moment was short. Natasha wiped her eyes, stepped outside and whistled for Alexia, who wasted no time backing the van up to the front door steps. Alexia started moving boxes without a word of instruction, almost as if she'd been waiting for the go-ahead.

It took half an hour to cram the van with crystal candlesticks, silver platters, and English china. Penny wasn't sorry to see any of it go. She'd been surrounded by superficial (flat) things her whole life, and felt more pleasure giving them away than she ever had in owning them.

"Maybe you'll find a nice Muscovite man and get married again. A real marriage this time," said Penny as they closed the van doors and locked them tight.

Natasha got in the passenger seat and said, "I don't feel love the way you do, Penny. Something is missing in me. I can't let a man in. I don't want to try. Your mother was like me. I see these last days she is changing. I'm a bad influence on her. Besides, she doesn't need me anymore. Neither do you. A twenty-three-year-old woman can tie her own shoes."

Boris climbed onto Natasha's lap. He stuck his little head out the window. Penny kissed him and Natasha one last time. Then Alexia drove away, taking Natasha, Boris, the wedding gifts, and untold other items away forever.

At the bottom of the driveway Natasha leaned out of her window and called out, "Penny! One more thing. Call exterminator!"

Chapter 34

"There must be a hundred of them," said Esther, standing next to Penny in the control room. Through the mirror, the two women watched a horde of squirrels twitching around the playroom, swarming over the remnants from Bram's final feast, gnawing the furniture.

"They came in through the skylight," said Penny. "Same way Bram got out."

"I've got to give him credit," said Esther, rubbing the bruised spot on her ass where she'd landed in the hotel hallway. "Dismantling the bookshelves, the makeshift ladder. Takes ingenuity."

"Jumping off the roof? That was idiotic," said Penny, watching the rodents frolic.

Esther nodded. "Stupid, yes. Moronic, even. But daring, too. Brave. You've got to admit, you're impressed he escaped."

"Now you want me to like him?" asked Penny. "And, for your information, I let him go."

"You said he jumped off the roof," said Esther.

"Into the pool. Where I could have recaptured him. But I granted Bram his freedom—from your clutches, and mine."

Esther said, "If that's what you really want."

"It is," said Penny, a mite too forcefully.

"Perhaps you let him go to see if he'll come back."

"Bullshit," said Penny. "Natasha took off not five minutes ago. I wish she'd waited for you."

Esther frowned. She would miss her companion. For all Natasha's unswerving loyalty, she'd expected her to leave one day. As well she should've. What kind of life did Natasha have here with her? "Natasha made her great escape today, too," she said.

"I gave her my wedding presents," said Penny. "It seemed like the right thing to do. You probably wanted me to return them. That's the proper etiquette when a wedding is called off."

Esther shrugged. She knew she'd once cared about what was proper, but now she couldn't imagine why. "Send a letter to the guests," she advised. "Thank them for their generous gifts. Say you've taken the liberty of donating them to the Natasha Molotov Freedom Fund. And be sure to mention that their charitable gift is one hundred percent tax deductible."

"Excellent idea, Mom!" said Penny. "Look at that greedy beggar! He must weigh five pounds."

The fat squirrel sat on the TV, tail jerking. He seemed to realize he was being watched, and faced the mirror as if he could see through it.

"He's cute," said Esther. "Let's poison him."

The control room phone rang.

Esther pushed the button to take it on speaker. "Hello?" she said.

"Penny!" squealed a high-pitched voice.

"Vita?"

"I've killed Bram!" said the hysterical soap star. "And Morris, too! They're both dead! I'm looking at their dead bodies right now!"

"Well, that takes care of that," said Esther.

"Mom!"

Vita's howls and sobs poured through the speakers.

"Where are you?" demanded Penny.

Vita blubbered, "The Plaza. Room 1224."

"We're coming," said Penny, hanging up. To Esther, she said. "Car keys."

Esther looked at her daughter's empty palm. "Absolutely not," she said.

Penny slapped Esther. Not much of a wallop. More like an aggressive pat. "Please, Mom," she insisted. "Two men are dead."

"They are *not*," said Esther, touching her grazed cheek. "You know how Vita exaggerates. If she says 'they're dead,' she means they have a cough. Or the sniffles."

Esther saw that her daughter wasn't amused. Penny raised her hand again. Esther snagged her wrist and said, "You don't need to repeat yourself."

"But it felt so good the first time," said Penny.

Esther nodded. "You must be furious at me."

"You should have hugged me more," blurted Penny.

Esther sighed dryly. "All right," she said, reaching into her purse and rummaging for her keys. Dangling them, she said, "On one condition."

"For God's sake," said Penny.

"I'm coming with you."

"I'll drive," said Penny, snatching the keys.

The two women went downstairs, out to the driveway, and into the Volvo. "There must be grooves in the road between here and the Plaza at this point," said Esther. "Back to the scene of the crime."

"Which crime?" asked Penny.

"I suppose there are a few to choose from," said Esther.

"And you're right. I should have hugged you more. I had a problem with showing affection. Always did. I'm just not a demonstrative person. And I'm sorry."

"Don't cry, Mom."

"I really am so fucking sorry!" she sobbed.

Esther had never cried in front of her daughter before. And there had been times, many of them, when not crying in Penny's presence had required superhuman strength. The dregs of last night's makeup running down her chin, Esther let her tears run. She tried to remember why she'd been determined to hold back in Penny's presence. To appear strong? Unscathed? The constipated emotional approach seemed absurd in hindsight. Why not show her feelings? Why not let herself have them?

Penny rubbed Esther on her back and said, "There, there." Then her daughter zoomed toward the Plaza.

Chapter 35

Bram flew out of his father's hotel room. Livid, inflamed, hot as a poker. Groping along the hallway walls, he remembered that his oldest and best friend was also located somewhere in this hotel.

He took the elevator down to the lobby and found a house phone. He asked the operator for Morris Nova and was connected.

"Hello?"

Bram nearly cried upon hearing his friend's voice. He croaked, "What's your room number?"

"Twelve twenty-four," said Morris. "Who is this?"

Bram hung up. His childhood friend didn't recognize his voice, but he still gave out his room number. Morris had never been the brightest bulb in the house.

He decided to burn off some of his anger by taking the stairs back up to the twelfth floor. After being locked up for days, it felt good to exert himself. By the tenth floor he'd burned off his rage.

When Bram found Room 1224, he kissed the door. It was

the portal through which he'd enter a sane world, safe from Bracket women and their allies. He rattled the knob, calling to Morris. He banged until the door opened.

"Bram! Dude!" said Morris, naked except for the sheet wrapped around his waist.

Bram stumbled into his friend and clung to him. "Morris," he exhaled. "Man, is it good to see you!"

"What's going on?" asked Morris, who seem oddly stiff.

"I've been to hell and back," said Bram. "And hell ain't pretty."

"I believe it!" said Morris, trying to extricate himself from Bram's desperate grip. "Have a seat."

Bram took the chair. He'd give up the hug. He didn't really want to be so intimate with Morris's chest hair anyway. Rubbing his nose, Bram smiled at his friend. Morris was pouring him a glass of champagne from an open bottle. Also on the table, strawberries in a dish. Chocolates in a box.

"So, to hell and back," said Morris, sitting on the edge of the bed. "Where were you? South Jersey?" He glanced nervously at the closed bathroom door.

"You need to take a leak, go ahead," said Bram.

"I'm good."

Bram paused, studied his friend. "Dude, you look different."

"I got a haircut," he said.

"And a shave. And earrings. And—are you wearing mascara?"

"Just a little," said Morris. "An experiment. No biggie."

"Dude, when a man starts wearing earrings and makeup, it's a biggie."

"Forget it, man. It's . . . a girl did it." Morris glanced again at the bathroom door. "She likes men with mascara. She said it reminds her of her punk rock roots. So I let her put it on me. She's an actress. Likes to experiment. And she's very persuasive. If you know what I mean."

"And Little Miss Blowjob is in the bathroom right now?"

"Showering," said Morris. "She takes long fucking showers. Like forty-five minutes. I have no idea what she's doing in there."

"Have you looked?" asked Bram.

"Not a chance," he said. "She locks the door, stuffs a towel under the crack."

Bram said, "Maybe she's really a he."

"I've taken a complete inventory of her parts," said Morris.

Bram's entire body relaxed in the good company of his old friend. "It is really great to see you," he repeated. "You're the only sane person left. Everyone else has gone crazy on me. My dad. Penny. Esther Bracket is a complete psycho. I always knew she was a lunatic. Like I wrote in that letter."

"What letter?" asked Morris.

"The letter I left for you at my apartment. You were supposed to meet me there yesterday morning. You didn't go?"

"I . . . you weren't there?"

"Neither were you, I guess."

"Bram, I'm sorry. I got caught up with this girl. And your dad practically beat the truth out of me. You didn't see him at your place?"

"You told my father where I was?" Bram's head spun. "I can't believe this."

"He gave me the whisper treatment," said Morris. "I had to give it up."

"So you blew me off and sent my dad in your place? Did *he* read my letter?" asked Bram. Not possible. If Keith had read it, no way would he be lolling in bed with Esther Bracket. Bram popped out of his chair. "I asked you to do one simple thing. Meet me at my apartment at ten on Sunday. And you blew it, man!"

"I'm sorry," protested Morris, looking not very convincing

in his sheet. "Technically, you asked two things. One, to give Penny the note to cancel the wedding. Two, to meet you at your apartment."

"Pathetic," said Bram.

"It's this girl," said Morris. "She's fucking my brains out. Literally. Every time we do it, I get stupider. I think I'm falling in love."

"Not you, too," moaned Bram. "Who is she? Some slut you scraped off a bar stool?"

"Did you say *slut*?" squealed a voice from the bathroom.

Morris cringed. Bram looked at the squealer, her grapefruit boobs stuffed into a frilly peignoir with ostrich feathers at the hem. Her hair was damp from the shower, water trailing down her shoulders. Her bow-shaped lips were pursed with disgust.

"I can't believe this," said Bram. "Vita Trivoli? Penny's best friend?" This was as bad as his dad screwing Esther Bracket.

"Where the hell have you been?" shrieked Vita, swooping in on Bram with her ostrich feathers. "I could kill you for what you did to Penny! You heartless, gutless, dickless—"

"That's the last time I trust you," said Bram to his ex-friend. "You probably told her everything, too."

"What could Morris possibly tell me?" screamed Vita. "He didn't know anything about your despicable plans."

"So you managed to keep your mouth shut *with her*," said Bram snidely. "Fuck you very much for that."

With full throat, Vita said to Morris, "You swore on your own grave you didn't know where Bram was hiding. You lied to me! And to Penny. In her hour of greatest need!"

"Please shut up, Vita," said Bram, his head splitting.

"Don't you tell me to shut up!" she bellowed.

"Morris," said Bram. "Can't you control your woman?"

Vita did not like that. She lunged at Bram, her puny arms

flailing. He pushed her away. Gently. And yet she fell on the floor.

Bram groaned. Now Vita would tell Penny that he'd thrown her across the room. He closed his eyes and pinched the bridge of his nose. And then he heard the resounding thud. Suddenly slack, Bram collapsed out of the chair and onto the floor in a heap.

His vision blurred. He heard yelling, another thunderous crack. A heavy weight landed on his ankles. Then everything went black.

Chapter 36

"Here we are," said Penny, pulling into the Plaza drive. "I changed my mind," said Esther, cowering in the passenger seat, afraid of being spotted by Keith Shiraz. "I'm not going in. You don't need me."

Her daughter said, "If I'm not back in fifteen minutes, you'd better come looking for me."

"Call my cell when you get upstairs."

"Okay," said Penny as she exited the Volvo.

Esther admired her daughter's graceful jog up the hotel's front steps. She was so leggy and muscular. Bouncy. Penny could do better than Bram Shiraz. Even if he wasn't a lawyer or a batterer, she still hated the kid. For one, he thought she was a murderer. That had a way of kiboshing her positive inclinations. Penny seemed to have made her peace with his rejection. Good thing, since with him dead and all, they wouldn't get another opportunity to clear the air.

Looking out the car window, Esther watched the valet parking attendant walk toward her. Through her open window, she said, "I'm just sitting for a minute."

"No problem, ma'am," he said without a trace of interest in her or her purpose. Ten years ago, she thought, any man would give her a flirtatious smile, an extra three seconds of eye contact. Since she was fourteen, she'd been an object of desire, and considered the attention a nuisance. Now, sitting alone in her car, Esther felt old, invisible. Her feminine powers were waning, with younger men, at least.

She still had the goods with older men. Keith made love to her three times last night. He'd been plenty attentive. When he entered her, she felt lit from the inside, as if his penis was light itself, shining and gleaming out of her every pore. She'd been switched on by him. She still felt the glow, although she knew it would soon dwindle.

If he ever touched her again, it would be with a truncheon. If Keith didn't kill her (or have her killed), and Bram (*please be dead*, she thought) didn't have her locked up, she would try to be more open to a relationship. Although the idea of letting a strange penis into her body was gross. She didn't want sex. She wanted Keith. And therein lied (laid?) the rub.

Another car pulled up, a Porsche. The valet liked this driver a lot more than he liked Esther. He snapped to his full height and doffed his cap at her. He helped the driver out of her seat. She soaked up the sycophancy. She would. Ashley Longmead had always relished an ass-kissing.

Esther scrunched low in her seat, not wanting to be seen and forced into small talk. What on earth was Ashley doing here? she wondered. Inching upward, peeking out her window, Esther watch Ashley in her miniskirt and spaghetti straps—dressed like a lamb, not the mutton she was—as she sauntered up the steps of the hotel, shaking her posterior, which had not, given its jiggle, been surgically tightened (yet).

Esther waited three minutes. Then she exited her car and marched over to the valet.

Slapping the key and a twenty in his hand, she said, "Keep it close." She took the steps two at a time and pushed the revolving door with the palms of both hands, sending it spinning like a top.

She'd bet her fortune that Ashley was all dolled up to visit Keith Shiraz. "Like a rat to cheese," she muttered to herself (although people in the lobby heard and gave her a few eyebrow tilts). Her face was streaked with makeup. Her hair was a tangled mess. She appeared to be a ranting middle-aged freak. And maybe she was. When a man squinted at her as she waited by the elevator, she said, "What're *you* lookin' at?"

Flustered, he scurried away. She rode the elevator solo to the twelfth floor. She'd find them in Keith's room. Together. It was only too predictable, she thought, pushing the button again and again, even though the car was rising steadily (like her blood pressure). Despite her jealousy and anger, Esther still had the presence of mind to appreciate how her emotions had become spectacularly unlocked over the last few days, ever since she hit Bram on the head. Her theory was holding up. That strike *had* dislodged the plug in her own subconscious. She should consider pummeling someone else, make even more emotional progress. A wicked grin spread across her face. She knew exactly whom she'd like to cudgel.

At twelve, Esther pounded down the hallway, footsteps muffled on the carpeted floor. When she got to 1214, she put her ear to the door and tried to listen. Muffled sounds, voices. More than one.

Testing the knob, she found the door unlocked. She would fling it open and make her dramatic entrance. She counted to three. Then she turned the knob, leapt into the room and yelled, "Ah-ha!"

And there they were. Ashley and Keith on the bed. He was

in a bathrobe, and she was sitting on top of him. A compro-
mising position if there ever was one.

Esther blinked. She'd been hoping for a comic scene. That
she'd burst in, say her "Ah-ha!" and find them playing pi-
nochle or tiddlywinks. They'd look at her with affectionate
tolerance, she'd stammer about her "stupid jealousy," and
then they'd all laugh and be friends.

Honestly, the idea of actually catching them with their pants
down (and/or skirts up) seemed farfetched. Paranoid.

"I'm gone for half and hour, and you're already screwing
someone else!" she screamed at Keith.

He said, "How did you get in here?"

Esther rushed the bed, swatting at Ashley with her purse.
"Get off of him!"

Ashley rolled away from Keith and stood up. She circled
wide to avoid Esther's purse. Reaching for her bag on the desk,
Ashley removed a tube of lipstick. "Esther. So wonderful to see
you. You look . . . you look wretched, darling." She smeared
the peach wax on her mouth.

"How long after I left did you wait before you called her?"
Esther demanded of Keith.

"I didn't call anyone," he barked. "And you didn't leave. I
threw you out!"

"Yes, but you didn't mean it," said Esther.

"You kidnapped my son!" he said. "And you lied to me
about it. For days. And nights. Well, just the one night."

"One great night," she corrected.

Keith smiled against his will. "I am nowhere near forgiving
and forgetting, Esther," he warned. "That said, Ashley arrived
here five minutes ago—uninvited and unexpected."

"She took the liberty of coming over?"

He nodded. "I guess so."

"And she took the liberty of sitting on you?" Esther asked.

"My God, Esther, don't you ever stop complaining?" asked Ashley with the precision of a German-engineered razor. "I've been listening to you whine and moan for more than twenty years and I'm sick of it! If I have to listen to one more word, I'll tear your throat out."

Bug-eyed, Esther stared at her neighbor and (until now) dear friend. "I'd better shut up then," she said.

Keith said, "Don't talk to Esther like that!"

He's defending me, she thought warmly. Perhaps he wouldn't have her intestines removed after all.

Ashley said, "I couldn't help myself, Esther. I wanted him. Seducing Keith is all I've been thinking about since I saw the two of you together in your garden."

"What's the big attraction?" asked Esther. "He's kind of chubby. He's not rich—not by your standards."

"Hey!" said Keith.

"No offense," said Esther.

"I know he's fat and poor . . ." said Ashley.

"The word is 'portly,' " he protested.

". . . but I wanted him anyway. Because he wanted you," said Ashley. "Whenever a man had come on to you, I've tried to take him away. You must have noticed. I did it dozens of times since Russell died."

"I thought you were protecting me," said Esther.

"You are a naive, clueless rube," said Ashley. "Always were. I could not *believe* it when Russell brought you home. A twenty-year-old secretary? From Ohio? You didn't know anything about anything. And yet, he chose you over a far superior woman."

Esther babbled, "He divorced his first wife a year before we met! A year before."

"I don't mean *Shirley*," snarled Ashley, still fiddling in her purse.

"Then who are you talking about?"

Ashley groaned with annoyance.

Keith, now standing next to Esther, said, "Wild guess: I think she's talking about herself."

"*You?*" Esther said to her neighbor. "But you were married to Lawrence."

"Who I was going to leave," she said. "Russell and I had been lovers for two years already by then. We made plans to escape together. He had one last business trip, and when he got back from Ohio, we were going to run away. It was agony, waiting for him to come home. I watched his house with my binoculars, every day. And then his limo finally pulled up the driveway. Through my binoculars, I watched Russell climb out of the car and cried for joy. But then you and your long legs and blond hair got out of the car. I knew instantly that Russell had changed his mind about me. I threw up where I stood, right on my bedroom windowsill. He dumped me for you, just like he dumped Shirley for me. I swore I'd get revenge on Russell. And you."

Buzz. Esther's cell. On automatic pilot, she answered it. "Hello?"

"Mom!" said Penny breathlessly. "You've got to get up here! It's an emergency!"

"Hang up," said Ashley.

"I'll have to call you back," said Esther, closing her phone, looking straight into the barrel of Ashley Longmead's gun.

Chapter 37

Penny stared at the phone in disbelief. Esther just hung up on her. In-fucking-credible.

Vita said, "What am I going to *do*?"

"We have to call 911!"

"We can't," pleaded Vita. "I'll be arrested for murder. Or manslaughter. Men slaughter."

"That might be true," said Penny, "if they were dead, which they aren't." Penny had already confirmed with a finger to both men's throats that Morris and Bram were still alive, if unconscious.

That meant two concussions for Bram in the span of three days, she realized. She bit her lip, not wanting to upset Vita any more than she already was, if that was possible.

"They're dead!" her petite friend raved, tearing at the feathered hem of her lingerie, beating her bony chest with her tiny manicured fists.

"Here, feel for yourself," said Penny.

The soap star fell to her knees and groped Bram about the chest, her hand rising and falling with his breath. "Bram has a hot bod," she observed.

"I made good use of it last night," said Penny, grinning. "In the cabana by the pool."

"What, he just showed up at your house?" asked Vita, confounded to hear it.

Penny paused, not wanting to get into the whole kidnapping story. "He surfaced, yeah," she said.

Vita investigated the rise and fall of Morris's chest, the pitter-patter of his pulse. "Morris. Wake up!" she said, holding his chin and rolling his head from side to side. "I like this Morris," she announced. "He's got a permanent erection. He'd come—and stay hard. He's the privates investigator. He examined me with a penlight. And he certainly gets to the bottom, if you know what I mean."

"Did you try ice?"

"Up the butt?" asked Vita.

"To *revive* them," said Penny. She checked the silver champagne bucket. It was half full (not half empty) of icy water. "I'm going to enjoy this." Then she doused Bram in the face.

He stuttered, shaking his head from side to side. His eyes flickered and then he went back under.

Morris, meanwhile, had started to move. "Look!" said Vita, pointing at the sheet tenting across his hips. "Do I lie?"

"He must be dreaming about you," said Penny.

"If he has any doubts that I can play a tough broad," said Vita, "I'll just hit him with the champagne bottle again."

"You might be the first actress in New York to assault her way to the top. Or, in your case, the bottom," said Penny. She looked down at Bram's slack expression. She hadn't seen him as serene in months, even in his sleep. She checked the pulse again at his wrist, and saw that he was wearing her ring on his pinkie.

Penny's heart dropped to her guts. It would have gone all the way down to her feet, but she was kneeling.

"I'm worried about Bram," she said. "We have to call for help."

"Try your mother again."

Penny scoffed. "Like she'd do anything for Bram."

"Who else can you call? Not hotel security!"

Keith Shiraz was residing at the Plaza. Penny said, "I'm going down the hall to get Bram's dad."

"And bring him *here*?" asked Vita, scrunching her nightie to her throat in a show of modesty.

With Vita, everything was a show. "I'll be right back. Don't hit them while I'm gone."

With one final glance at Bram, Penny stood up and left the men alone with Vita, who was already tearing through her suitcase for something decent to wear.

Chapter 38

Esther had seen Ashley's gun many times before. It was a pearl-handled .22, made by Smith & Wesson. The limited edition model, as Ashley proudly told Esther when she first got it years ago, was called "Girl's Night Out." It was a lightweight revolver with a feather trigger, designed and marketed to women. Esther knew she carried it wherever she went. But when Ashley pulled it out of her alligator purse and pointed it at her, Esther couldn't believe her eyes.

Keith said, "You can't be serious."

"Both of you, in the bathroom," said Ashley.

Esther held onto Keith's hand. She was spinning back in time. The Christmas party when Russell slipped Ashley the tongue under the mistletoe. The day she went into labor, calling Ashley in a panic because she couldn't find Russell, then Russell running up the driveway two minutes later, his shirt untucked.

"You never stopped sleeping with him," said Esther, her arms raised as she walked.

"Into the tub," ordered Ashley.

"Don't worry, Esther," said Keith as they stepped over the rim of the bathtub. "I've got this under control."

"I can see that," said Esther.

"We broke up for a couple of years," said Ashley, "but he came back to me when you got pregnant. He was disgusted by the changes in your body. We started making plans again. He said he wouldn't leave you until the baby arrived. I didn't understand why, but I was willing to wait. Penny was born. And then Russell didn't want to leave when she was so small. And he was worried. You were a damned incompetent mother. He was afraid you'd harm his daughter. So he hired that British nanny to help you. I approved. If it made him more comfortable about deserting you, fine. When Penny was three, Russell told me his brilliant idea. That, to protect me, he'd say he was running off with the nanny. Jemima would pretend to be his mistress in exchange for $20,000. When he officially divorced, he'd come back for me."

"But he really did love Jemima," said Esther.

"He was stringing me along," said Ashley. "He needed me to keep an eye on you during the settlement battle."

"So he betrayed you. Twice," said Esther. "I didn't do anything to you."

"You married him!" said Ashley. "You had his child!"

In a bathrobe blur, Keith surged forward, grabbed at the barrel. His feet slipped on the tiles and he fell backward, his head hitting the edge of the tub. He slid onto the bathroom floor.

Esther screamed, "Keith!"

"Don't move," said Ashley.

"He has nothing to do with this!"

"He rejected me," said Ashley.

Esther's brain clicked. "You pushed Russell off the balcony at the mall."

"I didn't push," she said. "I tripped him."

Esther, suddenly frozen, said, "Penny's kidnapping."

Ashley said, "My idea. I suggested it to Russell. He'd have you declared incompetent, and get custody of Penny. Russell bribed the mall security guard. I hired the Dominican woman through a maid service."

"You masterminded the worst day of my life," said Esther. "I blamed myself. I hated myself. That shaped everything, decades of my life. It tainted my relationship with Penny."

"You'll never have to worry about it again," said Ashley, raising the gun.

TWACK! A crack resounded against the bathroom walls.

Ashley's body, boneless, crashed to the floor, her head bloodied.

Esther looked up, and saw Penny standing in the bathroom threshold, a champagne bottleneck in her fist.

"When life gives you lemons," said Penny, "make pulp."

Chapter 39

"It seems higher today," said Penny, leaning over the second floor balcony railing at the Short Hares Mall.

"Higher than what?" asked Esther.

"Than before."

"You come here often?" asked her mom.

They were standing at the exact spot, outside the Pottery Barn, over the fountain, where Russell Bracket took his final flight.

"You can't blame me for being curious about him," said Penny, who had visited this spot frequently. "He was my father. And you never told me anything."

"I'm sorry about that, too," said Esther.

Penny both loved and loathed her mother's new *mea culpa*-itis. She soaked up the acknowledgments and apologies, since she'd been waiting to hear them for quite some time. On the other hand, her mom seemed fragile and overly sensitive, a stark contrast to Esther's previous untouchability. Penny had a mother now. But she'd miss the tough broad she grew up with.

She watched the action on the ground floor below, the people in clusters of three and five strolling aimlessly; women ducking into Victoria's Secret; teenage boys loitering outside Tower.

"I wonder if he saw Ashley before he tripped and fell," said Esther.

Penny said, "I wish I'd known Russell was such a shit."

"Me, too," said Esther.

Esther should have done a bit more research before marrying the guy after a way-too-short romance. Penny had known Bram for over a year before getting engaged. At the moment, as far as she knew, he was still at the Short Hares Memorial Hospital, where he, Morris Nova, Keith Shiraz, and Ashley Longmead had taken up residence. Penny had bashed Ashley hard enough to crack her skull (oops). She was in intensive care, under the guard of the Short Hares police. Vita hadn't done as much damage to the thicker skulls of Bram and Morris, but both had sustained concussions. Keith Shiraz had a minor head contusion and a broken arm. He'd fallen funny.

Head injuries were notorious for appearing minor, only to worsen suddenly and dramatically. The men were advised to remain under doctor's watch for forty-eight hours. So Keith and Morris traded neighboring hotel suites for adjoining hospital rooms. Bram was in another room he couldn't walk out of.

Penny assumed their hospital accommodations were comfortable. Not that she'd seen them. Although Keith, Bram, and Morris had declined to press charges against any of the three bottle-wielding loony women of their acquaintance, they'd also filed orders of protection against Penny, Vita, and Esther. Individually, and collectively. Unless they were bleeding or broken, the women would be arrested if they crossed the hospital doors.

"I know you were young, looking for an escape from your

family," said Penny. "Dad was impressive, older. Rich. You didn't have an inkling that he was amoral?"

Esther put her elbows on the railing. "I've asked myself that question a million times. I wished I'd seen something, or listened more carefully when he told me about his first divorce. Or noticed the clues—all too obvious now—about Ashley. I was dazzled. So were Shirley, Ashley, Jemima. Who knows how many others?" She paused, looked all the way down at the fountain below. "He must have been terrified when he fell. I never felt sorry for him until this moment."

And Penny had *always* felt sorry for him—until now.

Esther continued, "As horrible as the end was, the beginning with Russell was wonderful. When I got pregnant, we were both overjoyed. I'll try to remember him that way."

"Good luck," said Penny.

"If I could go back, I'd marry him again. I'd be smarter about it, of course. I'd get a better lawyer."

"That's insane," said Penny. "You could have married some nice, decent guy. A man your family would have approved of. Someone who could've made you happy."

"But then I wouldn't have you," said Esther.

Esther touched Penny's hand on the railing. Penny inched closer to her mom, slipping an arm over her shoulder. Esther mirrored the movement, and suddenly they were in a tentative grapple.

"Don't look now, Mom," said Penny. "We're hugging."

"Get a room," said a female voice behind them.

"Come here," said Penny, reaching for Vita. Her friend was back from Mrs. Field's with a bag of hot chocolate chip cookies.

"I don't group hug."

"Neither do I," said Esther.

Penny said, "Then hug each other. I'll watch."

"You're sick," said Vita.

"Shake hands, then," begged Penny. "If Vita hadn't clobbered Bram and Morris, we wouldn't have gone back to the hotel, and then you wouldn't have followed Ashley into Keith's room and learned the truth about her. I wouldn't have come looking for Keith, and neutralized Ashley. Thanks to Vita, your good name has been cleared of any suspicion, Ashley is handcuffed to her hospital bed, and we're all eating cookies at the mall."

"Thank you, Penny, for the summary," Esther said, "And thank you, Vita, for bashing skulls."

"You're welcome, Esther."

Penny said, "I'm kvelling."

"Sweetheart, you're not Jewish."

"Excuse me?"

"I've been meaning to get to this," said Esther. "Your father was Jewish. But I was raised Catholic."

"I knew it!" said Vita. "No one with hair like that could be a Jew."

"My father was an adulterer," said Penny. "And I'm only half Jewish. What next? Was I born with a second head?"

"No, but you did have six toes on your right foot," said Esther.

Penny blinked. "You're full of shit."

Esther said, "Ever notice how none of your baby pictures show the feet?"

"That's not funny," said Penny.

Vita said, "Are we going shopping, or what? You promised to lavish us with gifts, Esther."

"Wait one second," said Penny, fishing in her pocket for change. "My ritual," she explained, tossing a one-cent coin into the fountain, watching it sink in slow motion—into the sphere's hole.

"You got it in!" yelled Vita, clapping her hands.

"First time," said Penny, grinning. "In about ten thousand tries."

"You've thrown a hundred dollars' worth of pennies at that fountain?" asked Vita. "Doing the math in my head, I'd like to point out."

Esther said, "Have you really, Penny?"

She had, although she stopped counting after five thousand tosses when she was fifteen. She used to bring rolls of pennies to this spot, flipping them one by one into a watery grave.

"Do you make the same wish, or was it different each time?" asked Esther.

"Always the same gist," said Penny.

"Well, since you got it in the hole this time, it'll come true."

"Tell me it's not something boring," said Vita. "Like health and happiness."

Penny said, "I wished I had another puppy." Although she had something else entirely on her mind.

"I was wrong," said Esther. "It won't come true."

Chapter 40

Vita returned to New York and her daily soap-sudsing schedule at *The House of Blusher*. Esther and Penny went home to the mansion to find it eerily empty. Except for the squirrels. And the half a dozen turkey vultures that were perched on the roof by the skylight.

Esther said, "Weird here without Natasha."

"I can't believe she'd just leave," said Penny. "I thought she loved us."

"She did, as much as Natasha could love anyone," said Esther. "Which wasn't too deeply. She was looking out for herself."

"You can do that and still love someone," said Penny.

"I've decided to host a few dinner parties," announced Esther. "Widen my social circle."

"Invite me," said Penny.

"You won't be here?" asked Esther. "I thought you were moving in?"

"And give up my apartment in the Village? No way."

Esther was glad, even if the mansion would be frighteningly empty with her daughter and the Russian gone.

"I haven't seen Natasha's empty room yet," said Esther.

Together, they walked up to the red room. Esther took in the stripped bed, the naked nails, the bright squares on the walls where pictures used to hang. She opened the dresser drawers, just to see if Natasha had left a single item. Unlikely. Esther was surprised she hadn't taken the dresser itself.

But she was wrong. Natasha did leave something behind. In the middle dresser drawer, Esther found a white envelope.

"What's that?" asked Penny.

"Another note?" said Esther. "I can't read it."

Penny took the envelope and opened it. She removed its contents and fanned the papers to examine them.

"Two electronic plane tickets and a car service voucher," said Penny.

"Let me see," said Esther. She examined the stack. Sure enough, she held two e-tickets for a flight to Hawaii, departing tomorrow morning. One was registered to Penny Bracket. The other to Bram Shiraz. The car service voucher was good for a one-way trip to Newark International Airport.

A note was paper-clipped to Bram's ticket. Esther immediately recognized Natasha's boxy letters. She read, " 'Dear Esther and Penny: I find tickets in Penny's room. I was going to use with Alexia. But then fax came from mama. You two go to Hawaii. Have fun. Get tan. While you are on beach, think of me, shivering in Moscow, cooking meat on a stick over a pile of burning garbage. Love, Natasha.' "

"She was going to steal my honeymoon tickets!" said Penny.

"So she was planning to go, before the fax," said Esther. "I suppose we owe it to Natasha to take her advice. To have fun. Get tan. Think of her cooking meat over a pile of burning garbage." Esther did her best Russian impression.

"You sounded like the cartoon Natasha. 'Kill moose and

squirrel,' " said Penny. "Speaking of which, if we're going to
Hawaii tomorrow, we'd better call the exterminator today."

"Where is the car?" asked Esther for the fifteenth time.

She and Penny were beyond ready to leave. They stood on
the (desquirreled) mansion front steps with their suitcases.
The car service was supposed to arrive twenty minutes ago.
Even with the cushion of time Esther had allowed, they'd be
cutting it too close for comfort if the car didn't materialize in
the next thirty seconds.

"Here it is," said Penny as the black sedan pulled in the
driveway. "And if you're going to be neurotic, maybe we
should stay home."

"I'll relax when we get through security," snapped Esther,
who didn't travel well.

The driver pulled the Town Car to a stop. He stepped out
and put their suitcases in the trunk while Esther and Penny
took seats in the commodious rear compartment.

The black glass panel between the driver and the passenger
seats was down. When the chauffeur got in, he said, "Good
morning, ladies. I'm Charlie. If you need anything, please let
me know."

"We need to get moving," said Esther briskly. "Newark Airport. American Airlines. If you please."

"Yes, ma'am." The driver turned the ignition, pushed a button. The black glass between the seats rose.

Penny said, "He likes you."

"Shut up," said Esther.

The Town Car started moving at a decent clip toward the
highway. With a metallic clunk, the car doors locked.

"Stuffy in here," said Esther. She pushed the button to open
her window. It was locked. "Try your window."

Penny did as she was told. "Locked," she said.

Esther rapped on the glass panel. "Charlie. We'd like to open the windows."

No response. Penny said, "He can't hear you."

Esther found an intercom switch and repeated her request.

He didn't respond, but the air conditioner suddenly went on.

Esther and Penny looked at each other, perplexed.

They reached the entrance to Newark Airport. But instead of taking the exit ramp, the driver proceeded to the New Jersey Turnpike entrance.

On the intercom, Esther said, "You're going the wrong way!" To her daughter, she said, "Can he hear us? I can't see anything through the glass."

Penny said, "I have the feeling we're being watched."

Esther jabbed the intercom and said, "Pull over. Right now!"

But the driver kept going north toward the swamps of the Meadowlands.

"Don't worry, Mom," said Penny. "I can take him."

"Take him where? To dinner?"

"I know some karate moves."

"That man weighs three hundred pounds!"

"I'll use his bulk against him," said Penny.

"Your martial arts magic will make him punch himself?"

"Do you think we're really being kidnapped?" asked Penny.

"If we survive, I'll kill Ashley for this!"

"Mom, she's in a coma."

"She could plot my destruction from the grave!"

"He's slowing down."

"Get your karate ready," said Esther. "In case this is the end, I want you to know that I love you. I live for you. I hope you'll fall in love again."

"I still love Bram," said Penny. "I should admit that to my-self, if this is my final hour."

"Then I hope you'll get him back," said Esther.

"You'll support the relationship?"

"Sure," said Esther. "I'd even pay for a second wedding. Smaller, of course. No catering. And no cake. Petits fours, and passed hors d'oeruves. Champagne toast, but no wet bar."

"That sounds perfect," said Penny. "You agree, then, that love is a worthwhile pursuit?"

"Of course it's a worthwhile pursuit," said Esther. "But what about after you catch it?"

Penny said, "Force feed it shrimp cocktail?"

"Don't forget the broiled salmon," said Esther. "He's park-ing. Where are we?"

"Looks like a rest stop." It was the Vince Lombardi Memo-rial rest stop.

With a sudden report, the locks clunked open. The car's weight shifted. The driver opened Penny's door.

Leaning low, he said, "This is it, ladies."

Esther asked, "Do you mean that in a metaphorical sense?"

He said, "The ride is over."

"On the road we call life?" asked Esther.

"Please, just get out of the car," he insisted.

"I'm moving," Penny said, and winked at Esther. She swung her long and muscular dancer's legs out of the car.

Then she unleashed her killer right knee into Charlie's groin.

The three hundred-pound gorilla folded like a paper doll. Penny started kicking him in the ribs. Esther was out of the car now, joining Penny in the full foot attack, landing pointy-toe kicks on Charlie's back and thighs.

"Stop!" screamed Charlie.

"Just try to rape and murder us!" screamed Esther.

"I took you for a drive!" yelped the writhing man on the pavement.

"To the end of the road we call life!" replied Penny, a swift sneaker finding the jelly of his belly.

The sound of running footsteps. Then Penny and Esther were pulled away, lifted off their feet, legs churning in the air.

Chapter 41

B ram drove one of his dad's company's Mustangs. The car was brand new, black, gleaming, a showpiece. "I feel like a new man," he said, tapping the gas, the engine responding beautifully.

"Slow down," said Keith. "The cops will pull you over in a heartbeat. Given your turban."

Bram looked at himself in the rearview window. His cap of white bandages did make him appear to be a highway risk, an escaped lobotomy patient, or an Islamic extremist on a getaway. "The doctor said it could come off in two days. He gave me permission to drive. I've got the note in the glove compartment."

"Christ, not another note. No more notes, okay?" said Keith, himself elaborately bandaged, his arm in a white cast and sling. "That means our pen pal tradition. We did a lot of writing, but not a lot of telling it like it is. Let's make a vow. Or is that a categorical impossibility for you?"

Bram knew when to shut up. Since their release from the hospital last night, Keith had been making his feelings about his wedding flake-out clear. Bram said nothing. He knew he'd fucked up. He didn't need his father to rub his nose in it.

"Right up here," said Keith. "That rest area."

Bram took the exit ramp and parked in the truck stop. "How long?" he asked.

"A few minutes," said Keith.

"You really think this will work?"

Keith shrugged, which made him wince.

"You should shrug with just the left shoulder, Dad."

"I'll make a *note* of it."

The two men looked out the windshield. Bram cleared his throat. He fidgeted in the driver's seat. He cracked his knuckles.

"Out with it," said Keith.

Bram said, "When Mom died, I knew you'd date again. I pictured you with younger women. The type you'd date a few times, have fun with, and move on to the next. You deserved it, after what you did for Mom when she was sick. I thought you'd take a long vacation from a serious relationship. I just couldn't picture you with a woman your own age. I must have been afraid of you replacing Mom, or my having to deal with a stranger who'd take over your life. When I saw you with Esther Bracket—"

"You objected to Esther for other reasons."

"But at that moment, when I saw you in bed with her, what made me mad was that you'd choose her over me. When Mom died, I thought we'd spend a lot more time together. And then I met Penny. I kind of abandoned you when you were down, didn't I?"

"I was thrilled for you," said Keith. "Parents want their kids to be happy."

Bram nodded. "I understand why Esther Bracket snapped on the wedding day. She was standing up for her daughter.

Although, considering what Penny did to Ashley Longmead, I think she can stand up for herself."

Keith laughed. "I wish I'd been conscious to see the hit."

"So Esther's not a murderer. I guess she's got that going for her." Bram paused. "What I'm trying to say is that I'm okay with you and her."

Keith smiled and Bram soaked it up. His dad tried to pull him in for a fatherly hug, but then Keith yelped in pain. "The arm," he said.

"Just as well, Dad," said Bram. "Here they come."

The black Town Car, the finest in Keith's company fleet, pulled into the rest stop. Charlie stepped out. He waved at the Mustang, parked twenty feet away. They watched Charlie open the back door. Bram smiled as one of Penny's legs emerged. Then the rest of his once and future bride's body was revealed. Bram thought he knew her body so well, but had only just begun to understand her. They watched Penny smile beautifully at Charlie, and then she plowed her knee into the old man's balls.

"Ooooff," said Bram and Keith.

Penny proceeded to thrash the poor bastard, screaming at him, her cheeks glowing. Esther Bracket soon joined her daughter, hurling kicks and invectives.

Keith used his walkie-talkie. "George. Come in, George."

Squawk. "Yeah, boss?"

"Send a backup for Charlie."

"Same location?"

"Yup," said Keith. "And hurry." He clicked off.

Keith cringed as Esther landed a savage blow to Charlie's backside. "Another man they'll send to the hospital."

"You can't take the Jersey out of the girl," said Bram.

"We're going to have to stay on our best behavior with these two," said Keith.

"Otherwise, they'll kick our asses," agreed Bram. "Again."

"We'd better stop them," said Keith.

The two men left the safety of the Mustang and rushed toward the rest of their lives as fast as their bruised bodies would carry them.

Chapter 42

Esther felt herself being lifted and dragged away. Her hair was in her eyes as the man grabbed her from behind. She tried to kick backward, but the man swung her horizontally and carried her under one arm like a bag of laundry.

"Stop struggling," he said. "Every time you squirm, I get a shooting pain in the shoulder."

"Keith?" she said. What was he doing here? And, more importantly, had he arrived to save her or collude with Charlie in the abduction? She said, "Put me down."

He dropped her onto the rear bumper of the Town Car. She looked back and saw Penny in conference with Bram (who was sporting a bright white bandage headdress).

"Charlie," whispered Esther. "Oh, God. Is that"—she pointed at the prostrate man on the pavement—"is he *your* Charlie?"

"I'll go check on him now," said Keith.

Esther nodded. She watched Keith, whose sling and cast did nothing to detract from his masculine aura of competence. He helped Charlie to his feet. The man stumbled a bit and seemed to be biting back tears. Esther's stomach churned at what she'd done. She called, "Can I help?"

Charlie cried, "No!"

Keith held up his good hand. "Stay where you are."

He gingerly helped Charlie into the rear compartment of the Town Car. She heard Keith tell him that another driver was on the way to take him to a safe place away from these women—or to the hospital if need be.

Then Keith returned to Esther. She said, "We thought he was kidnapping us."

"I got that," said Keith. "My fault. I told Charlie not to tell you where he was taking you."

"You told Charlie . . . I don't understand. Penny and I were going to the airport." She reflexively checked her watch. They'd never make the flight now. "How did you know we hired a car?"

Keith seemed flummoxed. "You told me."

"As per the order of protection, I have not come within two hundred feet of your home or place of business, nor have I attempted to make contact."

"You called my car service last night to make a reservation," said Keith. "I was there, checking on business. I took your call! You didn't realize you were talking to me?"

"ABC Limo is your company?" asked Esther.

"You were very polite on the phone," he said. "I assumed you knew you were talking to me but were pretending not to so you wouldn't be violating the court order, but letting me know you wanted to."

Esther said, "Huh?"

"So I sent Charlie to pick you up and bring you to neutral territory. Sorry for the confusion. It should have dawned on me that you might think kidnapping."

"I'm always polite on the phone, no matter whom I'm speaking to," said Esther haughtily.

"About the order of protection," said Keith. "Tempers were a bit hot that day."

"How is Bram?" she asked. "And Morris?"

"They're both fine," said Keith. "Bram isn't angry at you. He gave me his blessing."

"He's a priest now?" asked Esther. "First a lawyer, then a carpenter. That kid had better make up his mind."

"He has," said Keith, "as you can see."

Esther turned around. Over by a black Mustang, Bram and Penny were having an intense conversation. He appeared to be begging.

Esther said, "I gave Penny my blessing."

"So you're a priest now?"

"Don't be stupid," she said tartly. "We both know women can't become priests."

Keith smiled, and Esther couldn't help returning it. He really was a devastatingly handsome man.

"Explain what you intended," she said. "To have Charlie pick us up, bring us to the turnpike's most exclusive rest stop, and then what?"

"I was going to take you away," he said.

"Where to?"

"Wherever."

"*Wherever?*" she said. "I absolutely *love* Wherever. It's one of my favorite places! How did you know?"

He shrugged, and winced. "I just knew," he said. "Slide down from there. Let's get your luggage."

As Keith lifted the suitcases out of the trunk, another Town Car pulled into the rest area and parked. Keith rapped its trunk with his good knuckles, and the driver popped it open. Keith put Esther's suitcase inside and slammed it shut. Penny's bag remained on the pavement. Keith walked to the car's front window and had a brief conversation with the driver. The man got into the driver's seat of Charlie's car, waved goodbye, and drove off, Charlie sprawled in the backseat.

Keith said, "Would you like to take the wheel?"

"I'll take the whole car—with you in it," she said. "If that works for you."

His eyes shone, and Esther's heart sang.

"So it's your way or the highway," he said.

"My way *and* the highway," she said.

"Then there's one more thing I need to know."

"What?"

He smiled naughtily and asked, "Which exit?"

Chapter 43

Penny watched as Esther and Keith got into the second Town Car and drove over to where she and Bram stood. Her mom rolled down the driver's side window to talk. Bram, at the passenger side, conferred with his dad.

Penny said, "Where're you going, Mom?"

"We're being spontaneous," said Esther with a shrug. "Where are *you* going? In the metaphorical sense."

"I don't know," said Penny. "Both roads end at the same place, regardless."

"And that place is?"

"A fresh start," said Penny.

Her mom's chin quivered and her eyes took a teary shine. Penny would never get used to the sight of her mom emoting.

"Are you sure about this? About Keith?" she asked her mom.

Esther smiled. "Yes, I'm happy."

And just like that, after ten thousand tosses, Penny finally got her wish.

Esther said, "It's not enough for me to be happy. You have to be happy, too. I'd do anything for that."

Penny said, "You've done enough, really. If I ever need your help, I promise I'll ask."

She stepped away from the window. Esther waved frenetically at Penny as the Town Car inched forward, and then she burned rubber out of the rest area. Bram held onto his bandage turban as the car sped away, which elongated his torso and pulled his shirt tight against his chiseled chest. It would be easier for her, in their negotiations, Penny thought, if Bram were short, fat, and ugly.

"You lost the playroom pounds already," she observed. "Hospital food that bad?"

"Don't change the subject," he replied.

He looked sternly at her. Reproachful. As if she were purposefully toying with his emotions, now that he'd flung himself at her feet. She enjoyed having the upper hand. The power created an electrical surge under her skin. She liked the sensation, the crackle. It felt like a protective force field that Bram couldn't penetrate.

She said, "I'm not ready to get married."

"You didn't think that four days ago."

"I was much younger then."

"And now you're a wizened old hag?" he asked.

"Four days ago you didn't want to get married and I did. Now we're reversed."

"You're wrong," he said.

"How so?"

"You didn't want to marry me, either," he said. "You would have gone through with it, but you were scared."

He was right. She had been anxious and uncertain. She remembered staring at herself in the mirror at the Plaza's bridal prep room, willing herself to muster her guts and have faith that it would work out in the end.

Another car pulled into the rest stop. It drove right by her duffel, narrowly missing it.

Penny said, "I should get my bag before someone runs it over. Or steals it."

She walked over and picked it up. The plane tickets were tucked into a mesh side pocket. Penny checked her watch. If they got lucky, avoided all traffic, cruised through security, and ran like cheetahs through the terminal, they could still make the flight.

Penny returned to the Mustang and showed Bram the tickets.

"Our honeymoon trip," he said, frowning.

"We can make it if we rush."

"Two hours at the airport. A ten-hour flight. An hour drive to the hotel. Is this what you want?"

"You don't?"

"Thirteen wasted hours," he said. "I'm thinking of another romantic destination. There's this cool poolside cabana I know, with this awesome lounge."

Penny smiled, thinking of the cabana, and the mansion, completely empty, full of food. "I've always preferred the comforts of home to the stress of traveling," she said.

"Your ride," he said, opening the Mustang door for her.

She slid inside. He put her suitcase in the back and folded himself into the driver's seat.

He said, "Before we go, I need to be completely honest with you."

Penny felt a flicker of fear. She said, "I can take it."

Bram unwound the bandage strips around his head. Underneath, he was completely bald.

"Now who's exposed?" he asked.

She laughed at the sight, and then felt like crying. Of all his features, Penny most adored his mink brown hair. "It'll grow back," she said, gently rubbing his cue ball cranium with the two bruises.

"Will you be around to see it?" he asked, serious now. "Where are we headed, Penny?"

"To my house," she said. "To that cozy little cabana with the minifridge and heated towel rack."

"That's not what I meant."

She was well aware. "We'll know where we're going when we get there," she said. "Meanwhile, let's just drive."

A+
AUTHOR
INSIGHTS,
EXTRAS, &
MORE...

FROM

**VALERIE
FRANKEL**

AND

AVON A

The Top Ten FAQs (Four Are About Sex) From Readers, Writers, and Fans

1. Where do you get your ideas?

Idea generation is like meat grinding. The day's events, the people you meet, creative influences (art, movies, music, books) are stuffed into the funnel of the mental grinder. Then the subconscious cranks the handle, and out of the spout comes . . . sausage. Or, as sausage is otherwise known, ideas.

The basic idea for *I Take This Man* was cranked out on a typical day in the life of a working mother. My daughter came home from school and announced that some little girl in her first-grade class made her cry. A flash of anger flooded my brain. After a minute or two I calmed myself down. Lucy and I discussed what had happened, and worked out an appropriate response. But that flash of maternal rage got my meat grinder going. Any intense emotion is a kick-start. It made me wonder: What offense against one of my daughters would actually move me to lash out with violence against another human being? (The offense itself would have to be nonviolent. I won't write about rape, incest, assault, murder, torture, mutilation. I'll gladly relinquish such themes to other writers, and stick with comedy, what I prefer to write—and read.)

It's like the oft-trotted-out cocktail party question, "How would you most like to die?" (I guess I go to some strange parties.) Any number of novel plots can be generated by asking theoretical questions. For example, a thriller writer could probably devise a decent novel called *Killing You Softly* about a secret agency that guarantees its exorbitantly wealthy clients a death in the manner of their choosing. Except, the secret agency is a shady (as well as shadow) organization. They somehow arrange to steal all their clients' money and off them prematurely. The beautiful and brainy daughter of one of the victims finds a loose thread, tugs at it, and then the whole deception starts to unravel, putting her in dire straits until an FBI hunk joins the investigation . . . You get the idea.

Back to the night of the first-grade cat fight: I fixated on the question, lay awake in bed, wondering what indeed would make an otherwise controlled, rational woman thirsty for blood? I imagined being the mother of a jilted bride who, in a fit of vengeance, attacks the runaway groom. From there I asked more questions: "Why did the groom cancel the wedding?" "What did the mother do with the groom after she bashed him?" "How would the bride find out what happened?"

Five hours later, at three o'clock in the morning, I had the framework of a plot.

2. Are you saying novel ideas are a dime a dozen?

Well, yeah. I'd bet that most novelists have a file on their computers called "Book Ideas" that contains a list of five to twelve loosely-plotted outlines. Ideas are a dime a dozen. Great ideas are a bit more precious.

I test the quality of plots on close friends and family—people who won't lie and say they love everything. If my audience seems bored by the storyline, I immediately strike the idea from my list. If the idea goes over well, and the audience laughs a few times, I move it to the top. The test subjects for *I Take This Man* were three friends from *Mademoiselle*—the late, great magazine we worked at together before going our separate ways. The four of us regularly meet for dinner to catch up, laugh, drink, eat and conspire to help each other as best we can. On one such evening, I monopolized the entire meal by describing the plot of *I Take This Man*. These three (*very*) chatty women listened in rapt silence with expectant "go on" and "what next?" expressions as I told the story. By the end of the dessert course (we always order dessert), I knew I was onto something good. That meal stands out as the best feedback experience I've ever had. Hence, I've dedicated this book to Lauren Purcell, Jeanie Pyun and Daryl Chen. Ladies: I will *definitely* see you next Tuesday.

Sometimes, what might seem like a top-of-the-list novel idea is really just a short story or a long joke. I often cannibalize myself by folding smaller ideas into full-length novels. For example, I once believed that the travails of Edina Spanky—Privates Investigator, she gets to the bottom, etc.—was not only a fantastic cross-genre novel idea, but the stuff of an entire series. About two hours later, however, I realized I was wrong. I liked the puns so much, though, I worked them into *I Take This Man*.

3. Do you "write what you know"?

More than *what* I know, I write *where* I know. "Place" is always crucial to me. Location sets the tone since people are always products of their environment. Most of my books unfold in and around Brooklyn, New York, where I've lived for nearly twenty years. *The Girlfriend Curse* is my homage to the state of Vermont, my summer home. *I Take This Man* is a love letter to my natal state of New Jersey (only in NJ could a concussive blow to the head feel like a tongue kiss). I was born in Newark in 1965. My family lived in West Orange until 1974, when we moved to Short Hills. I graduated from Millburn High School in 1983.

Much like the fictional Short Hares, my hometown is famous for its mall. The Mall at Short Hills is a mere five-minute drive from my parents' house. I have spent absurd amounts of time (and money) at the mall since it was built in the mid-1970s.

My high school friends and I all had jobs there, got our prom dresses from Laura Ashley, had our first cigarettes in the parking lot, shoplifted there, were busted there. Ah, sweet memories of youth. A few years ago I heard about a man committing suicide by leaping off the second-floor balcony at the mall (he must have been depressed about how much money he'd just spent). He didn't crash head first into the fountain like Russell in *I Take This Man*. I believe the jumper went splat on the marble floor.

4. Have you always wanted to be a novelist?

Except for a brief sixth-grade fantasy of being a rock star (before I realized I had zero musical talent), I've always wanted to be a novelist. I started out writing little redemption pieces in junior high (cheerleaders waking up deformed, etc.), moved on to full-blown mopey "Who Am I?" novellas in college (which no one will *ever see*). *I Take This Man* is my eleventh novel. God willing, I'll collapse of a sudden heart attack at ninety immediately after typing "The End" on my one-hundredth. (And that is, incidentally, how I'd like to die.)

5. If, for some reason, you couldn't be a writer, what would you be?

A homeless person/drug addict. Other than writing, I have no other marketable skills. I suck at math. I can't sell. I'm not even a proficient buyer. Professional reader would be nice work if I could get it. Otherwise, it's a one-way ticket to skid row.

6. You write a lot about sex. Is this an area of particular interest?

Sex is an area of particular interest to *everyone*. I'm not special in that regard.

I started writing about sex in my early twenties at *Mademoiselle*. I was responsible for a Q&A sex advice column (my pseudonym was "Sandra Hollander"; I claimed to be Xaviera Hollander's love child), and provided answers to readers' burning sex questions. Are ejaculation-delaying creams safe and effective? Would excessive dildo use permanently stretch out one's vagina? Could a vacuum cleaner be used to simulate a blowjob? (The answers are: yes, no, and sort of.) I learned a lot, suffice it to say. I applied my newfound knowledge to my own sex life, which improved dramatically, sparking further study. Over the last fifteen years, I've written about sex for over a dozen magazines, covering the G-spot, multiple orgasms, female ejaculation, sexual compatibility, foreplay, afterplay, intercourse, outercourse. I've coauthored a book called *The Best You'll Ever Have*. I do radio interviews about sex, have talked about it on TV, am accosted on street corners by friends and neighbors looking for tips and advice.

I always try to incorporate what I've learned about sex as a journalist into my novels. In *I Take This Man*, I hit on the thorny subject of female performance anxiety. I'd written an article for *Self* about women's body conscientiousness in bed, and learned about "spectatoring," the textbook term for when a woman is so anxious about her jiggly thighs or her partner's responses, she mentally leaves her body, as if floating near the ceiling, and watches herself have sex. Penny Bracket, the main character in *I Take This Man*, is such a proficient spectator, her entire sex life becomes one big show.

How does she break her bad habit? Glad I asked (myself). The following are the four most popular Qs I've been asked as a sex advice columnist. Starting with:

7. How can I stay focused and in-the-moment?

This goes to spectatoring, above, as well as plain old mind drifting. According to a survey on foreplay I wrote for *Glamour* last year, about half the women responded that their minds wander during sexual preliminaries. *So what?* you might wonder. Is it such a tragedy to think about taking your cat to the vet while snogging your boyfriend?

If you aren't mentally attuned to what's happening to your body, you won't process the stimulation. That sensory input (as it were) has to go through the brain before it careens to your nerve endings (women have complicated wiring). Say, for example, you're wondering what to have for breakfast while your partner labors away on you. Your mind engaged elsewhere, your body will stall along the sexual response cycle (arousal, plateau, orgasm, resolution). If you get stuck on a plateau, you'll never get off. Directly put, you will NOT have an orgasm. He can lick you until he's blue in the face. But, unless you're paying attention, your partner might as well be sucking on the rusty storm drain outside.

A lot of mental distraction comes from body insecurity. You can't relax into sex because you're worried about jiggle. I interviewed Barbara Keesling, Ph.D., professor of human sexuality at California State University at Fullerton and author of the best-selling book *The Good Girl's Guide to Bad Girl Sex,* on this subject for another *Glamour* article last year. "It's a cruel irony that we look best flat on our backs, but that's the *least* stimulating position," she said. "We think we look worst on top, but that's the *most* stimulating position. The reality is, your boyfriend thinks you look better than you do. And he wants to do positions for how they feel, not necessarily how you look doing them." Keesling pointed out that avoiding rear entry is an example of fear overriding fun: "The truth is, your ass looks better up in the air than it does, you know, sitting or standing." Of course, women should have total body acceptance. But, when that's not possible,

"Move right along into lingerie and lighting," she said. "If you haven't already, paint your bedroom walls a Tuscan orange. Get orange sheets. It's a very flattering color."

Thus, staying mentally present and alert is crucial. In *Hex and the Single Girl*, Emma Hutch, the main character, learned to stay in the moment by keeping her eyes open during sex. Experts usually recommend the practice of "sensate focus," in other words, focusing on the sensations. How does this, that, and the other thing *feel*? Are his hands warm, soft, rough? Does his skin feel hairy, smooth, scaly? A running mental commentary about how you feel might seem weird at first. But it does work.

8. How can I best communicate to my boyfriend/ husband what I want in bed?

Poor communication is the bane of sex. In seminars I've been to with Shannon Mullen, the coauthor of *The Best You'll Ever Have*, a sexual information lecturer and sex-toy purveyor, I've heard women complain that their husbands and boyfriends don't know what they're doing, or are too rough, too gentle, too *whatever*. Shannon then asked, "Do you tell him how you'd like _____ (fill in the blank) performed?" The women are loath to give direction to their mates. They're embarrassed, don't know what to say, don't want to be demanding or critical.

Men are dying to know what women want in bed! Male respondents of a *Glamour* foreplay survey said they long for specific instruction from their partners. They said that is the one thing they want more than any other. The conventional wisdom—that men don't like getting directions—is one hundred percent WRONG. They won't take it personally (as a woman might). Give them a hint, for Christ's sake. Men aren't selfish pricks. In fact, they're desperate to be generous pricks.

So, how to communicate "harder, softer, faster, slower, deeper"? Shannon said, "Speak up. Use your voice. When he does something you like, say so. In fact, talk a lot during sex. Talk the whole time. It's jarring to be silent for twenty minutes and then to come out with, 'To the left.' Instead, keep the patter going from the beginning. 'Ohhh, that feels good. Ahhh, you're the best. That's sooo gooood—just a little to the left.' "

This comment from Shannon made us both laugh out loud. We started going, "Ohhh, I've got call waiting." "Ahhhhh, I'll call you back." "Ohhhhh, that would be soooo goooooood." But she does make a valid point. Women tend to be too timid and closed-mouthed during sex. We need to speak up. Grunting and groaning—alternatives to comprehensible language—will only get you this . . . close to what you really want. Men are not mind readers. Most of them don't speak Grunt. Nonverbal cues, moving his hand, etc., are also useful. But they still leave room for misinterpretation.

If words and physical cues fail you, I've got two other suggestions to try. I showcase one in *I Take This Man*, when Penny and Bram have their night of sexual truth in the cabana. She used a strategy called "mirroring." It has to be agreed on ahead of time, just so your partner is in on the game. Simply mirror each other's moves. What you want him to do to you, you do to him. Have him mirror your pace and intensity. This technique has the added benefit of keeping your head in the right place. It's mutual sensate focus.

Technique number two, one I recommended many times in *Mademoiselle* columns, is called "marking." If you can't bring yourself to tell your partner what you want, you can show him. If you've got a favorite romance novel passage you'd like to re-enact in your own life, leave the book open to that page on your boyfriend's pillow with a note that says, "Let's do this." Or dog-ear a page in a porn magazine. Or leave a porn DVD on pause at just the right moment. Not only does that help you "show not tell" your boyfriend exactly what you want him to do, the stimulation of leafing through dirty books, magazines, and DVDs will vault you into the arousal stage before you've gotten anywhere near the bed.

9. Do most women have multiple orgasms?

Multiple orgasm is the Holy Grail for women. All women have the physical capacity to do it. That said, only eleven percent of women have multiples. So they're possible, but not probable.

Here's how multiples work. After the initial orgasm, continued stimulation of the clitoris (but MUCH SOFTER—the clitoris with its eight thousand nerve endings is *extremely sensitive*, never more so immediately following an orgasm) can lead to additional orgasms of lesser intensity. I've compared the experience to skipping stones on a glassy pond. The first stone hop makes the biggest ripple, and each hop to follow is smaller than the one before.

Those in search of the Holy Grail of orgasms should realize that the harder you try to have it, the more elusive it'll be. Striving to achieve a multiple is perhaps the surest way not to have one. It's not a contest. No one's keeping score. If it happens, awesome. If it doesn't, you still get the one orgasm, which ain't exactly chopped liver. And I don't say that lightly. Personally speaking, I love chopped liver.

10. How can I give a better blowjob?

You can't believe how many "tricks" about blowjobs have filtered in over the years. Altoids in the mouth, ice cubes, hot tea, tongue gymnastics, thumping on the frenulum (the small bundle of nerve located at twelve o'clock on the bottom side of the penis in the notch where the head meets the shaft), humming, slurping, burping, prostate stimulation, ball scratching, the list goes on. But, the truth is, all those gimmicks feel good/bad/indifferent, depending on the guy, and most men would rather receive a meat and potatoes (ahem) blowjob that lasted twice as long compared to a short, contrived experimental maneuver.

Best-selling author of *How To Be A Great Lover* Lou Paget

spoke to me on this point for a *Glamour* piece: "Most women have two issues with oral sex: swallowing and gagging. Only twenty-five percent of women swallow. So do it, don't do it, doesn't matter much to him. On gagging: If you control the motion, and if you use your hand along with your mouth, the penis will only go in so far. Beyond those concerns, you should set ground rules first. No hands on head, you'll do it for a limited amount of time, etc. Explain that you consider yourself a beginner and hope he'll be patient with you. He can guide you gently, which will be a huge turn-on for you both."

According to a local expert, my husband Steve, "The only thing that makes a blowjob great is enthusiasm. No matter what trick a woman tries, if her heart isn't in it, it'll only be good. If she's into it for her own sake, then she could do anything and it'd feel amazing."

Bill Maher, host of *Real Time* on HBO (who I once made eye contact with at Newark Airport at 1:00 A.M.), said it best. On his show, he held up an issue of *Cosmopolitan* magazine, read the coverline that said, "101 Sex Tips that Drive Him Wild," or something to that affect. "A hundred and one sex tricks?" he said. "There's only one sex trick. It's called a blowjob. Do it a hundred and one times."

Stephen Quint

VALERIE FRANKEL is the author of twelve novels, including *The Accidental Virgin*, *The Girlfriend Curse*, and *Hex and the Single Girl*. Val is quite proud of her new novels for teens, *Fringe Girl* and *Fringe Girl in Love*. When not writing fiction, Val peddles her essays and journalism at *Self*, *Glamour*, *Parenting*, *Q*, and *Marie Claire*, among other magazines. A Jersey girl from way back, Val currently lives in Brooklyn, New York, with her two tweenage daughters, three cats and husband, the opera singer Stephen Quint.

Valerie Frankel